EVERY
MISSING
GIRL

Also available by Leanne Kale Sparks

A Kendall Beck Thriller

The Wrong Woman

EVERY
MISSING GIRL

A KENDALL BECK THRILLER

LEANNE KALE SPARKS

CROOKED
LANE

NEW YORK

Published in the United States by Crooked Lane Books, an imprint of The Quick Brown Fox & Company LLC.

Crooked Lane Books and its logo are trademarks of The Quick Brown Fox & Company LLC.

Library of Congress Catalog-in-Publication data available upon request.

ISBN (hardcover): 978-1-63910-230-3
ISBN (ebook): 978-1-63910-231-0

Cover design by Melanie Sun

Printed in the United States.

www.crookedlanebooks.com

Crooked Lane Books
34 West 27th St., 10th Floor
New York, NY 10001

First Edition: February 2023

10 9 8 7 6 5 4 3 2

For family who are best friends and
best friends who are family.
It is the best of both worlds.

1

Friday

F BI SPECIAL AGENT Kendall Beck knew she'd been to one too many crime scenes when in the midst of the bloodiest she'd walked into lately—this one in a convenience store—she wondered who had the tedious job of washing off all the blood smeared on the cellophane of a five-pack of Donettes. Or did they throw all the blood-splattered items away because, well, they were covered in blood? Maybe they put them on a clearance rack. But did they then have to disclose they were part of a murder?

Probably the best thing would be to send the tainted snacks back to the station with the patrol cops currently swarming the small store. None of them cared if the bag of Cheetos had some spatter on the front. Free food. No law enforcement officer would pass up gratis chips and donuts.

Mmm . . . donuts . . . What she wouldn't give for a jelly right about now.

"Can I help you?" a cop asked, sidestepping around her as she stood in the middle of the doorway.

"Yeah." She flashed her badge. "Can you point me to who's in charge of the investigation?"

The cop peered around the store and pointed to a man at the end of the checkout counter. "There he is, dark suit, talking to the balding old guy."

Kendall didn't need to see the lead investigator's face to know it was Adam Taylor. The two had met and worked together on a case, one near and dear to Kendall's heart—the murder of her best friend. During the investigation, Kendall and Adam had grown close, and she counted him among her tight-knit posse of confidants.

"Thanks." She signed the crime scene log and strode toward Adam and one of his sidekicks, Saul Chapman.

"Don't think for one fucking second that catching this case means you won't be helping me move," she said by way of greeting as she sidled up next to Adam.

"Oh, goody, they sent *you*." He gave her a sideways glance. "I've been looking forward to your wit and charm all morning. What took you so long? Decide on a bubble bath before coming in?"

"Full-body massage with a hot Swede."

"How was it?"

"Hard." She tipped her head toward the body splayed on the floor in the middle of a large pool of blood. "What's the story here?"

"Dead guy," Saul said, pointing out the obvious.

Kendall wrinkled her nose. "I don't do dead guys. I do kids."

"Got one of those too."

"Dead?" Kendall hated starting any day with a dead body, but a dead kid made it ten times more revolting.

"No," Adam said. "But potentially a missing one."

"Elaborate."

"Bad Guy"—he pointed to the splayed body—"was trying to rob the store. Apparently had the child with him. There was another customer at the back of the store by the coolers, minding his own business. He hears a ruckus at the front of the store. Bad Guy is demanding money from the cashier, who grabs for a gun under the counter and aims it at Bad Guy. Things go sideways, Bad Guy gets a shot off, cashier goes down. Bad Guy kicks cashier's gun out of the way and puts another round in cashier's head."

"Meanwhile"—Saul picks up the story—"the kid is screaming, so the minding-his-own-business guy becomes a Good Samaritan, picks up the cashier's gun while Bad Guy is trying to empty the till. Bad Guy sees Good Sam, lifts his gun to shoot him, but Good Sam shoots Bad Guy first. Decent shot—looks like it was center mass. But Good Sam is apparently so freaked out by killing someone, he runs out of the store with the little girl in tow."

"Cops found them down the alley. Some neighbor called about a guy with a little girl hiding behind his garage," Adam said.

"Hiding from what?"

"Not clear on that," Adam said. "I don't do lost kids. I do dead guys."

* * *

Kendall mulled over the information Adam had given her as she walked across the parking lot of the convenience store to where police were talking to the Good Sam. The sun was breaking through the cloud cover, beams of light bouncing off windows and illuminating the city. This would be considered a rough part of town. Boarded-up warehouses covered in graffiti and store-fronts that hadn't been painted since they were first constructed competed with the fast-food conglomerates that always seem to thrive in any community regardless of the socioeconomics.

The Good Sam, who looked to be midforties, possibly skirt-ing fifty, slouched against the back end of the police cruiser, one hand grooming his closely trimmed gray beard. He wore jeans, a light-gray button-up shirt, and tan canvas shoes. Seemed to be a normal guy, which always set off Kendall's warning bells. Most "normal" people she met in her line of work tended to be the low-est forms of life. Shit dipped in gold. Shiny on the outside, just don't scratch the surface.

As she approached the car, the officer stepped forward. She flashed her badge; he nodded and stepped out of her way.

"Hi." She stuck her hand out for the man, who was now standing upright in front of her, an eyebrow raised. "I'm FBI Special Agent Kendall Beck. I was wondering if I could ask you a few questions?"

"FBI?" The man asked as he scanned her badge, then met her gaze while shaking her hand. "I already told the police every-thing about the shooting."

"I understand, Mr. . . . ?"

"Craig," the man said. "Melvin."

"Melvin. I know it's hard to keep repeating a story that's sure to give you nightmares, but I'm more interested in the girl who was in the store with you."

"She wasn't in the store *with* me," he said, placing emphasis on the word, most likely to ensure Kendall understood there was a difference. "She was with that scum of the earth who shot the cashier."

"I was told she was found with you."

"Yes, that's true," he said, drawing out the words. "But I just happened to be in the store. And she was in the store. But she came with the other guy. That's all. I don't know who she is."

Kendall smiled, hoping to put the man at ease. She didn't want the man on the defensive when it appeared he was trying to help the girl. She had learned a long time ago to start soft. Bring out the barbed-wire-covered bat only as a not-so-gentle means of persuasion when necessary. "Perhaps you should start from the beginning."

Melvin pulled his hand down his face and stroked his beard while letting out a long sigh. "I stopped by to get a Mountain Dew and a breakfast burrito—my usual breakfast. I was standing at the back cooler when the guy came in with the little girl. He looked sort of sketchy—"

"What do you mean by that?"

The man scratched along his jaw, his eyes squinting just slightly. "Well, he wasn't the kind of guy you expected to have a little girl with him. His clothes were dirty, his hair was long, and he looked a bit scraggly. Probably could've stood to shower, you know what I mean?"

Kendall nodded. She'd met many a sketchy dude in her line of work.

Craig returned the nod and continued. "And the little girl looked scared. So I kind of hung back and just watched them. Then the guy tells the cashier to give him all the money from the register. Next thing I know, both of those idiots had guns, and then the shooting started."

"So, just so I understand, both of them were shooting and you decided to get the girl?"

Craig looked up and away, as if trying to recall the scene in his mind. "I don't remember if they both were shooting—I think the guy shot the cashier first and she dropped her gun."

"And is that when you decided to pick it up?"

"Yeah—I don't know what I was thinking—the little girl was screaming and I was afraid the guy was going to shoot her. So I just . . . acted on instincts, I guess." He shrugged and looked down at his feet as he rocked from one to the other.

Kendall gave him a moment. It was never easy to kill people. Even law enforcement agents had a tough time dealing with taking a life. This guy might have only ever shot a gun at a range, taking out a paper man on a target. Not even close to the same experience. Paper men didn't bleed. And they didn't cry out in agony. It was a whole different ballgame when the shooting involved live flesh and blood. "What happened after you shot the man?"

Craig looked at Kendall, then swallowed, staring over her shoulder at the front of the store. "I just took off. I knew I had to get the girl out of there—she had already seen too much." He ran his hand over his beard again, and Kendall decided it was a nervous tic he probably didn't realize he was doing most of the time. "Truth be told, I was a little shaken up as well. I've never seen anyone die. And there was just . . . so much blood."

There was a great deal of truth to the statement. She had been to many violent crime scenes during her career with the FBI, and it was still unnerving to actually see how much blood the human body contained. "So why were you hiding when the police started canvassing the area?"

He inhaled through his nose and rocked back on his heels. "Honestly, I think I was in shock or something. I truly thought they were trying to hurt us." He shook his head, seemingly somewhat disgusted at the memory. "I know it sounds silly, but I was just really freaked out."

"It doesn't sound silly at all," Kendall reassured him. "Even the most seasoned veteran on the force gets shaken up in a gunfight. You did just fine." She glanced back at the store. "You said it's your routine to come here every morning, is that right?"

"Not exactly," he said. "I am not usually in this part of town. I live in Arvada and go to the store there."

"Where is that store? Do you know the cross streets?"

"Yeah, it's off Kipling and Ridge."

Kendall made a note. "So why were you on this side of town this morning?"

"I had a meeting with a client, but he didn't show up. So I decided to go into the store and grab breakfast before heading back to my office."

"What do you do for a living?"

"I'm a small business owner. Sort of a courier. I do all the running around for businesses who still deal in documents and stuff. Mostly lawyers, but today I was supposed to pick up some paperwork for a general contractor."

Kendall hadn't really considered there were still businesses out there that didn't do everything electronically. Didn't seem as if there would be enough work to make a living out of it. But then again, if he was one of only a few who did that type of work, he might be highly sought after by businesses who needed that service.

"And you're certain you don't know either of the people in the store?"

The man shook his head and dropped his gaze. "No. Like I said, I'm not usually on this side of town."

"And you don't know the little girl—at least you didn't before this morning?"

"Don't know anything about her," he said quickly and firmly, looking Kendall in the eye.

"Okay, thank you," Kendall said, fishing a business card out of her pocket and handing it to him. "If you think of anything else, please give me a call."

"Am I free to go now?" There was a slight edge of irritation to his voice. Weird, but perhaps the day's events were starting to catch up with him. There were many instances where a person went through stages—killing a man was one of them. Craig was probably going through the stage where he was getting pissed at everyone associated with this event, especially the person he shot. But it was difficult to get angry at a dead guy, so he was going to turn it on the next available living human.

Kendall was not up for being in his line of fire. It was too early in the day.

"Best to check with the officer," she said, and turned away. She wasn't going to get into a pissing match with Melvin Craig, and she had no idea whether Adam still needed to talk to him. Let the uniform deal with Craig and his attitude. It was good for young pups to learn how to overcome adversity.

As Kendall walked back to the c-store to find Adam, she hit the speed dial for her partner, Jake, and listened to her phone ring until he answered. Loud chatter and children's squeals nearly covered his "Hello."

"Where the hell are you?" she asked.

"I had to drop the kid at day care."

"They let you in with a gun?"

"They're not happy about it. I get lots of dirty looks."

"That's not necessarily because you have a gun."

"Did you call for a reason beyond damaging my fragile male ego?"

"Yeah, I'm at a crime scene. Looks like we found a possible missing girl."

"Alive?" His voice was tentative. It sucked having to start the day finding a dead kid.

"Yes, but I haven't had a chance to question her. Apparently, she's not talking. Adam had her taken to the PD, so I'm heading over to see if I can at least get a name and inform her parents."

"What do you need from me?"

"I'm going to send you some info on the guy she was with. It appears he's the reason we're not investigating her murder. I need you to do some background on the guy, see if the info he gave me checks out."

She heard the sound of a car door closing and a vehicle engine starting. "Heading to the office now."

CHAPTER

2

ADAM STOOD INSIDE the doorway of the convenience store, watching the medical examiner as she rolled over the dead body and looked for an exit wound. The air was pungent with the smell of burnt coffee and hot dogs (who ate hot dogs this early in the morning?) and the acrid odor of death. The scene was unnecessary. Death could've been avoided. Adam would never understand why people died for money.

The first rule of working at a convenience store: If you're asked to give all the money in the cash register to someone with a gun, do it.

Rule number two: See rule number one. Don't be a hero. That will get you dead.

Dr. Francis Ward—Fran to Adam—stood up, said something to her assistant, and waved Adam over. She was all of five feet tall, bubbly personality despite the grimness of her profession, and damn good at her job. "Okay, Dead Body One has a gunshot wound to the chest. Early assessment is he died within minutes after the bullet entered his body. No exit wound, so bullet appears to still be in the body."

She moved around the counter to the other body. The pools of blood were starting to dry, but it looked as if someone had spilled paint on the floor. The unmistakable metallic scent served as a reminder of the carnage. "Dead Body Two," she said on a sigh. "Three gunshot wounds—one to the left side, through and through. You'll have to check with the techs to see if they found a casing. This was not a fatal shot—which is probably why two more bullets were put in her, one in the chest and the other to the head."

Adam stepped from behind the counter to make room for the crime scene techs, in full Tyvek coveralls, who were trying to get by. Once Adam and Fran were out of the way, they carefully lifted the body of the woman and placed her in a body bag. The sound of the bag being zipped always gave Adam a bad taste in his mouth. It was unlike any sound he knew. Or maybe it was because the zipper was long—the length of a body—and seemed to take forever to get to the top. He couldn't recall anything that took as much time to zip as a body bag. And he associated that sound with death. And not just any death. Typically a homicide. A needless waste of human life.

The bodies were wheeled past him and out to the coroner's van. A cold shiver worked its way down his spine. Death was always a bad way to start the morning. The uselessness of this one added a dull gray to the day.

"Why do they think they should protect a damn cash register with their lives?" Fran muttered under her breath and gave a final look around the store. "And with that, I turn the crime scene over to you." She took off her gloves and placed them into an evidence bag.

"Thanks, Fran. Any idea when you'll get to the autopsies?" Adam asked.

She grimaced. "I wouldn't think until tomorrow, at the earliest. Probably not until the day after, but I'll shoot you a text."

They said their good-byes, and Adam refocused on the crime scene. It was a bloody mess. And to think a child had been in there, witnessing the violence. Absorbing the sounds of gunfire, enveloped by death. Adam shook his head slowly. He hated the thought of the little girl, within a year or two of his niece's age, having those memories for the rest of her life.

"Detective." A uniformed cop pulled him from his reverie. "The owner of the store is here."

"Thanks. Tell him I'll be right with him." Adam turned his attention to Saul and Fletch. "Saul, head back to the station. Let's make sure we can get ballistics going on the guns. And start checking on our kidnapper-turned-robber."

Saul nodded and headed for his car.

Adam pointed at the other lanky member of his investigative team. "Fletch, you're with me."

The uniformed cop was standing next to a short man with black hair, midfifties, mouth open, pained expression on his face. Adam approached and put out his hand.

"Adam Taylor, Denver PD."

The man shook Adam's hand nervously and a bit too vigorously, his gaze fixed on the storefront. "Lyall Osborne."

"You own this store?"

"Yes." His eyes were wide, and his voice dropped to near a whisper. "Is it true? Ashley is dead?"

"Who is Ashley?"

"My employee. She was scheduled to work this morning."

"And what is her last name?" Fletch asked, pen poised above his notepad.

"Collins," Mr. Osborne said, seeming to notice Fletch for the first time. No small feat; Fletch was about six foot three and rail thin, but surprisingly muscular and strong.

"Can you describe her for me?" Adam asked.

The man closed his eyes tight. "Brown hair, kind of long, maybe to her shoulders. Average height. Not fat, but not skinny—she still has some baby fat." He looked up at Adam, eyes pleading with him not to tell him what he already knew. "She just had a baby a few months ago," he added, as if the information could bring the young woman back to life.

"We don't have a positive ID on the victims, but it does appear the woman who was killed was your employee Ashley."

The man paled, took a step back, and bent over at the waist, as if Adam's words came with a herculean punch to the gut.

"I'm sorry for your loss," Adam said, his voice serious with a hint of sympathy. And he was sympathetic, but this was not new for him. Or personal. And he needed answers to questions in order to further the investigation.

"Do you have an employee file on Ms. Collins?" Adam asked.

"Yes, yes." The man pointed a shaky finger toward the store. "In the office." He looked at Adam, bottom lip slightly trembling. "Will you be telling her boyfriend, or do I have to do that?"

Adam grasped the man's shoulder, urging him toward the front door of the store. "We'll do that."

The man exhaled. His shoulders dropped as if a heavy weight had been lifted. Adam got it—he hated giving death notifications too. Nasty little perk of the job.

When they passed through the doors and into the store, Osborne gasped, his knees going weak, as he took in the sight of all the blood. Adam quickly grabbed the man under his arm and directed him down the first aisle toward the back of the store.

"Office back here?" he asked Osborne in an attempt to get him to focus on something other than the macabre display at the front of the store.

"Yes," Osborne mumbled, and pushed through a heavy swinging door into the back storeroom. Large panels, not unlike what Adam had for walls at the station, partitioned off a small office cubicle. Inside was a desk with a computer and printer on top, a large file cabinet, and a rolling chair. No frills. Not even personal pictures up on the corkboard.

Mr. Osborne took out a key ring, slipped a key into the file cabinet lock, and opened the top drawer. He shuffled through some files before pulling one out. Placing it on the desk, he opened the file, flipped through the papers until he found the sheet he was looking for, and handed it to Adam. "That's all her personal information—including emergency contact."

"Can I have a copy of this?" Adam asked.

"Of course." Osborne reached for the paper and placed it on the printer.

"What can you tell me about Ms. Collins?"

Osborne pushed some buttons and then looked at Adam as the paper slowly slid into the printer with a whir, followed by the rhythmic sounds of ink being placed on paper in the proper places to create words. Modern miracles to make life easier. Sure beat carbon copying. "She's a nice girl. Had some hard times growing up—her mom was on the crack pipe and not very maternal, from what I gather. Ashley got into drugs and alcohol at a young age. Dropped out of high school. Something happened—not quite sure what, but she hit some sort of rock bottom and decided to get herself together. Found a nice man with a decent job; they have a baby together. She works here in the morning and goes to school in the afternoon to get her GED."

"Any reason to believe she might be involved in the robbery attempt?" Adam asked.

"No." Osborne shook his head vehemently. "She was determined to give her daughter a better start in life than she'd had." He passed the copy to Adam and looked him straight on. "She wouldn't have done that."

Adam shrugged. "Sometimes money can get tight—maybe someone offers to share in the take if she helps with a 'robbery.'" He used air quotes on the last word.

"I really can't believe Ashley would do that. Vincent, her boyfriend—the father of her baby—he has a good job as an electrician apprentice. I don't recall her ever mentioning they had financial problems."

"Would she tell you? That's a bit personal, and you're her boss." Adam never divulged personal information to his boss. Hell, he avoided talking to the man as much as possible. But maybe Ms. Collins had a better relationship with her boss.

Osborne dry washed his hands, his face reddening a bit, and seemed to consider the question for a moment. "Perhaps not."

Adam made a mental note to check on Ms. Collins's finances. Sometimes, no matter how hard someone tried to leave a bad situation and make a better life for themselves, they just couldn't seem to make a clean break. A sad but true story a majority of the time, Adam had discovered throughout his career.

"Do you know if she was close to any of the other employees?"

"I don't know." There was a sudden air of irritation coming from Osborne, but Adam supposed he was considering whether his employee had tried to screw him over. "Typically there is only one person working in the front of the store. Deliveries are dealt with back here." He pointed to a large door leading to the back of the building. "But it's possible she made friends with whoever was stocking during her shift." He took in a deep, calming breath and released it through his nose. "And there is some overlap on shifts. She might be friendly with the person who works in the afternoon."

Adam rubbed his hands together to generate some heat in the cold storage room. "I'm going to need a list of employees and their contact information. Do you know if there were any deliveries this morning?"

"Yes," Osborne said, hitting a key on the computer to bring it to life. A spreadsheet filled the screen. Osborne traced his finger across the screen until he came to the information he was looking for. "We got a delivery from our bread supplier." He peered around the stockroom and then pointed to a stack of plastic pallets. "That's probably them."

"Would Ms. Collins have handled the delivery?" Adam asked, walking closer to the pallets.

"Oh, no. We have a couple of stockers who accept the deliveries and get everything checked in."

"Was there a stocker here this morning?"

Osbourne's posture stiffened, and his mouth dropped open. The question seemed to take him by surprise. No doubt he was just realizing his employee was not at the scene and wondering where he was. Adam was curious about that as well. Osborne walked back to the computer. "Alex Martinez should've been here." He glanced around as if he had missed seeing the man when he came in and expected him to announce his presence.

"Any reason to suspect he might have something to do with this?" Adam asked.

Osborne's hands rested on his hips, his gaze down. "Before today, I would've said no way. But with everything that's happened—and he's not here—I just don't know what to think."

Adam knew he had sown the seed of suspicion in the man's mind, but two people had died during the commission of at least one crime—potentially two, with the discovery of the missing girl—so Osborne was going to have to shed his belief that his employees were above illegal activities in his store. Adam had learned long ago that *anyone* could be a criminal. It was all a matter of incentive.

"Why don't you give me a list of all the employees, and we'll see if we can track him down." The owner printed off a list of names, addresses, and phone numbers and handed it over to Adam.

"I noticed you have surveillance cameras throughout the store," said Adam.

"Yes, well, only two of them are operational." Osborne's face reddened, and he scowled. "The company I purchased them through has been telling me for weeks they are sending someone to repair the ones that aren't working, but they haven't shown up yet."

"Are they digital?" Fletch asked.

"No, we haven't made the switch to digital yet . . . it wasn't a priority."

"How 'bout now?" Fletch asked.

Adam flashed him a warning glance. Fletch was young and still needed to learn when to push and when to play nice.

"We'll need the tape, then," Adam said. "Are you here most days?"

Osborne fumbled with the machine on top of the file cabinet, pushing the eject button several times in an attempt to coax the tape out. Once it finally popped out, he handed it to Fletch. "About every other day. I own another store about five miles from here. I split my time between them."

"So is there a manager here when you're not?" Adam asked.

"Yes, Janet Gross, but she has a regular shift—she's not here working when the others are. But she coordinates the deliveries when I'm not here, talks to the employees to make sure things are going all right. Handles the deposits on my off days and makes up the employee schedules."

Adam searched through the employee list for her name. She would be the top priority to talk to next. "How long has she been here?"

The man blew air out and ran a hand down his face, staring up at the ceiling in contemplation. "Gosh, damn near from the start, I'd say. I think she was my first employee at this store."

Adam put a star next to her name to denote that she was the manager. If she'd been there since the beginning, she probably knew more about what went on than Osborne. "Have you noticed anyone strange hanging around lately?"

Osborne guffawed. "Detective, most of the people in this neighborhood are a bit strange."

Adam smiled. "Stranger than usual, then?"

"No, but I probably wouldn't notice unless I happened to see them on the security camera. I stay back here most of the time doing work on the computer. Janet would be the better person to talk to—she seems to have a bead on what is going on around here."

Adam glanced at Fletch with an unspoken *You have anything?* Fletch gave a slight shake of his head. "Okay," Adam said, handing Osborne a business card. "If you think of anything, give me a call. We'll be back in touch."

Fletch and Adam made their way back to their cars. "I want to see if we can get as many of the employees to come to the station for questioning as possible," Adam said. "Let's decrease the amount of running around we have to do."

Fletch nodded. Adam pointed to the list of employees. "But first, see if Saul can find our disappearing stock boy. Let's make sure he's not another victim we haven't found, or if he has any involvement in what went down here."

"You got it, boss." Fletch jogged across the parking lot to his car.

Adam leaned against his truck, contemplating the various scenarios that might have taken place that morning. It wasn't unusual for a convenience store to be robbed. It was probably a daily occurrence across the city. The girl, though. She was the oddity.

Why had she been here? And what connection did she have to the dead guy?

CHAPTER

3

KENDALL WASN'T USED to giving good news to families, so when it happened, she tried to soak up every ounce of happiness she could. Store it away for those dark days when finding a missing child wasn't a happy occasion.

Watching Savannah Hawley reunite with her mother was a better start to the day than Kendall thought she was going to have. A glance over at her partner, Jake Alexander, caught him stealthily swiping at a tear.

Softy . . .

She knew the job tugged at his heartstrings in ways Kendall couldn't fathom. He had a gorgeous—if not precocious—little girl, and his wife was expecting their second child.

Kendall loved her job. Loved working to reunite children who were abducted with their families. Sometimes, oftentimes it seemed, children were returned in a manner that only allowed the family to have closure. But on days like today, she got to see joy and love and gratefulness on the faces of the families. Kendall had sworn off long ago ever having children of her own, so this job, these kids she helped—it was the closest she would ever come to motherhood.

"Ms. Hawley," Kendall said, hating to interrupt, "if we could ask Savannah a few questions, then you can take her home."

"Please, call me Karen," Ms. Hawley said, her voice soft and raw with emotion. "Can I stay in here with her?"

"Of course." Kendall knew it would've been virtually impossible for Karen to be very far from her daughter for fear she would disappear the minute she took her eyes off the girl. To Savannah's mom, this was likely still just north of a dream she might wake from, only to lose everything all over again.

Kendall motioned to two couches. The kids' room, painted a soft pinkish purple, was less stark and uninviting than the rest of the police department. There were toys and crayons and coloring books. An old TV on a metal rolling cart had a DVD player attached, and there were a few kid-friendly movies in a basket on the shelf.

Kendall had agreed with Adam that the PD was the best place to reunite the girl with her mother. Trying to get them cleared to enter the FBI building would've been a nightmare and unfair to Karen, who had been waiting a few months to see her child.

Kendall retrieved her cell phone from her jacket pocket, set it up to record the interview, and slid it onto the table, making sure it was as close as possible to Savannah. Children had a tendency to speak low or whisper during interviews, and Kendall wanted to get every word the child spoke. Though it was possible the man she had been with at the convenience store was the one who'd kidnapped her, it seemed unlikely. And Kendall wanted to find out who it was and bring them down. It seemed unfair the robber had died. After all, criminals who hurt children didn't fare well in prison. And this scum was due some painful justice over many years of incarceration. He got off easy in Kendall's estimation.

"Okay, Savannah, I need to ask you a few questions, and then you and your mom can go home. But I need you to answer honestly, even if it's embarrassing, okay? We have to have all the information, and even stuff you think isn't important is really important." Kendall kept her voice soft but authoritative. "Do you understand?"

Savannah wiped her tearstained face with the back of her hand, brushed the hair from her face, and nodded.

"Do you remember the day you were taken?" Kendall asked.

Savannah glanced at her mom and shrugged.

"You won't get into trouble for anything you say, okay?" Kendall glanced at Karen to get her to back her up.

The woman smiled at Savannah and nodded. "It's okay, sweetheart. Tell Agent Beck what you remember. Nothing you say will upset me."

The girl sent her mother a meek smile and glanced at Kendall.

"Were you inside your house?" Kendall asked.

"Yes." Savannah glanced over her shoulder in the direction of where Jake sat just out of sight, then toward the door.

Interesting, but not unexpected. Life was now one uncertainty after another. Hopefully, that would change over time, but chances were good some of it would stay with her forever.

"Alone?" Kendall pulled Savannah's attention back on her.

She picked at a scab on her arm. "Yes, no one is allowed in the house while Mom is gone."

"Okay, tell me what happened."

She slid her hand into her mother's and gripped so tight her knuckles were white. "I got home from school and got a snack, called Mom like I'm supposed to, and started my homework." She sneaked a peek at her mom and swallowed. "And turned on the TV."

Karen smiled at her daughter and kissed the side of her head. Kendall assumed there was a no-TV rule until homework was done.

Savannah's lip began to tremble. Her mother handed her the water bottle, and Savannah took a small sip, the bottle shaking in her hand. Kendall's heart clenched. Savannah was too young to have this type of trauma in her life. "Someone knocked on the door, so I looked out the little window beside the door and saw a woman standing there."

"Did you know the woman?"

Savannah shook her head.

"We're new to the neighborhood," Karen interjected. Kendall had read in the file that Savannah's parents had just gone through a somewhat nasty divorce.

"And you opened the door?" Kendall said, focusing on not sounding accusatory.

Tears slipped over the girl's cheeks, and she looked at her mom. "I'm sorry, I know I'm not supposed to open the door to strangers."

Karen wrapped her arms tight around her daughter. "It's okay, sweetie. Mommy's not mad at you, and you're not in trouble."

"Why did you open the door?" Kendall asked. "Did she say something to you to get you to open the door?"

Savannah nodded. "She said she lived a couple of houses away and her dog got out of her yard and another neighbor said the dog was in our backyard, and could she come through the house and get it."

"Do you remember what the woman looked like?"

"Like a grandma—her hair was kinda gray and she had it pulled up into a bun and wore grandma clothes."

"And what are grandma clothes?"

"Like ugly pants and a sweatshirt with a big white cat face on it."

Kendall wanted to chuckle. *Yep, those would be grandma clothes.*

"Was anyone else with her, or was she alone?"

Savannah exhaled shakily. "She was alone."

"Okay, so you let her in?"

"Yeah." Savannah still had a death grip on her mother's hand, tracing the outline of her mother's manicured nails. "She seemed nice, and I wasn't scared of her. I felt bad 'cause she seemed sad her dog was missing, and I wanted her to get her dog back."

"But you've never seen her before? Around the neighborhood?"

Savannah shook her head and reached for the water and took a small sip.

"What happened after you let her in?"

"I walked to the kitchen to open the door to the backyard."

"And she followed you?"

"Yes." Another glance back at Jake. Savannah was checking her surroundings and apparently not comfortable with someone being behind her. Jake took the hint and moved around so Savannah could see him but stayed far enough away so as to not be a threat.

"Was there anyone with her?" Kendall asked.

"Not that I saw."

"What happened next?"

"She went out into the backyard, calling her dog's name."

"Did you go with her?"

Her eyes bulged. "No, I stayed in the house. I don't like dogs, and I was scared it might bite me."

Kendall nodded in agreement. "I get it. Big dogs kind of make me nervous sometimes too. What happened when she went outside?"

She picked at the corner of the label on the water bottle, keeping her eyes averted. Kendall hated having to make the girl relive being kidnapped, but it was a necessary evil. "I was standing in the kitchen, just watching her look for her dog."

"Did you ever see the dog?"

"No, but that's because I heard something behind me." She threw a quick side-eye at Jake. "I turned around, and an old man was in the doorway. I thought he was the lady's husband or something."

Kendall could see where this was going. She'd seen scenarios similar to this many times over her career. Adults who used their authority and a child's trust to lure them away. Among the many traumatic things a child who had been abducted had to deal with, one of the worst had to be a loss of trust in adults. There was a negative trickle-down effect that stayed with them their entire lives, and through every relationship.

"Did he say anything to you?" Kendall asked.

"No, I don't think so." Savannah looked up at her mom, tears welling in her eyes. "I don't remember."

"That's okay, sweetheart," Karen said, giving Savannah a reassuring squeeze around her shoulders.

"You're doing so great, Savannah," Kendall said, reaching over to pat the girl on her knee. "I know this isn't much fun, but just a few more questions, okay?"

Savannah gave a half-hearted nod, and Kendall knew she was close to losing the girl's attention. The day had already been long and traumatic for her, which was just the icing on the cake of what she had experienced since being abducted from her home. The best thing Kendall could do was take the information Savannah provided—which now indicated there was a child sex ring and not some random guy kidnapping a little girl—and get her the justice she deserved.

And prevent whoever these people were from kidnapping any other children and forcing them into a life of sexual servitude.

Karen rubbed her daughter's arm but glanced up at the clock on the wall. Kendall was about to lose the mom as well.

"What's the next thing you remember after the man came into the house?"

Tears tipped over the edge of Savannah's lower lids and rolled down her cheeks. "I woke up in a dark room on a mattress."

"Could you sit up or stand?"

"Nuh-uh. My legs and arms wouldn't work and my head felt weird—like when I have a cold and I'm all stuffy."

So she'd been drugged. Typical. The best way to control someone and keep them quiet.

"Could you see out of the windows? See what was outside?"

The little girl shook her head. "The windows were all covered with that silver stuff"—she looked up at her mom—"the stuff you use to cover leftovers in the fridge."

"Aluminum foil?" Karen asked.

"Yeah," Savannah said. "The foil stuff, so the room was always dark."

That was actually useful information. The house would most likely be in an older neighborhood where there was no home-owners association. Most HOAs had rules against placing aluminum foil over windows. Ruined the neighborhood aesthetics.

"Was there anyone else in the room with you?"

"I don't think so—I can't remember. Maybe there was another girl, but I was so sleepy all the time. I couldn't stay awake."

"But you didn't see her?"

She shook her head.

"Do you remember seeing anyone else?"

"Just the man—he brought me food and took me to the bathroom."

"Did you see the woman who was looking for her dog again?"

"No, but I heard her yelling at the man one time."

"Could you tell what she was saying?"

Savannah shook her head again and yawned.

"Did you stay in the room the whole time?"

"Yeah, until today. The man woke me up and took me to a different bathroom and told me to get cleaned up in the bath-tub." She looked down at her dress—blue with bunnies and cher-ries that came just above her knee—and pulled it away from her body. "They gave me these clothes to wear."

Paired with white sandals and barrettes holding her hair back on each side of her head, the dress gave her the appearance of being younger than she was, and more innocent. A calculated move on the part of her kidnappers. The younger and more innocent, the higher the price tag.

"Is that when you left the place you were being held?" Kendall asked.

"Uh-huh. The old man put me in the back seat of a car and told me to lie down and not move or say anything."

"Did he get into the car?"

"No, the guy from the store was driving. He was mad—he was yelling at someone on the phone."

"What was he angry about?"

Savannah shrugged and pulled at a loose string on the hem of her skirt. "I think he wanted money. He said a lot of bad words."

"Did he go anywhere else before you stopped at the store?"

"No, just there."

"What happened when you got to the store?"

"He pulled me out and grabbed my arm"—she placed her hand around her upper arm, where a bruise was forming—"and shook me really hard. And he had a mad face and told me not to say a word in the store and to stay right next to him."

Kendall glanced up at the clock on the wall. Savannah had her head resting against her mother's chest. The poor girl looked wiped out. Kendall would love to get the entire interview done in one shot, but Savannah had been through enough for one day. Besides, the next part—the one where she'd witnessed two people being shot to death—might be better handled with a mental health professional observing.

"How about we stop there so can you go home?" Kendall asked.

The girl nodded and stood up, dragging her mother toward the door.

"Thank you," Karen said, trying to shake Kendall's hand as she went by, but Savannah was not slowing down. She wanted out of the police station. To return home. Find some semblance of safety and normalcy. Kendall prayed she would.

"The police will need to talk to her about what happened inside the store, but I'll suggest setting up a time when a therapist who specializes in this area is on hand to help guide the interview," Kendall said.

Karen nodded and strode toward the exit, mother and daughter clinging to each other as if their lives depended on it. Kendall knew that was bound to be the way it was for a while.

4

Saturday

THE THUNDERSTORMS THAT had drenched the front range of the Rocky Mountains the previous night had moved out of the area, leaving pleasant weather in its wake. Kendall was thankful, yet a little disappointed at having to spend such a beautiful day moving. In some ways it hurt her heart to be leaving the house she had shared with her best friend. Gwen had been murdered but had managed to continue looking out for Kendall even from the grave, bequeathing her the house—which Gwen had owned—as a living estate. It had been hard for Kendall to live in the house, though. Nothing had felt the same after Gwen died. Every inch of the house was still filled with her presence, her perfume, her soul.

So when Gwen's brother, Noah, had requested Kendall allow the family to sell the house, she agreed. Gwen's family, of which Kendall had been a part when Gwen was alive, blamed her for Gwen's murder. She hadn't seen any of them since shortly after Gwen's funeral. Once it had been discovered the serial killer who had been stalking Kendall had exacted some sort of revenge by killing Gwen, the family had closed ranks and pushed her outside their close-knit circle. They couldn't get past the fact Kendall had been the cause of them losing Gwen forever.

Kendall could barely get past it herself.

"Earth to Kendall," Adam said, yanking her from her memories. "Wanna grab the other end of this so we can get it into your place?"

"Don't get your knickers in a knot," Kendall said, lifting the opposite end of the mattress box.

"You know, you're not very appreciative of my time on my day off. I didn't have to help you move," he grumbled.

"Sure you did," she said with a smile. "How else were you going to get free beer and pizza?"

Adam let out a grunt as they stepped down from the truck. "By the way, where the hell is nerd boy, and why isn't he here helping?"

Quentin Novak, the remaining amigo, was a computer gaming-tech guy. Adam and Q tolerated each other for Kendall's sake—but just barely. And Adam never passed up an opportunity to insult Q.

She pressed the button to call the elevator. "Business trip."

Adam scoffed. "That was well timed."

"I thought so too, but he swears this has been in the works for a while. Apparently, he is the mastermind behind some new game that's gone viral or something, and the company has him going to all these gaming conventions. I think he's in Missoula, Montana, this weekend."

"Huh. Hard to believe he'd go along with that for too long, being adverse to crowds—and people."

"Yeah, he's loosened up a lot. Seems to actually enjoy traveling around and meeting with like-minded gaming geeks."

"Probably a good fit for him—hanging around other socially awkward people."

"Yeah, and I think he's getting laid, so there's that."

"Thanks. There's an image I won't be getting out of my mind's eye anytime soon."

When they arrived with the mattress box, Jake was standing in the middle of Kendall's new condo. It was in a more industrial area of Denver, atop a warehouse. The innovative owner had taken the second floor and fashioned out six nice-sized condos. Kendall had snagged a corner unit, so she had windows on two sides, along with a balcony overlooking the parking lot. But she also had a decent view of the Rocky Mountains. And who didn't like waking up to the purple mountain majesties of the Colorado front range?

"Is that it?" Jake asked, chugging a bottle of water.

"The very last thing," Kendall said.

"Where's my beer?" Adam demanded.

"Fridge," Kendall said, pointing to the kitchen. "Grab me one while you're at it."

"This is your place. I'm the guest. You should be getting me a beer."

"Yeah, okay," Kendall laughed. "We'll be on the balcony."

Jake grabbed a folding chair and sat, letting out a groan of satisfaction after a few hours of heavy labor. "This is a pretty cool place," he said. "If I were single, this is where I'd live."

Adam handed a beer to Kendall and pointed to the parking lot. "Hey, isn't that your real estate agent?"

Kendall peered over the edge of the railing. "Hey, Señor Jimmy!"

The man glanced up and waved his arm over his head. "Buzz me in."

Jake raised an eyebrow. "Señor Jimmy?"

"Yeah, he mentioned one time he was on vacation in Mexico and had a little too much tequila, which made him rather jolly, and he began dancing and buying shots for everyone in the bar. The locals dubbed him Señor Jimmy."

"Nice."

"Yeah, I think he got a sombrero out of it too."

Kendall got up and headed inside, hitting the button that unlocked the security door below.

"And ever since he told you this story, you've called him Señor Jimmy."

"Well, you're sort of obligated at that point."

"Agreed."

Within a minute, the real estate agent walked inside. "Hey, I just wanted to drop off the key to your storage unit downstairs." He glanced around. "All moved in?"

"Yep, just finished. Want a beer?"

"Uhhh"—Señor Jimmy checked his watch—"sure, I've got some time."

"Great." Kendall motioned toward Adam. "Get another beer."

Adam opened his mouth to protest being ordered around like the hired help, then closed it and returned to the kitchen.

"So, I saw you on TV," Jim said. "The murders at that gas station. And then finding the girl who'd been kidnapped?" He took a long draw of his beer. "It's a small world. My colleague sold the girl's mother their house. And I just had a sale fall through not long ago on the same street. A guy and his daughter were all set to buy, but then he had issues with his ex-wife. He pulled out of the sale and moved out of town."

Kendall looked at Adam, who, judging by the quirk of his eyebrow, was just as intrigued by the information.

"So, are you pretty familiar with that neighborhood?" Kendall asked.

"Yeah, we like to keep tabs on houses that come on the market there. It's an older established neighborhood, but a lot of young families are moving in and renovating the houses."

"Are there old people living there?"

"Not as many anymore—and not any that I can recall living on the little girl's street. The yuppies are offering good money for the houses, and many of the original owners have long since paid off their mortgages. They make a lot of money on the sale and move to Arizona to live out their days."

"And you're sure there's not an older couple who lives on that street?"

"Not a one. I think the closest empty nesters are one street over and about five blocks down."

So the couple who'd abducted Savannah had to have come into the neighborhood to kidnap her. Was it random? Had they followed her home from school and taken advantage of her being alone? Or had they planned this?

And how many other girls had they done this too?

CHAPTER

5

Tuesday

THE COOL AIR of the ice arena hit Adam in the face as soon as he opened the door. Kendall had beaten him there and was sitting with his sister-in-law, Poppy. Damn . . . he owed her a six-pack of beer. He hadn't seen much of her since helping her move on Saturday. They'd both been busy with their cases. For Adam, it had been a couple of days of running down leads and realizing in frustration that the case was moving closer to cold while he tried to figure out what had happened at the convenience store the day two people had lost their lives and one little girl had found hers. Adam hoped Kendall's part of the investigation was going smoother than his.

Adam glanced around the rink. Where the hell was Mark? He figured his big brother was giving his twelve-year-old daughter some last-minute coaching. The Taylor boys had grown up on the ice, and Mark had played for Colorado College. So it seemed only natural he would have his kid on skates with a stick in her hands as soon as she learned to walk.

Climbing the steps to where Poppy and Kendall were sitting, Adam gave his sister-in-law a one-armed hug and a kiss on the cheek before moving past her to sit next to Kendall.

"Where's Mark?" he asked.

Poppy's cheeks blushed slightly, and she glanced toward the hallway leading to the concessions at the front. "Uh, he should be here any minute." The look on Adam's face must've mirrored the confusion he felt. Mark and Poppy *always* came to the games together.

"He had some work to do at the station," she said.

A woman slid onto the bench next to Poppy. Adam recognized her as Mark and Poppy's neighbor, Cora. He was a little surprised to see her. Her daughter, once a good friend of Frankie's, was no longer with her. Adam would've thought it might be too hard on the woman to be around things her daughter had once been involved in so soon after losing her. But then again, maybe it helped to do familiar things, to see that life was still going on and she could take comfort in activities her daughter had once enjoyed.

Just before the start of the game, Mark lumbered up the stairs but cut short of his wife, giving her a tight smile and a curt "Hey," before stepping over the bench and sitting next to Adam.

Adam gawked at his brother. He couldn't recall a time when Mark and Poppy hadn't greeted each other with a kiss. And they without exception sat next to each other. It was uncommon to see them not holding hands, unless Mark had his arm around his wife. They were almost gross in the amount of PDA they exhibited. Gross, that is, in the way single people who'd been without a significant other for a while and were wholly jealous would define it.

Maybe it was because Cora was sitting next to Poppy? Mark would never be rude and squeeze between them. But then what was the dirty look he'd given his wife all about?

"Everything okay?" Adam whispered to Mark.

"Yeah," Mark answered, without further elaboration, effectively shutting down the conversation.

Adam glanced at Kendall, but she just shrugged. A few months earlier, after they had worked their first case together, Adam had brought her along to dinner at his parents. Kendall's only living family was her father, who was about three hours south of Denver in Cañon City. She had been folded into Adam's family and one of them ever since. He was pretty sure everyone actually preferred Kendall over him, but he was getting used to that.

The national anthem blasted through the speakers as the teams lined up on the blue lines. Frankie—short for Francesca—was a left-winger and lightning quick on skates with more than decent stickhandling skills. One of only two girls on the team, the other being the backup goalie, Frankie was the second-highest goal scorer on the team.

And always a starter. Except for today.

"Is Frankie not feeling well or something?" Adam asked Mark.

"Not that I know of." He leaned forward and glanced at his wife with a questioning scowl on his face. Poppy shook her head and shrugged.

To everyone's surprise, Frankie had limited ice time during the first period, only playing on the fourth line. Adam figured she must have spouted off to the coach or something and was being knocked down a peg or two to remind her who was player and who was coach. Adam had received a lesson or two like that when he was young. Down by five goals after the first period, however, the coach must have realized he'd made a poor choice in punishment, because at the start of the second period the goalie was replaced and Frankie was back on the first line, quickly scoring two goals.

By the end of the game, Frankie had added three more goals and her team had decimated their crosstown rival for the win. The arena buzzed with the chatter of happy parents and the clang of a hundred feet on the metal steps as they all made their way down the stands and into the front concessions.

Adam and Mark followed Kendall and Poppy out to the lobby to wait for Frankie so they could celebrate at the girl's favorite ice cream shop, as was customary. The coolness between Poppy and Mark had shifted into an ice storm, erecting a thick wall between them.

It was odd—and completely disconcerting. This was a couple who never fought without making up. Who seemed to have the perfect marriage and the perfect family. The perfect life. Adam hoped to one day emulate them.

But this was so contrary to anything he had ever witnessed in their fifteen-year marriage, and Adam was almost heartbroken at the realization they were simply human after all. He had always looked up to his older brother, had always thought of him as superhuman, and that had extended to Mark's wife once he married. After all, how could a superhero not have a superheroine as his life partner?

It was juvenile thinking, of course, but some things from childhood, even when tempered with reality and experience, were hard to completely dismiss.

"Adam, are you investigating that murder at the gas station?" Poppy asked, thankfully filling the awkward silence that had settled around their circle.

"Yep." He nodded toward Kendall. "With the FBI wonder child."

"Really?" Mark asked. "How come you're involved?"

"A missing girl was recovered at the scene," Kendall said.

"Oh, I heard about that," Poppy said. "Poor little girl. I hope she wasn't . . ." Her voice trailed off, but they all knew the unspoken thought.

Raped. Tortured. Molested.

They fell silent again. Mark looked at his watch, tapped out a text message on his phone, and mumbled, "Where is she?"

"Maybe the coach is talking to her," Poppy answered, glancing back toward the rink. "She was in a foul mood when we got here."

"Why?" Mark asked, an atypical hint of pissiness in his tone.

"No idea," Poppy said, not looking at him. And the ice wall thickened.

Kendall shifted uncomfortably from one foot to the other, eyes wide, eyebrows raised. Adam had no answer, so he stared at his feet and prayed for Frankie to appear. She would be in a good mood. Always was after a win.

Fifteen minutes turned into twenty. Every other player had left with their parents. But Frankie still hadn't appeared.

"I'll see what the holdup is," Mark said. "You try to get her on her cell phone," he directed his wife.

Adam and Mark walked briskly to the top of the ramp, an unnerving sense of urgency pushing them to move faster. An empty rink only served to ramp up Adam's concern. Even the Zamboni had finished clearing the ice and been put to bed for the night.

"Where the fuck is she?" Mark asked, running toward the locker rooms. He yanked open the door and stepped into the dark room.

Dread washed over Adam. His heart rate kicked into overdrive. Visions of his niece lying on the floor of the locker room, unconscious and injured, rapid-fired through his brain.

What the hell had happened? And how had they not known something was wrong?

Mark flipped on the light, and they moved in opposite directions. Mark headed for the locker bays; Adam turned toward the showers. He tugged back the shower curtain on each stall, a little more frantic as he moved down the line, only to find all of them empty. He did the same with the toilet stalls, pushing open each door to no avail. He was one part happy not to find her, one part scared he hadn't.

He met Mark back at the door.

"Anything?" Mark asked.

"No sign of her," Adam answered.

Mark burst out of the locker room, anxiety rolling off him in waves. He jogged toward the skate rental counter. The gate was pulled down and locked, the rows of skates dark.

"Hey!" Mark yelled, shaking the metal gate. "Anyone back there? Coach Turner?"

Eerie silence.

Adam searched the empty metal stands, hoping to see the black hoodie Frankie wore after every game. "It's tradition," she'd say. "It's superstition," he'd counter.

The ice was as smooth as glass, devoid of all remnants of the hard-fought victory.

The team benches. The penalty box. The back door.

They bolted toward it at the same time. Adam hit the release bar and flung the door open. It hit the exterior wall with a clang. Two vehicles were parked back there. A man was getting into an older-model Jeep, the engine roaring to life as the headlights illuminated part of the lot.

Mark made a beeline toward the Jeep, the rear lights indicating it was in reverse.

"Hey," Mark bellowed, waving his arms over head. "Coach!"

They were close enough for the driver to hear Mark's voice booming the coach's name over and over. But the Jeep pulled forward and turned out of the parking lot.

"What the fuck?" Mark's face was ashen, stricken with fear and anger. "Where is she?"

"I don't know," Adam said, forcing the fear that gripped him out of his voice. His skin prickled with apprehension. He had a bad feeling. "Let's head back inside. Maybe she's with Poppy and Kendall."

The back door was locked, so they jogged around the building to the front. Adam forced himself to believe Frankie was safe. She would be waiting, shifting restlessly from one foot to the other, hands thrust in the kangaroo pocket of her sweatshirt, whining about wanting to go. She had no patience when there was a waffle cone of chocolate fudge caramel swirl only a short drive away.

He prayed the fire in his gut was him overreacting. But he knew the truth without needing confirmation.

Something was wrong.

* * *

Mark tore through the door and into the lobby. Kendall was talking with the ice arena manager. Poppy stood next to her, arms wrapped around her midsection, tears streaming down her face.

Mark grabbed her elbow and turned her toward him. "What's happening? Where's Frankie?"

Poppy shook her head. "I don't know." She pointed at the manager. "He says she's not in the building. Kendall went with him to look in the back where the skates are and the offices, but she wasn't there." The last words were choked out by a sob.

"Did you check the location app?" Adam asked. Like most parents, Mark and Poppy had an app that would tell them where Frankie was—or at least where her phone was.

Poppy nodded, opened the app, and handed the phone to Adam. "It says location services are turned off."

Why would Frankie turn off location settings? Adam handed the phone back to Poppy, that sinking feeling turning into a raging storm of fear and uncertainty.

"She has to be somewhere," Mark said, his hands around Poppy's upper arms. "She can't have just disappeared into thin air."

Adam agreed—at least about the thin-air part. But he knew how easily children disappeared, especially since becoming friends with Kendall. The stories she had told him were the stuff of nightmares.

Mark turned to Adam, anguish etched into his face. "What do we do?"

Kendall stepped away from the manager and joined them. Her eyes were glued to Adam's. As soon as she was close enough, she said, "Call it in."

Adam's heart dropped into his gut, and dread washed over him. He called dispatch to report his niece as a missing child and requested backup at the scene.

Within an hour, the arena was swarming with cops. Saul and Fletch were taking statements from Adam, Kendall, Mark, Poppy, and the manager, Mick Donahue.

Saul joined Kendall and Adam. "Manager swears he didn't see anything unusual but can't recall seeing Frankie leave either."

"Something is definitely off with the coach," Adam said. "It's hard to believe he couldn't hear Mark—or at the very least, see us waving our arms and running towards him. We were practically close enough to bang on his windows."

"Think he could've had her in the vehicle?" Kendall asked.

"I think it's a possibility. I know I don't want to wait until morning to interview him. Care to take a drive to his house with me?"

"Absolutely," Kendall said, pulling her keys from her coat pocket. "Let the others know what we're doing, and I'll pick you up in front."

She jogged to the door and disappeared into the night.

"Where's Kendall going?" Mark asked, a hint of irritation in his tone.

"We're going to take a drive over to the coach's house," Adam said.

"I'm coming with you."

Adam placed a hand against his brother's chest to stop him. "No, you're not."

"Like hell. She's my daughter. I want some answers from that shithead. How could he leave without making sure Frankie was with us?"

"Big brother, I know you're worried, but going after him is not going to help. We need him to talk to us. If you're there, intimidating him, he'll shut down. Then he won't give us anything."

Mark opened his mouth to protest, but Adam raised a hand to silence him. "This is my job, Mark. It's what I do, so let me do it. Take Poppy home in case Frankie or someone else calls. Saul and Fletch will go with you, just in case something weird comes up."

Mark forced air through his nose, his jaw clenched tight, the vein in his neck pulsing. He poked his finger into Adam's chest. "You let me know what that prick says. I want to know what the hell is going on. Understand, little brother?"

"You're my first call."

Adam gave Poppy a quick kiss on the cheek and darted out the door.

With any luck, Frankie would be waiting for them at home, wondering what all the fuss was about.

6

Tuesday night
1:11:34 hours missing

COACH JASON TURNER was a twenty-six-year-old former hockey phenom from the University of Wisconsin who'd had his NHL hopes dashed when he took one too many headers into the boards. Scouts weren't interested in a kid who might have brain damage retiring before making it through his rookie season. Returning home to Colorado, Turner accepted he would never play hockey again, so he did the next best thing and joined the coaching staff of the Colorado Elite Hockey School. He also moonlighted as a Parks & Rec hockey coach for Frankie's team.

Turning off Sheridan Boulevard, Kendall and Adam slowly made their way through the residential area where Turner lived. Many older neighborhoods in Denver were getting facelifts. This was not one of them. And while it was difficult to see the houses in the dark, there was little doubt that Turner's was an eyesore even in this little subdivision. The front stoop had a large crack down the center of the cement slab. A bag of trash sat on the ground just outside the door. Adam told Kendall that the Jeep in the driveway looked like the one he had seen at the rink earlier that night. She pulled in behind it to block it in. Just in case Turner decided he didn't want to talk to them and tried to bolt.

They got out of the SUV and made their way onto the stoop. Kendall knocked on the door and listened for movement inside.

Just as she was poised to knock again, the door swung open. Jason Turner, sweatpants hung low on his hips, beer in hand, stared at the badges Kendall and Adam flashed at him with wide, bloodshot eyes.

Kendall took the lead, since this was in her bailiwick. Adam should've probably recused himself from the investigation, but she knew that wasn't going to happen. She hadn't been able to remove herself from investigating her best friend's death.

"Mr. Turner, Special Agent Kendall Beck, and this is Detective Adam Taylor. We'd like to ask you a few questions."

He leaned out the door and looked out toward the street, then back at Kendall. "What about?"

Kendall placed her foot on the threshold. "Do you mind if we come in?"

"Um . . ." He glanced over his shoulder into his living room. "Sure, come on in."

The room was dark, the only light coming from a single lightbulb in a fixture on the ceiling missing the glass dome covering. Empty beer cans littered the wood pallet table. The sweet scent of pot lingered in the air, almost masking the stench of body odor. Turner snatched something off the table and shoved it in his pocket. Grabbing a T-shirt off the back of the threadbare couch, he pulled it over his head.

Kendall and Adam took seats on the love seat adjacent to the larger couch, and she tried not to wonder what the lump under her left butt cheek was. Some things were better left unknown. There was a metal dining table with two chairs just beyond the couch that Kendall assumed had been procured via a dumpster dive. A door to the left led into a kitchen with an olive-green refrigerator that had to have been original to the house. On an old wooden desk with two drawers missing was an obnoxiously large flat-screen TV. The absurdity of it was not lost on her.

For a twenty-six-year who was probably making decent money, the guy still seemed to live like a frat boy.

"Can you tell us the last time you saw Frankie Taylor?" Kendall asked.

"Why?" Was that a hint of fear mixed with curiosity in his voice? "Has something happened?"

Kendall forced a smile and kept her tone level and patient. "This will go a lot easier and quicker if I can ask the questions and you provide the answers. I promise I will answer your questions as soon as we get through mine."

"Yeah, okay." Turner ran his fingers through his nearly shoulder-length brown hair. "Well, just about an hour ago, I guess. She was at the hockey . . ." He pointed at Adam. "Aren't you her uncle or something?"

"Yes," Adam responded.

"Did you see her leave?" Kendall asked.

"No, I parked in the back lot and left through that door. The players meet their families out front by the concession stand."

Somewhere in the house a faucet was dripping, each droplet making a plopping sound as it hit the sink basin. It was distracting enough that Kendall thought about getting up and turning the faucet off. "Can you recall what she was doing when you saw her last?"

"Uh . . ." Turner's eyes went to the water-stained ceiling. "She was grabbing her bag and heading to the lobby, I think." He looked back at Kendall. "I'm pretty sure, anyway. I didn't really pay attention."

"You don't ensure your players are safely out of the building before you leave?" Adam asked, his tone clipped.

Turner narrowed his eyes and glared at Adam. "I saw her parents there and figured they could probably be trusted to take responsibility for her, especially since the game was over and my job was pretty much done for the night."

Kendall gave Adam a sideways glance, hoping it conveyed that he needed to shut his trap before he screwed everything up. Turner wasn't a suspect. His failure to stop and talk to Adam and Mark in the parking lot did not equate to probable cause in Frankie's disappearance. Turner was under no obligation to answer their questions. And if he got pissed off, he could throw them out. There wasn't enough evidence to initiate a search of the property under exigent circumstances. They needed a warrant, and that had zero chance of happening. At the moment, they didn't have a shred of evidence there was any foul play. Most missing teenagers turned out to be runaways, and the majority of those showed up within a couple of days.

"So you left through the back of the building and into the parking lot," Kendall reiterated, hoping to get Turner's attention back on her and away from Adam. "Then what happened?"

"I got in my Jeep and left," he responded, his tone just north of uncooperative.

"Did you come straight home?" Kendall asked.

"Yes."

"Didn't stop anywhere along the way? Get gas? Run through a drive-through for fast food?"

He rolled his eyes. "No, I came straight here."

"And you haven't left since you got home?"

He leaned forward and rested his forearms on his knees but clenched his hands into fists. "No, I've been right here. In my home. In front of the TV, relaxing with a beer. Is that suddenly a crime?"

Kendall could seriously kick Adam's ass for putting the young guy on the defensive. She was going to have to play especially nice if there was any hope of getting information out of him.

"No, Mr. Turner, it certainly is not," Kendall confirmed, mentally berating Adam. "Before you left the parking lot, did you see or hear anything?"

Turner paused and then shook his head. His leg started bouncing, and his tongue darted out and licked along his lips. "No, I just got in my Jeep and left. There was no one in the lot when I left."

"Were there other cars in the parking lot?"

"Yeah, Mick's car—the rink manager. He was still there, locking up."

Adam shifted next to her, subtly indicating she should follow up with questions about Turner not seeing or hearing him and his brother yelling for the man to stop.

"And you're positive you didn't see or hear anyone in the parking lot. Maybe someone yelling? Or anyone in the lot besides yourself?"

"Positive," Turner said, but then he shrugged. "But I probably wouldn't hear anyone. I usually turn my music up loud when I'm driving. So I wouldn't've have noticed anyone trying to get my attention or anything."

That was interesting. Kendall hadn't said anyone was trying to get his attention. Had he just assumed that by the question? Or had he seen or heard Adam and Mark and intentionally
ignored them? And if that was the case, why? Because he had
Frankie stashed in the back of the Jeep?

"Frankie didn't play much in the first period—and not on
her usual line. Was there a reason for that?" she asked.

"Are you kidding me? You came all the way out here to harass
me about my coaching choices?"

"I can assure you that is not why we are here. Can you answer
my question?"

The leg was bouncing double-time, and he was doing a real
number on his cuticles. "No, just gave Sam a shot at the position."

"Why tonight?" Adam asked, thankfully keeping his tone in
check. "Big game against a tough rival."

Turner took a deep breath. His leg stilled. "I've been catching
some heat from Mr. Farmer about Sam not getting enough ice
time. The man is like a tick burrowing into my ass, so I gave in
and put Sam on the first line."

"How did Frankie feel about that?" Kendall asked.

He snorted. "Not happy."

"Did you let her know what was happening before the game
started?"

Turner paused. His tongue darted out again. "Uh . . ." And
there went the leg back into full bounce mode. "Yeah, I did."

"Was she upset?"

"Of course." He looked at Adam. "Your niece can be a real
ballbuster."

A sly smile crossed Adam's face.

"But I assured her it wouldn't be for the entire game."

"Why were you so sure?"

"Because unlike his dad, I'm quite clear on Sam's talent. He's
an average player at best. There was very little chance he would be
able to keep up with the caliber of play on the first line."

The lightbulb flickered above their heads.

"What do you mean?" Kendall asked.

"Lack of speed, shit stickhandling skills." He tossed his head
back to move the hair from his face. "Okay, I've answered your
questions. Tell me what's going on."

"Frankie Taylor has gone missing. No one has seen her since the conclusion of the game. She never came out of the rink into the lobby, and she is nowhere in the building. All attempts to reach her through her cell phone are going straight to voice mail. And the GPS has been disabled."

"Whoa." Turner raked his hand down his face. Unless he was faking—and Kendall had a better-than-average bullshit detector—the man looked genuinely surprised. And shook. "That's horrible. Is there anything I can do?"

"You can let us take a look around your house," Adam said.

And just like that, Turner shut down. Kendall was definitely going to kick Adam's ass now.

"You got a warrant?" Turner asked.

"No, I just thought you wanted to help." Adam bowed up. "If you have nothing to hide, then there shouldn't be a problem."

"And if you want to look around, you can come back with a warrant." Turner got up and stalked to the door, yanking it open. "Now, if you don't mind, I've had a long day."

Kendall and Adam rose and walked to the door. Kendall fished a business card from her pocket and handed it to Turner. "If you think of anything, no matter how small or insignificant, give me a call."

Turner took the card, shoved it into his pocket without looking at it, and closed the door with a bit more force than was probably necessary.

Kendall turned on Adam, ready to pound him into the ground for fucking up her interview.

"I know, I'm sorry," he said, hands up in surrender. Or self-defense. "But that guy is hiding something."

"And if you would've let me handle it, he may have agreed to let us look around."

Adam exhaled loudly through his nose. His shoulders dropped and he hung his head. Kendall hit the unlock button on her key fob as they walked to the Range Rover, and got in.

"Look, I'm sorry, but this is my niece. And if she's in that house, there's no telling what he's doing to her. I mean, why not let us take a quick look just to get us off his back?"

"Well, judging by the smell of pot when we walked in, it could be that he doesn't want us to find his stash or discover he has an illegal growing operation in his basement." She backed out of the driveway and headed out of the neighborhood. "All I know is we don't have probable cause to obtain a search warrant, and it could be a while before we get one. And he's been tipped off that we suspect him. If Frankie is in there, he now has time to move her."

Adam crossed his arms over his chest and stared out the window.

Kendall hit her hands-free phone button on the steering wheel. "Call Brady."

Her boss answered on the third ring. "This better be good, Beck."

"I have a missing child, twelve years old. Last seen at a hockey game. Parents were waiting for her to meet them in the lobby, but she never came out. I just questioned the girl's hockey coach, and he seemed on edge. At this time, with the information I have, he may be the last person to see her. Refused a consented search of his residence. I'm requesting we place him under surveillance."

"Assigning your own cases now?"

"No, sir," Kendall responded quickly—and reverently. She didn't need another man indignant and pouting because she'd bruised the fragile male ego. "I happened to be at the hockey game. The missing girl is Detective Adam Taylor's niece. As time is of the essence, I decided to question the coach while Denver PD handled questioning other parents at the game and the rink manager. They've also initiated an Amber Alert."

"Has Denver PD requested our help in this matter?"

Kendall glanced over at Adam. "Unofficially."

Brady sighed. "Text me the details, including how to get in touch with Taylor's boss, and I'll have a couple of agents sit on the coach's house. You'll need to brief me and the team in the morning."

"Yes, sir," Kendall said. "Sorry to bother you this late at night."

There was a click on the line.

CHAPTER

7

Tuesday night
2:14:03 hours missing

IT APPEARED ADAM'S entire family was at Mark's house by the time Kendall pulled up in front of the two-story, blue-gray house. She knew Poppy had inherited the house from her grandmother, but Mark had done a lot of work to get it to the modern beauty it was now. It wasn't big, but it was perfect for the three of them.

"Okay, we need to figure out the best way to do this." Kendall said before Adam opened his door.

"What do you mean?"

"I don't think it's appropriate for you to interview your family." Adam rolled his eyes. "There are questions that need to be asked that might make you and your family uncomfortable, which means they won't be forthcoming. Also, there's a very good chance you won't see things you might pick up on if you weren't questioning your family."

Adam's neck and face flushed deep red. "Why don't you just call me incompetent while you're at it, Kendall?"

"Don't play the martyr; you don't wear it well," Kendall said. "Besides, if you step back and think about it, you know I'm right."

"Don't be a bitch," Adam tossed back at her. He knew deep down she was right; she could read it in the way he avoided eye contact. Kendall wouldn't take offense—but if he started to make a practice of it, she had no problem throat punching him to even things up.

"Make you a deal," she said. "You can sit in on the interviews—except for Poppy. We both felt the tension between her and Mark tonight. If there is something going on between them, she won't open up about it in front of you."

He grimaced. "Agreed."

Kendall opened the door and stepped out into the cool spring night air. The sun had set long ago, but the moon lit up the night sky enough for her to see the outline of the Rocky Mountains. She inhaled deeply, hoping the magic of clean mountain air would help her get through the next few hours. These people had become family. But she had a job to do. Better to piss them off now and beg forgiveness after she brought Frankie home.

As soon as Adam opened the front door and they stepped inside, every eye in the living room turned in their direction.

Poppy bolted out of her chair and ran toward them. "Did you find her?"

"No," Adam said, wrapping his arms around her. "Anything from her friends, or other parents who were at the rink tonight?"

"No one remembers seeing her after the game," Mark said. "And she isn't with any of her friends."

"Did you talk to her friends' parents to corroborate that?" Kendall asked.

Mark nodded.

"None of her friends have seen her since school," Poppy said, tears streaming down her face.

"Saul and Fletch went to assist questioning her teammates," Mark said.

Not surprising they'd go in person. Seasoned investigators learned more from body language than spoken words.

Kendall softened her voice and looked directly at Poppy. "Let's find a quiet place to talk."

Poppy wiped the tears from her face, nodded, and headed up the stairs. She pushed open the first door and walked into the room. "We can use my office," she said with a shuddering exhale.

Kendall closed the door and took a seat on the couch across from Poppy. The walls were artfully decorated with black-and-white photos in matching black frames. The pictures showed Frankie at various stages of her life. A few had Mark or Poppy in them, too, but every single one had Frankie.

"Tell me about today, starting from when you woke up."

Poppy's hand went to the base of her neck, her eyebrows furrowed. "What? Why?"

"I know it feels silly, especially because it doesn't seem relevant. But I can assure you, sometimes it's the stuff you find irrelevant or redundant that will be the clue to unlocking everything and getting Frankie back home."

Poppy grabbed a tissue from the box on her desk and blew her nose. "Okay, well, Frankie's alarm was going off, so I went in and had to wake her up."

"Is that typical?"

"Lately, yes, but only the past couple of weeks or so. She's usually really good at getting herself up and ready for school."

"Why do you think she's having issues now?" Kendall asked, taking out her notepad and pen.

Poppy stared at the notepad for a few seconds. Kendall could see the slight shift in the woman's demeanor as it dawned on her she was being questioned by an FBI agent, not a friend.

"I'm not sure. I guess I figured it was puberty kicking in and she was more tired than normal. She's pretty active, so I wasn't really concerned anything was wrong."

"How has she been acting lately? Notice any change in her personality?"

Poppy stared at the wall just behind Kendall and slowly shook her head. "No, not really."

"Does she have a boyfriend or girlfriend?"

She flinched as if the words burned her. "She's twelve, Kendall."

Okay, so even if Frankie had a boyfriend, Poppy was clueless about it. Kendall would make a note of asking Frankie's friends; they'd have better information about any crushes or relationships.

"And there haven't been any issues with friends? School? Could she be getting bullied?"

"She hasn't said anything to me—and I think she would."

Kendall wasn't so sure. Her own mother had been in the dark about a great deal of things Kendall had going on in her preteen life. But perhaps Frankie and Poppy had a different relationship. "Okay, you went in to wake her up. What happened next?"

"I made sure she was out of bed before I left her room. I heard the water running, so I knew she was taking a shower. I got dressed and went downstairs to make coffee before Mark left, but he was already gone."

Kendall made a notation that Mark hadn't said good-bye to Poppy before leaving. Was it more evidence of marital discord? "Did he leave earlier than usual?"

"I'm not sure. I wasn't paying attention."

Kendall made a point of placing her notepad beside her on the couch before asking the next question. "How are things between you and Mark?"

"What?" Poppy asked, crossing her arms over her chest. "What kind of question is that? My marriage has nothing to do with Frankie being missing. How dare you ask that."

Kendall reached forward and placed her hand on Poppy's knee. "I understand your frustration, but it is relevant to the investigation. If Frankie was picking up on any tension between you and Mark, she may have run away and be hiding out at a friend's house." Kendall paused and smiled. "Please know that anything you say to me will remain between the two of us. But I need to know everything, Poppy. Everything. I'm not here to judge you or Mark. I'm here to find Frankie—that is my only goal."

"I'm sorry," Poppy said. She let out a long sigh and waved a dismissive hand in the air. "It just caught me off guard. I'm a little stressed right now, and I'm trying to hold it together. Apparently, I'm not doing a very good job of it."

"You're doing a great job."

Poppy nodded and wiped her nose with her tissue. "It was silly, at any rate, because Mark and I are fine."

Lie.

"No fights or disagreements lately? Nothing Frankie might pick up on and misinterpret as issues between the two of you?"

Poppy kept her eyes averted, balling up the tissue in her hand. "No, things have been great between us."

Big lie.

Why was she lying? Kendall had witnessed—and certainly felt—the chill between the couple earlier in the night. As if they couldn't stand to be around each other. Why was Poppy hell-bent on portraying them as happy and stable?

What was Poppy covering up?

"So, anyway," Poppy said, changing the subject as she dabbed tears from the corner of her eye. "The rest of the morning went fine. Frankie got through with breakfast. I dropped her off at school and came back home."

"What did you do during the day?"

She spread her arms out and glanced at her desk. A stack of files sat in one corner of the desk. "Worked."

Kendall already knew Poppy was a medical transcriptionist, which allowed her to work from home.

"All day?" Kendall asked.

"Until I had to pick Frankie up from school."

"And you didn't leave the house? Didn't run to the grocery store? Pick up dry cleaning?"

Poppy shook her head slowly, staring at the tissue in her hand as if she wasn't sure what it was. "Nope. Was at my desk all day."

There was something just enough off about Poppy to make Kendall wonder if she wasn't getting the truth—or at least not the full story. Which was alarming, given the circumstances. "What time did you pick her up?"

"I left the house at two thirty."

Kendall noted the time on her pad. "What happened when you picked her up?"

"Nothing out of the ordinary. We came home, she had a snack, started on her homework, and watched TV until we had to leave for her piano lesson." She finally looked Kendall in the eye.

"What time did you get home from school and then leave for the piano lesson?"

"It was around three fifteen. And then we left for piano at four forty-five. Her lesson starts at five and is an hour long."

"How was Frankie? Did she seem upset when she got out of school?"

"No, she seemed fine." Poppy was shredding the tissue in her hand. Was she avoiding eye contact with Kendall?

"And you drove her to her piano lesson?"

"Yes."

"Is this at a studio or in someone's house?"

"In a house. Her teacher works at the high school but has a few students she teaches out of her home."

"How long has Frankie been taking piano lessons from her?"

Poppy tossed the shreds of tissue in the trash can and blew a long stream of air out through her mouth. "A couple of years now."

"Was she having any issues with her piano teacher?"

"Not that I know of. She's never said anything to me about having problems with her." She let out a little chuckle. "I imagine Frankie is not a favorite student. She thinks I'm torturing her by making her continue to take lessons."

Kendall smiled. She didn't know Frankie that well, but she knew the girl was interested in sports and loved playing hockey. Just like her dad. "I'll just need the piano teacher's name and contact info."

"Okay."

"What did you do while she was at the piano lesson?"

"I grabbed a coffee at the Starbucks around the corner from her and read a book. Then I picked her up, and we went straight to the rink."

"What time?"

"Her lesson ends at six. It takes about ten, fifteen minutes to get to the rink, so we got there by six fifteen, give or take a minute."

"Did Frankie seem upset when you picked her up?"

Poppy shook her head, shrugging one shoulder. "No, just her normal self."

"Was she apprehensive about going to her game?"

"No, she seemed excited. She's so competitive. Nothing excites her more than checking boys twice her size into the boards."

Kendall couldn't help but smile, eliciting a small smile from Poppy, as well.

"Do you know if she's having any issues with any teammates?" Kendall asked.

"No, but she wouldn't talk to me about that. Mark would know if she was."

"What about her coach—how did she feel about him?"

"She liked him a lot." She pulled another tissue from the box, working it between her fingers.

"Were they close?"

"He's close to all the kids on the team, I think. He's really good with them. I know she really appreciated that he didn't make her sit the bench because she's a girl, so she may have a soft spot for him in that way. But she didn't have a crush on him or anything."

"And you know that? She would've talked to you about things like that?"

"Oh yes." The rapid head nods ensued. "We're very close. Mark is gone a lot—being a firefighter and all—so it's often just the two of us." She cleared her throat. "We're very close," she said again, as if to make the point stick. Kendall just wasn't sure which one of them she was trying to convince.

"I know at the game you indicated you didn't know why Frankie wasn't playing her usual position, but can you speculate?"

Poppy bit her bottom lip while shaking her head from side to side. "I really have no idea. She's been on time for practices and worked hard, as usual. I guess something must have happened after we got there, but I can't for the life of me figure out what it might've been."

"And you didn't see anything?"

"No." She was a bit sheepish. "I support Frankie playing hockey and I'm happy to be a hockey mom and all. But I don't particularly enjoy the sport. I usually read a book during practice and warm-ups or play a word game on my phone. Sometimes I chat with the other parents."

"So you're friendly with the other parents?"

"Yeah. We're around each other so much, we all get along pretty well."

"No issues with anyone?"

She shrugged her shoulder. "Well, Sam Farmer's father is a bit of a hothead—you know, those parents who are a little too into the game. Living vicariously through their kids. He takes it a bit far—yelling at the refs and the coach during the game. Stuff like that. He and Mark got into it one time, but Sam's dad backed down pretty quick. Mark's a big guy, at least bigger than Drew Farmer."

"Did they have a physical fight?"

"No, just a heated exchange of words."

Kendall ran through her notes to see if she had missed anything. A knot grew in her belly. Something seemed off. Poppy's answers were too perfect.

"Okay, I think that's all for right now. Thanks for being so candid with me," Kendall said, but she wasn't sure she believed her own words. Life was not as rosy as Poppy was portraying it. But why would the woman want to lie when her daughter's life potentially hung in the balance? "If you could just get me a list of all her friends, the team roster, and the piano teacher, that would help a lot."

"Of course," Poppy said as they stood and descended the stairs to the living room. Poppy was immediately wrapped in her mother's arms and steered away from the mean FBI agent.

Adam sidled up next to her. "How'd it go?"

Kendall shrugged. "We'll talk about it later. For now, let's see what Mark has to say."

Adam nodded, eyes narrowed. He grabbed his brother and whispered to him. Mark nodded, and the three of them went up the stairs and into Poppy's office and closed the door.

CHAPTER

8

Tuesday night
2:49:28 hours missing

Adam closed the door to Poppy's office. There was a tranquility to the room. It was soft and feminine, like Poppy, with its cozy couch and fluffy throw pillows. And it always smelled of gardenias, Poppy's favorite flower. It was comforting even in the midst of the fear consuming him.

One glance at Kendall with her *Keep your mouth shut or I will kill you* look on her face irritated him but also shamed him. He knew he'd blown a perfect opportunity to search Turner's house for Frankie. And Kendall was telling him in no uncertain terms that she wouldn't allow him to fuck this interview up too.

Adam gave her a quick nod to say he understood the rules and took a seat on the opposite end of the couch from her. Truth was, Kendall sometimes scared the shit out of him, and he wasn't altogether sure she wouldn't come out on top if they ever had a physical altercation. She had a reputation in her unit for having a quick temper and a killer uppercut.

Mark sat in the desk chair, his shoulders slouched, the weight of the world nearly crushing him. He'd aged ten years since they'd first discovered Frankie missing a few hours earlier. His daughter was his world. His little girl. His sidekick. His mini-me. And Adam knew this was ripping the man's heart to shreds. After all, he was her father and had vowed to protect her from every evil in the world only moments after she entered it.

"Mark," Kendall said, "I know this is hard—just sitting around waiting for something to happen. And I know you would much prefer to be out looking for Frankie, but the best thing you can do is help me coordinate a search. What we don't want to do is to waste time, and once I get all the info, we can make a plan that optimizes our efforts to find Frankie and get her home safely."

Damn, she was good. Kendall was brilliant at knowing exactly what to say to people to get them talking. She had read his brother perfectly. Mark was a man of action. He led by example. If there was a job to be done, he did it. And his number-one priority at the moment was to find Frankie. Sitting on his ass was not something he did very well in the best of times. But pitching in and actively searching for Frankie—he could do that. Being told to wait was not something he was apt to handle for long.

Elbows on knees, wringing his hands together, Mark nodded his understanding.

"Tell me how the day started, from the moment you got up."

He glanced up at the ceiling. "I woke at six, as usual, and left for work at seven."

"Did you see Frankie before you left?"

"No, she was still in bed. Poppy was irritated with her for not getting up on time and was yelling at her to get out of bed and get ready for school."

"So you saw Poppy this morning before you left?" Kendall asked, a slight hint of surprise in her voice. Adam tucked that note away in his memory to ask about later.

"Yeah, but we didn't really talk. I needed to head out to work, so I grabbed coffee and left. I figured I would talk to her later in the day."

"And did you talk to her later?"

He wrinkled his eyebrows, hands clenching into fists and releasing. "I tried calling her a couple of times, but she didn't answer."

Kendall's eyes narrowed slightly. Adam had seen that look before. She was trying to work something out in her head. "Is that unusual—for her not to answer?"

"Not really, if she's in the middle of transcribing something. But she always calls me back when she takes a break."

"And she didn't today?"

"Not until she was on her way to the hockey game. Which didn't help, because I was at home waiting for her to swing by and get me so we could go to the game together."

With a tilt of her head, Kendall asked, "Was that the usual routine?"

"The usual routine," Mark said, with a tinge of exasperation in his tone, "was for Poppy to swing back to the house while Frankie was at piano, then we would all go together to the game."

That explained why Mark had come separately, and why he was in a foul mood when he got there, barely acknowledging Poppy.

"Did she give you any reason why she hadn't returned your calls? Or had changed the routine?"

"I haven't asked her about it." He dropped his head. "All of this seemed to make it less important."

Adam knew Kendall probably didn't feel the same way, and he agreed there could be something there.

"Have you noticed any changes in Frankie?"

He inhaled deeply through his nose and raised his eyebrows. "She and Poppy seem to be going through some mother-daughter growing pains lately. A little more testy with each other than usual. More fights between them."

"What are the fights about?"

"I'm not sure. Poppy tells me not to worry about it—she went through this with her mother when she was growing up. Normal girl hormones, becoming a teenager."

"Makes sense," Kendall said. "Do you know if Frankie was having any issues with her teammates?"

"No. I mean, one kid was bitter about her taking his spot, but I got the feeling he didn't say anything to her, just talked about her behind her back."

"Did that bother her?"

A hint of a smile graced Mark's lips. "Didn't seem to. She thought it was funny because all the other guys on the team were happy she was playing."

"And this is Sam Farmer we're talking about?"

He nodded. "Yeah."

"I heard you and his father had an incident."

When did this happen? It was odd Mark hadn't told Adam about it.

"That was nothing—Farmer can be an asshole and takes shit too far sometimes, but he's all right. A little overexuberant about the game and thinks a bit higher of his kid's talent on the ice— but that's normal."

"So, no lasting animosity between the two of you?"

Mark shook his head. "Not on my part."

Kendall set her notepad aside and leaned in, clasping her hands together. "Okay, I need for you to be completely honest with me—I promise nothing you say will go any farther than this room. Are you and Poppy having any issues?"

Mark exhaled, raked his hand down his face, and looked back and forth between Kendall and Adam. "I think she might be having an affair."

Boom.

Shock burst through Adam's veins, kicking up his heart rate before lighting a fire in his gut. His mouth went dry. The absolute last thing he'd expected Mark to say was that Poppy was cheating on him. Adam never would've thought it possible. And his heart physically ached for his brother.

"Why do you think that?" Kendall asked, as if she'd already suspected.

Mark rubbed his hands along his jeans. "Up front, I want to say I can't prove anything. It's just a feeling."

Kendall nodded.

He released another long exhale, buying time. This had to be hard for him to admit. "She leaves during the day and lies about it."

Kendall scrunched her eyebrows together. "How do you know?"

"I'm not proud of it, but I check the mileage on her Explorer. There are more miles on there than usual. A lot more miles. Like she's going to the other side of Denver or something."

"Could she be going to visit her mother?" Adam asked.

Pain filled Mark's eyes as he peered at Adam. "Maybe, but why lie about it? I don't care if she goes back home. There is absolutely no reason to cover that up."

"And you don't think it could be running errands or anything like that?" Kendall asked.

"No, too many miles for just running errands."

"How many miles?"

He shrugged. "Varies, but around a hundred and twenty to a hundred and fifty miles are being added almost every week."

That was a lot of miles. Especially for someone whose farthest destination was usually ten miles away at most.

"Have you asked her about the extra miles?" Kendall asked.

Mark dropped his gaze again. "No."

"Why not?" Adam asked, not disguising his shock.

"I'm not sure I want to know. Right now, it's just speculation." He trailed off. Adam got it. If it was true, and confirmed, their lives would be changed forever. Possibly destroyed. And his big brother was desperate to avoid dealing with his dream life shattering into a million pieces. He wanted the picture-perfect family to remain intact, even if it was a lie.

"What made you decide to start checking her mileage?" Kendall asked.

"She's been very . . . edgy lately. Quick-tempered. Easily aggravated with me over small stuff. Some days she avoids me completely—like today. Other days it just feels like she's holding back." He took in a deep breath and exhaled. "And she's very secretive with her phone—when she never has been in the past. Suddenly, she's never without it."

"So you haven't been able to check to see if there are any odd calls or text messages?" Adam asked.

"No. She hides it from me." Mark scowled.

Kendall leaned forward with her elbows resting on her knees. "How is your relationship with Frankie?"

"Good." He smiled one of those proud-dad smiles Adam had seen a million times. "She doesn't seem to be having the preteen angst towards me that she has with her mother."

"Would she talk to you if she was having a problem?"

"I think so."

"Have you asked her about what's going on between her and her mother?"

"Yeah, but she just shrugs."

So that would be a no. Frankie did not talk to her father about her problems. That surprised Adam.

"Mark, I want you to really take a moment to think about this next question," Kendall said.

Mark nodded.

"Do you think Poppy could harm Frankie?"

He inhaled deeply through his nose, his lips pressed together, and slowly exhaled. "If you had asked me a couple of months ago, I would've said you were off your rocker—and I really doubt Poppy would ever hurt Frankie. But she is so different lately. I guess I'm just not one hundred percent sure what Poppy is capable of these days."

CHAPTER

9

Wednesday morning
9:30:43 hours missing

KENDALL TOOK A seat next to Jake and tossed a file onto the large conference table.

"So"—Jake leaned close and whispered—"there aren't enough missing children in Denver for us to search for; you had to make your friend's niece disappear to give yourself something to do on a Tuesday night?"

Kendall gave him a sideways glance.

"I'm just saying, if you're looking for excitement to fill your lonely nights, there are special toys you can buy to help with any sexual frustrations you may be experiencing."

"If you don't shut up, I'll use my vanishing powers against you and make you disappear. The only difference is, I won't look for you."

"No, the only difference is I'm not a child."

Kendall snorted. "Highly debatable. You still eat Cocoa Puffs for breakfast and play with little Star Wars men."

Jake scowled and raised a finger. "First, Cocoa Puffs are delicious, so fuck off." Another finger went up, as if Kendall didn't understand the ordering scheme. "Second, I do not play with the Star Wars figures—I collect them. And someday I will sell them for millions of dollars and buy an island in the Caribbean, and you are not invited to visit."

"Is that day coming soon?" Kendall asked, crossing her fingers and mouthing *please*.

"Just for that, I'm not giving you the jelly donut I brought for you. Instead, I'm going to offer it to Willis." He pointed to a rather rotund man across from them who should've retired from the Bureau about a hundred years ago and always managed to slop food down the front of his shirt. "And then you will have to spend the entire morning looking at the jelly that could've been yours displayed proudly on his tie, taunting you."

"Give me the jelly or I will shoot you where you sit." She was only half kidding. Kendall loved a good jelly donut. Raspberry was her favorite, but this morning she wasn't picky.

Their boss, Agent in Charge Jonathan Brady, walked into the room, and everyone went silent. Jake slid the napkin-wrapped jelly donut toward Kendall. Inhaling it would have to wait until after the briefing. Which pissed her off a little, because if Jake had given it to her when she first sat down, she could've had it polished off by now. Been happy and full, with a decent amount of powdered sugar and raspberry filling surging through her veins.

"Okay, listen up," Brady said, taking command of the room. "We have a twelve-year-old missing child from Berkely Ice Arena following her hockey game last night. Beck is going to brief us on the case so far. Pay attention. The MC is the niece of Detective Adam Taylor of the Denver PD, so this is personal. We will also be working in tandem with the Denver PD on this investigation. Beck is the lead on our end and a liaison between the agencies."

A low murmur filled the room. Many had met Adam—or at least knew of him—when he'd saved Kendall after she'd been beaten by The Reaper, a serial killer who had plagued the city for years. Kendall had shot and killed the man, but she'd been in pretty bad shape when Adam found her locked in a secret basement room.

"Beck," Brady said by way of introduction, turning the floor over to her. Kendall grabbed the file from the table and walked to the front. She taped Frankie's picture to the whiteboard, grabbed a black Expo marker, and wrote the girl's name under a picture, followed by her parents' names.

"Twelve-year-old Francesca 'Frankie' Taylor played a hockey game last night at Berkely Ice Arena. Her parents were waiting in the lobby for her following the game while she got changed out of her hockey gear. After a considerable amount of time went by and nearly all the other parents had left with their children and the arena manager was getting ready to lock up for the night, Frankie's father, Mark Taylor, and his brother, Detective Adam Taylor, went in search of her. Her mother, Poppy Taylor, and I searched the lobby, and the front parking lot. We questioned parents who were still there, along with their children—Frankie's teammates—to see if any of them had seen Frankie or knew if she had perhaps left with another family. No one remembered seeing the girl after the game or anything unusual."

Kendall wrote the name of the coach on the whiteboard. "The last known person to see Frankie was her coach, Jason Turner. I questioned Turner at his home last night, but he claims not to have seen Frankie following the game. He also admitted he did not ensure she had been picked up before he left. Furthermore, he stated he had not seen or heard Mark and Adam trying to get his attention as he drove away from the parking lot. I asked Turner if he would allow me to search his home, but he refused. At this time, we do not have probable cause to obtain a search warrant. According to agents who were sitting on the house last night, Turner was home all night and did not leave until this morning, when he drove to his day job at the Colorado Elite Hockey School, where he is also a coach. The agents tried to look in the windows at Turner's home, but what they could see was not unusual."

Brady held up his hand. "Who has the update on the Turner surveillance?"

Calvin Charles spoke up. "That's me. We got to Turner's about twenty-two thirty. Confirmed he was in the house—appeared to be alone. Approximately oh-thirty the interior house lights went out along with the front porch light. Presumably he went to bed. Callie made a trip around the perimeter of the house. Couldn't see in the windows—too dark—and didn't hear any noises from inside."

Callie, a slight redhead who had enough attitude to make up for her size and scared more than a few agents in the Bureau, picked up the report. "Everything was quiet when we turned the watch party over to Benson and Handley at five thirty. I checked in with them about"—she checked her watch—"fifteen minutes ago. Once there was light, Benson took a quick look around the exterior. Again, nothing of interest inside. No noises. Turner left the house approximately six, hit the drive-through at McDonald's, and drove to Colorado Elite Hockey and remains there."

Agents started tossing out thoughts. "The kid could still be there—if we're thinking he took her."

"Not enough for a search warrant," Kendall said.

"What else?" Brady asked.

"Can't rule out that she ran away," another agent said.

"It is a possibility," Kendall confirmed. "There are some issues between the parents. If she caught on, she could've run."

"Is this a ransom situation?" Willis asked.

Kendall gave a one-shoulder shrug. "It seems doubtful, since there hasn't been a ransom demand yet, but still a possibility."

"Are the parents wealthy?" another agent asked.

"Middle class—father is a firefighter, wife is a medical transcriptionist. Own their home outright, but we are still checking finances. It doesn't appear, at this time, there is a monetary motive. But, as I said, it can't be ruled out."

"Willis, you take point at the Taylor home in case there is a ransom call. Set up recording and talk to the family about how to answer any calls that come in. Beck, inform the family." Brady pointed at two agents sitting across from him. "Check the usual runaway haunts for our MC. I want updates regularly so we can keep the flow of information moving. Let's go find our girl."

10

THE HOMICIDE FLOOR of the Denver Police Department was like its own little world—ringing phones, fingers tapping on keyboards, the chatter of detectives sharing stories of the one that got away. Adam dumped his light jacket on the collection chair—so named because no one ever sat in it; it was there to collect all the shit Adam piled on it. Sticky notes covered his computer monitor. He pulled them off one at a time and determined which pile they went in: action required, trash, or payback. Payback was usually in response to an inappropriate drawing. Today's gem was a stick figure drawing depicting Adam with a limp dick and a sad face.

Fletch popped his head around the fabric dividing wall.

"From you?" Adam asked, holding up the dirty sticky note.

A shit-eating grin was his answer. "Burrows wanted to give you tits, but I thought that was too much."

Adam wasn't sure if he should thank him or be offended.

"The big man sent me over to retrieve you."

"What for?"

"I am but a lowly messenger," Fletch said, and walked away.

A cold sweat broke out over Adam's skin. He hated having to talk to his boss first thing in the morning. It usually meant the rest of the day was going to be shit. Inhale—*one, two, three, four, five*—exhale. Adam knocked on the doorframe.

"You're off the case, Taylor."

Lieutenant Dale Underwood did little more than glance at Adam before returning his attention to his computer screen.

Adam froze. He knew what case the boss meant.

"Lou, I can handle it."

"Nope, you're too close. I can't have you going off half-cocked and fucking shit up beyond repair. And before you make some lame-ass attempt at promising me you won't, save it. I don't have time for groveling or knob-polishing this morning. Budgets are due."

Budget deadlines to the boss were tantamount to having bamboo thrust under his fingernails.

"Then can I request Saul take the lead but keep the investigation within my team?" Adam asked.

Lou gave him a frustrated scowl.

"I promise I will only be there to provide information and guidance—when it is warranted."

Lou typed furiously on his computer. At any moment the machine was bound to start smoking and combust.

Finally, Lou stopped typing and fixed his gaze on the keyboard in front of him, releasing a heavy sigh. "Fine, the double homicide at the c-store is your top priority. Understand? And if I hear you're pushing Saul out of the lead and taking over, I will have you transferred out of here and back to traffic cop by the end of the week. Are we clear?"

"Yes, sir," Adam said, and left the office. He knew better than to thank the man. Get the answer and get out before pissing the big man off and getting the olive branch snatched away.

All in all, that had gone better than Adam had expected. Other scenarios had involved way more humiliation.

He entered the war room—the conference room where the team would meet to discuss and strategize his niece's case. Frankie's picture was up on the whiteboard, like the photos of so many victims before her.

Victim.

It was virtually impossible for him to conceive of having to place his niece in that category.

Above her picture, in the left-hand corner, was a crudely drawn box with *60* written inside it in red marker.

Frankie had already been missing for twelve hours. If they didn't find her in the next sixty hours, chances were good that either they wouldn't find her at all or, if they did . . .

Adam wouldn't let his mind go there. Maybe Lou was right: he was too close to this case. Any other child and he would've already been stating to his team that they were behind the eight ball. He would be mentally preparing to search for a body and not a child. And he wouldn't've thought twice about it.

All that was changing now.

Saul was sitting at the conference table, shuffling through papers. Fletch had his nose in his laptop. Neither acknowledged Adam as he came into the room and took a seat.

"What did Lou say?" Saul asked, still attending to his sorting task.

"We have the case," Adam said. "You have the lead, Saul. I'm an adviser."

Kendall entered the room, dropped her bag on the floor next to a chair, and pushed a carrier of Dunkin' coffee into the center of the table along with a bag of donuts. "Sorry I'm late. I had to brief my team."

Adam glanced at his watch. "Already? It's only eight in the morning."

"We feds like to get an early start. Very little need for sleeping in. Too many criminals, so little time."

Saul grabbed a coffee and tipped it toward Kendall. "Welcome back, Kendall. Looking forward to working with you again. We are open to all advice and suggestions." He took a sip of coffee. "And thank you for the coffee. It is much appreciated."

Adam wrinkled his nose. Saul was such an ass-kisser. Adam was sure the man had a secret crush on Kendall—the dirty old fart.

Fletch grabbed for the bag of donuts and pulled out a jelly donut, which Kendall promptly snatched out of his hand without apology. Fletch barely noticed, reaching again into the bag and pulling out two cinnamon sugar twists. He shoved an entire twist into his mouth.

Saul shook his head at Fletch. "Okay, Fletch, brief us on what you know so far."

He chewed and swallowed, and it was a miracle he didn't choke. "Overnight, we had officers canvassing the area around the rink. As you know, there are no houses or businesses close by, since the rink sits in the middle of the park. But they did knock on doors within a two-block radius. So far, nothing of interest. They will be widening the search this morning."

Saul continued the brief. "We were able to get video from the two stores that were open overnight: Walmart and the Kum & Go station—"

Fletch snickered and opened his mouth to no doubt make his standard crude comment. Saul pointed his finger at him. "If you value your life—"

Fletch flashed a shit-eating grin, shoved the other twist in his mouth, and raised his hands in surrender. "The IT geeks are doing their voodoo to clean up the video from the gas station. There are a few other businesses in the area we can visit today and see if they have security on the outsides of the buildings we can take a look at."

Kendall brushed powdered sugar off her blouse. "It's amazing to me that, in this day and age, there are businesses that still don't have CCTV. I mean, take the ice arena; there are so many kids around there on a daily basis. Why haven't they invested in *any* cameras?"

"I'm guessing that's in the works now," Saul said. "Reactionary security—great business model."

Fletch used the back of his hand to wipe sugar residue from his mouth and chin. "Uniforms did a cursory Q and A of the teammates and parents—nothing much there. Have a list of vehicles they were driving last night along with any others they own. Everyone let the officers look inside. Nothing stood out as abnormal or out of place. No obvious blood, but it was dark, so—"

Fletch took a swig of coffee before continuing. "Which brings us to the Farmers, who own a silver 2005 Toyota RAV4, which was not at the house when the officers asked to see it. According to Mr. Farmer, their teenage son took the vehicle to visit some friends. When asked if they could get an address for the friend, Farmer claimed he wasn't sure which friend the boy was visiting or how long he would be gone. Didn't seem very interested in asking the kid to bring the vehicle back, so there may be something there."

Strange. "How old is the son?" Adam asked.

Fletch searched his notes. "Just turned sixteen."

"And he's out visiting a friend that late? On a school night?" Kendall wrinkled her nose. "Some people's parents."

"A few of the teammates mentioned young Samuel Farmer is not a fan of letting girls play on the team, an opinion his father shares or, more than likely, encourages. When questioned, both Farmers said they hadn't seen Frankie before they left the rink, and that was pretty much it." Fletch rubbed his hands together, then wiped them on his pants. A stack of napkins sat six inches from his right elbow, untouched.

"Anything on her cell phone?" Adam asked. In most instances, even if the phone was turned off, the phone company could locate the general area where it was by tracking the cell tower pings.

"Nothing yet," Saul said. "We were able to get a warrant, so hopefully the cell phone company will shake a leg and send the full log to forensics."

"Should probably get warrants for Poppy's and Mark's phones," Kendall said.

"Could you add a request for Ashley Collins and . . . have we figured out our unlucky c-store robber's name?"

Saul pulled a folder from the bottom of his pile and flipped through it. "Darin Stevens."

"And him," Adam added, pointing to Fletch.

Fletch chuckled. "Still afraid of Sheri?"

Adam's ex. "The woman is scary."

"No worries, man; I'll submit the request. She likes me."

Not surprising. Sheri liked just about everyone except Adam.

"Additionally," Saul interjected in his scolding-dad voice, "the computer, laptop, and Frankie's iPad from your brother's home are all getting the once-over."

"Has anyone checked Frankie's social media?" Kendall asked.

Adam said, "I looked at her Facebook page last night and again this morning. Nothing new for a couple of months."

Kendall and Fletch looked at him as if he had three heads. "What?"

"Kids don't use Facebook, grandpa," Fletch said.

"Easy with disparaging grandparents," Saul said.

Adam was lost. "What do they use?"

"Instagram," Kendall said.

"Snapchat," Fletch added.

"TikTok," Saul said, and every eye went to him. He shrugged. "I'm a hip grandpa."

Adam felt seriously out of touch.

"Let's get someone on that too," he said. Saul nodded.

"If I could make a suggestion?" Kendall asked, looking at Saul. Adam knew she was trying not to step on any toes.

"I will defer to you, Agent Beck," Saul said, looking slightly relieved he didn't have to carry the entire burden of finding Adam's niece on his shoulders. "You are the expert in missing children cases."

Kendall gave Saul a megawatt smile. Adam wanted to gag.

"Let's have a mix of my team and yours go back and reinterview the parents and teammates—we may get more from them if trained investigators are asking the questions instead of uniformed cops. It's not a slight on the uniforms, just a mindset people have. There's an element of stepped-up importance when badges in suits show up on the doorstep. I have a team of five at your disposal. I'll provide contact info for them and let them know you're the lead."

A knock sounded behind her. Everyone turned their attention to the cop standing in the doorway.

"Sorry to bother you, Detective Taylor," Officer Caleb Young said, "but dispatch just got a call from a truck stop on north I-25. A cashier saw the Amber Alert flyer we faxed out and believes the missing girl you're looking for is there with a middle-aged white male."

Adam's heart took off like a racehorse out of the gate. Adrenaline surged through his veins. It took every ounce of self-control he possessed to stay calm. He wanted to get to the truck stop, wrap his arms around his niece, and never let her go. He wanted to call Mark and Poppy and let them know they could breathe again. He closed his eyes and slowly inhaled. He had to remain calm. When he opened his eyes, Kendall was staring at him, her eyebrows raised.

"Did they get the name of the cashier?" Saul asked.

"Yes." Young started to hand the paper to Adam, but Fletch intercepted it.

"Well, lookee here—the dude is apparently driving a silver Toyota RAV4." Fletch thrust a finger in Saul's direction. "I knew there was something sketch about that Farmer dude."

"Easy, Sherlock," Saul said, fixing his tie and tossing his coffee cup into the trash. "This might be nothing."

And just like that, warmth spread throughout Adam's chest, releasing tension he felt everywhere in his body. He was taking Fletch's side on this one. He had a feeling—a good feeling—this was his niece. He was going to be able to take her home and deliver her to her parents. Tears of joy would replace the pain that had been so rampant in the family since the previous night.

"Get in touch with the cashier, Fletch," Kendall said, not batting an eye at taking over the case. She already had her bag on her shoulder, keys in hand. "See if we can determine where the girl and the man are in the truck stop. Also, make sure she calls you if they start to leave."

Saul ended a call he was on. "I have a marked car on the way there. He knows to hang back and watch the vehicle from a safe distance."

"Great, let's go." Kendall pointed at Adam. "You're with me."

"I'll drive," Fletch said to Saul.

"Like hell. I want to arrive there in one piece," Saul responded, pulling his keys from his pocket.

Once in the SUV, Kendall headed for the ramp onto I-25 north, Saul and Fletch close behind. "You need to cool your jets, Adam."

"I'm cool," he said, unable to temper the elation in his voice.

"You're not." Kendall glanced at his bouncing knee. Adam placed his hand over his traitorous kneecap to force his leg to stay still.

"I saw that look in your eyes back there when you heard the news—you've already convinced yourself it's Frankie. And you need to stop. Right now. I need your head in the game, Adam. Whatever this is, I need for you to be a seasoned detective, not a member of the family who's going to go in, running wild, and get us all busted. That's not going to help Frankie."

He clenched his jaw so tight it was painful.

"I don't need a lecture on professionalism, Kendall. I can handle myself."

He didn't need this—didn't need her and her sanctimonious FBI arrogance telling him how to do his job. He needed her to shut up and drive. Frankie might be in danger, and she was going to lecture him on staying in his lane?

"Like you did last night with the coach?"

Adam inhaled noisily through his nose. His body twitched with rage. And recognition.

Fuck. He hated when she was right. A golden opportunity to search Turner's house for his niece had been pissed away. As it stood, they still had no idea if Frankie was stowed away at her coach's place and were no closer to getting a search warrant if this current venture turned out to be a wild-goose chase.

He released his breath. "My shit's stored," he promised her.

Kendall hit the hands-free button. "Call Saul."

After three rings, Saul's gruff voice came through the speakers. "Chapman."

"Saul, it's Kendall. I think we should have the four of us—you, me, Adam, and Fletch—go in and have a look around. Fletch, talk to the cashier, get an idea of where they are, and make sure she isn't obvious about it. We don't need him tipped off. I need you both to take an exit so they can't leave without us knowing. We're already going to be conspicuous."

Adam hadn't thought about that. People stopping at a truck stop were either truckers or, at this time of the year, families on spring-break vacations. Not people in business suits. Massive law enforcement tip-off.

"Let's be careful. I don't want the girl to get hurt, or anyone at the truck stop," Adam said.

Kendall ended the call and took the exit ramp, pulling into the parking lot of the truck stop. She drove slowly, each of them searching row after row of vehicles, looking for the silver RAV4.

Adam pointed out the front window. "There it is. One row over, fifth car in."

Kendall pulled into a spot three away from the Toyota on the opposite row.

Adam wished he could leave his jacket in the SUV, roll up his sleeves, and try to look less like a cop. But the gun holstered to his belt was more of a giveaway than the jacket.

"You ready for this?" Kendall asked.

"Let's see what's up," Adam said, glancing at the truck stop over his shoulder. "Maybe we can save a girl today."

CHAPTER

11

Wednesday morning
12:37:32 hours missing

THE GLASS DOORS slid open, and Adam was assaulted by the
sights, sounds, and smells of the bustling oversized convenience store—the buzz of people milling about, kids begging
their parents for sweet treats, large cups of coffee being filled.
Rows of everything from snacks to overpriced canned goods to
pain relievers and baby wipes lined the shelves. A woman passed
in front of them, a harried look on her face, arms loaded with
chips and chocolate bars and beef sticks and bottles of water held
precariously in place between her elbow and chest.

Adam caught sight of Fletch at the checkout counter talking
to an older woman in a red shirt with the truck stop logo on the
chest. Her brunette hair was long and frizzy, her nails painted hot
pink. She was pointing toward another part of the store.

Adam's phone buzzed with an incoming text. He pulled the
phone from his pocket at the same time Kendall glanced at her
screen.

Fletch had sent a text to the group. *Last seen in food court.*

The walk through the store felt like walking on a conveyer
belt the wrong way. Staying a few steps behind Kendall was the
only way Adam could keep from breaking into a run to find out
if his niece was there.

The food court was busy with young families getting break-fast as they set out on their spring-break destinations. Trying to be inconspicuous while looking through the throngs of people was nearly impossible. Adam settled on the idea that people would just think he was looking for a table, even though he had no food. At this point, it didn't much matter. He was intent on finding his niece. There was no other outcome.

He caught Kendall's eye on the opposite side of the food court, but she shook her head.

Damn! Where could they have gone?

His phone pinged with an incoming text from Kendall. *Check the restrooms.*

He saw she was headed toward the women's restroom as he moved toward the men's room. The pungent odors of urine and sweat assaulted him as he shouldered open the door. Men stood with their backs to him, legs apart, no one looking any-where but at the streams coming from between their legs. It was a well-known fact that talking at the urinal could result in an ass whooping. The second rule of urinal etiquette: keep a urinal between you and the next guy.

It was unlikely a guy could bring a young girl in here with the amount of men milling between the toilets and the showers, but that didn't mean the man didn't have her locked in a stall, hop-ing anyone who observed them would mind their own business.

Just as Adam was about to pound on the first closed stall door, he heard his name being called.

"Adam!" Kendall hollered.

All eyes at the urinal turned toward him as he crossed to the restroom door. A few of the men snickered at him. One said, "Adam," in a high-pitched voice. "Mommy's calling you, Adam."

Adam considered flipping him the bird but didn't think get-ting his face shoved into a filthy urinal by the 350-pound man would benefit anyone, especially him. He pushed through the door and breathed in the fresh deep-fried aroma of the food court.

"Fletch called." Kendall had started running through the food court. "They're on the move."

"How? We had exits covered!"

"Food court has exits."

Damn . . . hadn't thought of that. But then they hadn't had any time to properly plan this operation.

Adam broke into as much of a run as he could without plowing down customers in his way. They pushed the throngs of people out of their way, getting glares from most, and slipped through the sliding doors as they opened. Adam caught sight of a man with a young girl heading toward where Kendall had parked. They both burst into a full-out run through the parking lot toward the pair. A man burst past Adam, tall, lanky, and fast.

Fletch.

Kendall broke off to the left, the Range Rover beeping as she unlocked the doors remotely. He watched as she jumped behind the driver's wheel, the engine roaring to life. The man caught sight of all the excitement, yanked open the passenger side door to the RAV4, and forced the girl inside. Slamming the door, he rushed to the driver's side. Within a few seconds he had the car in gear and was driving toward the exit. They were too far away for Adam to determine whether the girl was his niece. The hair had been the right color. Possibly the size and build. But he hadn't seen her face. And now it was too late to get a look.

Saul was coming up behind him, out of breath, barking out orders into his walkie-talkie to the marked police cars. "Get the son-of-bitch before he gets on the interstate."

Adam's breath caught and his chest seized. Visions of the car entering the heavy morning commuter traffic and evading capture assaulted him. Bending at the waist, a full-on panic attack ensuing, he tried to get his breathing under control and his heart to stop beating out of his chest. He'd been a hairsbreadth away from potentially rescuing his niece, and she was slipping through his fingers.

And there was nothing he could do to stop it.

12

Wednesday morning
12:52:10 hours missing

K ENDALL THREW THE SUV into reverse, flipped on her emergency blinkers, and joined the chase for the vehicle getting
way too close to the interstate. That couldn't happen. Kendall
sat on her horn as she flew past the entrance to the store, hoping
to hell no one would step out in front of her. This was extremely
dangerous, considering how many people were at the truck stop,
but there was no other choice. A police chase on the interstate
could result in fatalities—including that of the little girl she was
trying save.

And Kendall had no doubt the girl needed saving. Why else
would the man have taken off so quickly? If there was nothing nefarious going on, he wouldn't have run. In fact, he probably would've assumed they were after someone else and looked
around for who was in trouble. That's what people who were
doing nothing wrong typically did.

This guy had not.

The man's car was racing toward the entrance ramp on the
opposite side of the parking lot from Kendall. She floored the
SUV and charged toward the ramp without looking at the speed-
ometer. Ignorance was often the smarter course of action in times
like this, and offered plausible deniability when she caught hell

from her boss and the highway patrol for her reckless behavior. Better to beg for forgiveness than err on the side of caution.

She made it to the ramp just ahead of the Toyota. The RAV4 flew in front of her vehicle wrenching violently to the left, nearly tipping the vehicle over. Kendall was forced to slam on her brakes to avoid hitting it. The man got his vehicle under control and made a break for the interstate.

No fucking way was this pissant going to get away from her. Kendall pressed the gas pedal to the floor, the V-8 engine catapulting her forward.

Blue and red lights flashed in her rearview mirror. Kendall glanced up and saw three marked cars coming up behind her fast. The end of the ramp was too near. If she had any chance of preventing him from entering the interstate, she had to make her move.

Getting as close to the rear end of the RAV4 as she possibly could, she swung to the right and passed the vehicle. Once she was ahead of the Toyota, she slammed on the brakes and wrenched the steering wheel to the left as hard as she could. The Range Rover came to a stop across the road, offering no chance for the other vehicle to get past her.

The Toyota's nose dipped dramatically as the man slammed on the brakes. She released the seat belt and braced for impact. If she was T-boned at this speed, there was no way of getting out through the driver's door. It would be jammed shut. She readied herself to climb over the center console and get out through the passenger side.

The Toyota skidded to a stop just short of hitting the Range Rover. Kendall threw open the door, yanked her Glock from the holster, and jumped out of the vehicle. As soon as her feet hit the ground, she saw the marked cars block the vehicle from behind, the cops exiting their vehicles as soon as they came to a stop.

The driver's door of the RAV4 flew open and the man took off toward the ditch separating the road from the interstate.

"Shit!" Kendall reholstered her gun and took off after the man. He lumbered—probably the first time he'd run in a few years—and Kendall quickly gained on him. Pumping his arms, he got to the edge of the ditch and pushed off the ground to jump it. He seriously underestimated his speed and landed at the bottom of the ditch. Groaning, he rolled onto his hands and knees and tried clawing his way up the opposite side.

Kendall leapt on top of him, landing with her knee in his lower back. She flattened him against the weeds and rocks, a loud grunt erupting from his lungs as all the air was released.

Kendall wrenched his arm back, slapping handcuffs on his wrist while reaching for the other arm. The man flailed underneath her. His hips bucked in an attempt to knock her off of him, his legs kicking as if he were butterflying to the finish line.

"Keep still, asshole, or I'll let the very trigger-happy cops behind me shoot you where you lie."

"Fuck you," he forced out as he tried to turn his head to the side.

"Is that the best you have?" Kendall asked. "I was hoping for something a little more original, perhaps with some color to it." She leaned in close to his ear. "If I were you, I'd save the sweet talk for your cellmate. I hear they love to make men like you— who kidnap little girls—squeal like a pig as they claim you as their bitch."

"I didn't kidnap nobody," he sneered.

"We'll see if the girl in your car has the same story."

She rolled off him and allowed a uniformed cop to lift the man to his feet and drag him to a patrol car.

Kendall climbed out of the ditch and jogged over to the Toyota. Adam was crouched by the open passenger door. The girl had her head in her hands, her body shaking with sobs. He glanced up at Kendall and shook his head.

She hadn't realized how much she had been counting on this being Frankie. But the ache in her heart emphasized the point.

Kendall leaned against the hood of the RAV4 and tried to catch her breath. She had known this was a possible outcome— that the girl would not be Frankie—but the truth felt like a knife stabbing her in the heart.

She pushed off the hood of the vehicle as Saul and Fletch approached.

"Let's get her to the hospital to be checked out," Kendall said.

"EMTs are on the way," Saul said. "What do you want to do with the dickhead?"

"I think we should take him to my office. It might intimidate him more if we have a chat with him there. No one likes dealing with the FBI."

CHAPTER

13

Wednesday morning
13:25:06 hours missing

KENDALL GLANCED AT the text message she had just received from Jake and had to do some quick maneuvering to make the exit off the highway.

"Where are we going?" Adam asked.

"They took the girl to Saint Joe's hospital to get checked out. I want to see if I can talk to her before we question the dickhead."

She followed the signs for the emergency room and parked in a spot reserved for law enforcement. Kendall put a placard with the FBI emblem on the dashboard. Adam met her at the back of the vehicle, and they walked silently to the entrance.

The sliding doors opened with a whoosh, and the air was suddenly thick with noise and the unmistakable smell of antiseptic and harsh cleaning chemicals. Coughing, crying, moaning, and a sense of desperation and frustration filled the waiting area. Emergency rooms—an oxymoron if ever there was one—were the last place to go if you had an emergency, unless you could manage to sit for hours with whatever ailment had sent you there in the first place.

Kendall flashed her badge to the woman at the registration desk. "Special Agent Kendall Beck." She threw a thumb over her shoulder at Adam. "Detective Adam Taylor, Denver PD."

"What can I do for you, Agent Beck?" the nurse answered with only a slight attempt to be cheerful over the exhaustion etched into her face.

"A girl was brought in by two detectives—"

The nurse reached under the counter and hit a button. A loud buzzing came from the door behind her. "Through there; see the nurse at the desk. She can tell you what room she's in."

"Thanks," Kendall said, moving quickly to the door. She loved efficiency.

By the time Adam caught up to Kendall, she was following a nurse down a hallway. They stopped in front of a room with actual walls and a solid door. The nurse knocked and poked her head inside the room. "There's an FBI agent here to speak to the patient," the nurse said. She turned back to them. "You can go on in. The liaison from social services is here as well."

Kendall turned to Adam and put her hand up. He stopped short of running her over.

"What?" His tone conveyed a high level of pissiness.

"You have to stay out here."

His eyes bulged and his nostrils flared, and Kendall prepared for a fight.

"Like hell I do. Give me one good reason I shouldn't go in."

Kendall wondered if she had been this obstinate when she was helping with Gwen's murder investigation.

"I'll give you three: First, she's a little girl who has been through trauma and will likely not respond to a male being in the room. Second, you're too close to this investigation. You reek of hostility and impatience." He wrapped his arms across his chest, his chin thrust out, proving her point. "And lastly, this may not have anything to do with Frankie's case, and it is therefore inappropriate for you to be involved in the interview."

His face softened, and he looked down at his feet. Kendall knew he hated when she was right. Especially when it involved his family.

"Now, sit in this lovely plastic chair here, and try to behave yourself." She pushed open the door and slipped inside the room, closing it behind her before he could object.

A girl lay in the bed, covers tucked tightly around her waist, TV remote in hand, flipping through the channels. And completely oblivious to the fact that anyone new had entered the room.

"Kendall Beck," Kendall said, reaching her hand out to the social worker sitting in the chair next to the bed, checking her phone.

"Sally Lewis, Child Protective Services." Lewis glanced at the girl in the bed and lowered her voice. "She says she lives in Pueblo with her mother, but we haven't been able to get in touch with her. Apparently, the mother doesn't have a cell phone, and she can't remember the address where they live because they just moved in—they move around often, sometimes staying with friends of her mother."

The perfect prey for an ACM—alleged child molester—a girl with no real ties and absent parental guidance. Why did people have kids if they lacked the ability or desire to care for them? The question haunted Kendall with every new case.

"What's the status of her health?" Kendall asked, certain the woman would understand that she was asking if the girl had been sexually assaulted or not.

"Seems to be in good health, although undernourished, most likely from lack of proper nutrition over the years, not from her abduction."

That might account for the girl's small stature and explain why the woman at the truck stop had thought she was younger than she was.

"Well, if there's any good news in this, at least she wasn't abused," Kendall said under her breath, so the girl couldn't hear. But that didn't make what had happened to her any less horrible. "Can I get her name?"

"Aleena Mayo, fourteen years old, no record. Was in foster care when she was two years old due to her mother's boyfriend creating an unhealthy, unsafe environment for the girls—she has an older sister who no longer lives with them, ran away at fifteen—and mom refused to leave the boyfriend when ordered to remove the children from the home. So the state did. Mom left the boyfriend and went into rehab. Three years later, she was able to get the girls back." Lewis handed Kendall the printout she was reading from. "You can have that."

"Jeez, what a way to grow up," Kendall said. "Okay if I ask her some questions?"

Ms. Lewis nodded. "I can't see why not. She seems to be more interested in what she's going to have for lunch, than what's happened to her."

Kendall moved to another chair on the opposite side of the bed and stood in front of the girl. "Hi, Aleena. I'm Kendall Beck. I work for the FBI. Can we talk for a few minutes?"

"Yeah," Aleena murmured, gaze still glued to the TV screen above Kendall's head.

"How about we turn the TV off. That way we can talk, I can get out of here sooner, and you can get back to watching TV. Deal?"

Aleena sighed and reluctantly clicked the button on the remote, shutting off the TV.

"Can you tell me how you came to be with the man you were with at the truck stop?" Kendall asked, taking a seat.

"I'm not sure." Aleena tilted her head to the side and pursed her lips. "I was supposed to meet my boyfriend at Home Depot so we could go"—Aleena's gaze darted to Kendall, a blush creeping up her neck and into her cheeks—"hang out."

Code for *have sex.*

"What's your boyfriend's name?"

"Aidan Pierce."

"How old is Aidan?"

"Seventeen."

Kendall nodded, hoping to put the girl at ease. "And how did you and Aidan meet?"

"Well, I haven't met him in person yet—that's what we were doing." Aleena picked at the fuzz on the blanket that covered her legs. "I've only talked to him over chat. The people's house where we're staying has a computer in the basement they said I could use."

Kendall inhaled. She knew where this story was headed but needed the girl to confirm her suspicions. "And did your boyfriend show up?"

"No. I was waiting for him at the back of the parking lot, by the trees, like we agreed. Then that guy pulls up and asks me if I'm Aleena. I said yes, and he said Aidan was trying to get out of his house but his parents were giving him shit, so sent that guy to pick me up." She looked up at Kendall, a mixture of experience and naïveté in her eyes. "I thought it was kind of weird, because Aidan is really rich. And this guy was kind of a creeper, and his car was old and gross."

"How do you know Aidan is rich?"

"He showed me pictures of his house. It's, like, a mansion. And he drives a Mercedes convertible. Plus his name just sounds . . . rich, you know?"

Kendall nodded, but every fiber of her being was awash with disbelief. Young girls were oblivious of danger and too often vulnerable to predators. This girl was no exception. She was so eager to get away from her life that she'd convinced herself "Aidan" was her millionaire knight in shining armor. "Why did you go with the man?"

" 'Cause he knew Aidan and he knew my name, and Aidan was the only one who knew my name." She shrugged and returned to defuzzing the blanket. "How would he know all that if he wasn't Aidan's friend?"

Kendall could count all the ways on her fingers and toes.

"Okay, so he gets you in the car—what happens next?"

"He gave me a Gatorade, and I drank it even though I wasn't really thirsty. But I didn't want to be rude or anything. We drove for a while. When I asked how far away we were from Aidan's house, he said we were getting closer. That the house was in the mountains. Then I got super tired and fell asleep. When I woke up, I was lying in a bed and the guy was there talking on the phone. I asked if it was Aidan, and he told me to shut up."

"Did he do anything to hurt you at all?"

"Do you mean, did he rape me?"

"Or touch you? Hit you? Force you to do things you didn't want to do?"

Aleena shook her head. "No, he got me some food from Taco Bell and another Gatorade, and I fell asleep again. I woke up just before we got to the truck stop, and I told him I had to pee."

Kendall opened the picture app on her phone and showed Aleena the picture of Frankie. "Have you seen this girl? Was she with you at any time?"

Aleena looked at the picture. "No, never seen her before. It was just me and El Creepo, unless she was around while I was knocked out."

"Okay, Aleena, I'll let you rest. I might want to talk to you later, though, okay?"

"Sure." She looked over at the social worker. "When are they bringing my food? I'm hungry."

Kendall nodded at Lewis, who gave Kendall a tight smile that said she wasn't looking forward to the next few hours, and opened the door.

Adam jumped to his feet as soon as the door closed behind her. "Well?"

"She says she didn't see Frankie."

Adam seemed to deflate before her eyes. She grasped his bicep and gave him a reassuring squeeze.

"Let's go see what dickhead has to say."

14

Wednesday midday
15:10:10 hours missing

FBI OFFICES WERE seriously swanky compared to the Denver PD. No years of grime smashed into the carpet on the floors. No hint of cigarette smoke in the paint from when it had been acceptable to smoke indoors and give your coworkers lung cancer. Everything was stark and bright and . . . clean.

Even the interrogation viewing room Adam was in felt cozier than the rooms he was used to. Comfortable seats; a large monitor on the wall so everyone could see. Notepads and pens provided, stacked neatly on a table under the monitor. There was even a coffee station set up with a Keurig and every type of gourmet coffee currently on the market. Adam half expected a guy in a white coat with a towel over his arm, silver tray in hand, to take his lunch order.

The interview rooms, however—those were the same everywhere. Small, so agents could crowd the suspect. Uncomfortable chairs. And the heat was usually turned up to make it even more excruciating. More conducive to wanting to spill one's guts just to get out of there and breathe fresh air.

But what was making Adam chuckle was the guy Kendall had chosen to assist her with questioning. Special Agent Marcus Thompson was a walking tower. Arms the size of a howitzer.

Adam had needed to tip his head back when he'd been introduced to the man and was still working out a kink in his neck.
He wanted to ask Thompson if he had to get his clothes custom-
made but was scared shitless to do more than greet him.

On the large screen, Kendall walked into the interrogation
room, set a file down, and slowly pulled out her chair, never once
looking at the man across the table from her. "Mr. Stalin, I'm
Special Agent Kendall Beck with the Crimes Against Children
unit. I am advising you that this interview is being recorded,
both through audio and video." She looked up from her file and
feigned a smile. "Can I call you Gary?"

"You can call me whatever you want, sweetheart." Stalin
made a point of trying to look around the table to see her body.
"If I had known the FBI had hot agents like you, I would've
joined up." A salacious smile slid across the creep's face.

"A missed opportunity indeed." She pulled out a document
from her folder and examined it. "Your extensive criminal record,
however, would most likely have precluded you from serving."

Stalin's grin widened, and he pointed at Kendall. "Hey, you're
the woman who jumped me in the ditch. I like the way you
moved against me." He thrust his pelvis out a couple of times.
"Made me horny."

Kendall glanced at Stalin's groin. "I didn't feel a thing. Are
you sure that thing works?"

"Oh, it works, baby. I'll show you how well it works; you just
find us somewhere private"—he glanced up at the camera in the
corner of the room—"where all your fed buddies aren't watching. I'll lay down some hot pipe on you."

"Smooth talker. Is that how you pick up all those prostitutes?
Sweet-talking them as you hand over your twenties?"

Stalin flipped her the bird.

Kendall looked back down at the papers in front of her. "But
let's talk about your lengthy criminal career. Arrested for solicit-
ing minors on several occasions. One charge of kidnapping—
how are you out of prison already?"

"Good behavior."

Kendall shook her head. "Tell me how you came to have a
girl with you over a hundred miles away from home."

"She's my niece."

"That's not what the victim is saying."

"What victim?" He leaned forward and put his arms on the table. "Look, she asked me if I could give her a ride. She was looking to get out of town."

"And you what? Decided to drive her two hours north, taking a rest overnight in the Springs, out of the goodness of your heart?"

Stalin patted his chest and opened his arms wide. "I'm a giver."

"Where were you headed?"

"Don't know; you'll have to ask her. She just said to drive north, so that's what I did."

"Very generous of you." Kendall kept her gaze on Stalin. Adam knew Kendall was good at her job, but this was the first time he had seen her interrogate a suspect. It was impressive.

"Like I said—"

"You're a giver." Kendall referred back to her notes. "And staying at the Colorado Adventure Motel last night?"

"Also her idea."

"At least you popped for a nice room. What did that cost you? Thirty-five dollars for the night?"

"Forty."

"Big spender."

"Part of that whole giver thing I do so well."

"And what did you do with her in the room you so generously sprung for?"

Stalin sighed and looked up at the ceiling as if irritated. "Read the sheet, Agent Beck." Adam pulled out his copy of the charging sheets. "I don't do little girls."

"Well, there's the moral high ground I was searching for," Kendall said.

"You can't help who you love," Stalin said.

Adam forced bile down his throat. The kidnapping conviction had stemmed from Stalin taking a nine-year-old boy from a Walmart. The police had found him several days later in the back room of a crack house. Adam stopped reading the report, unable to stomach the details of what the boy had lived through during his imprisonment.

Kendall stared at Stalin for a full minute without speaking. Stalin held his ground for about thirty-five seconds, but then the silence got under his skin, and he began to fidget.

"Look, I don't know what you want me to say." He picked at something on the tabletop. "I saw a girl who looked in need of assistance. She said she was trying to get away from an abusive mother and could I help."

Kendall continued to stare for a few more seconds, then drew a breath in through her teeth. "I just don't think you're telling me the truth, Gary."

Stalin leaned back in his chair. Arms across his chest, smirk in place. "Not my problem, Special Agent Kendall Beck."

"Oh, but it is, Gary."

The door opened, and the moment Adam had been waiting for did not disappoint. Agent Thompson stepped inside, and even from the viewing room Adam could feel all the air being displaced. Stalin sat up, eyes wide, mouth open, hands gripping the seat.

"Agent Beck," Thompson said in a deep baritone that conjured thoughts of darkness and pain. He handed a note to Kendall, then assumed his position between Kendall and Stalin, blocking the only exit in the room. His gaze settled on Stalin, who looked as if he was two seconds from crying.

"According to this note Agent Thompson just handed me . . ." She looked up. "Sorry, I guess you haven't been introduced. Gary Stalin, Special Agent Marcus Thompson. According to this note, you are not related to the girl who was in your custody at the truck stop today."

She pulled a notepad from under the file and clicked her pen. "Would you like to tell me what happened?" She glanced up at Thompson, then at Stalin. "The truth this time."

The sigh from Stalin indicated his resignation. "I got a text to pick up a girl and take her to meet someone."

"Someone who?"

"I don't know. I just get an address and a time."

"And I assume you get paid for this?"

"Yeah, I accept the job and then get a notification from Venmo that a transfer has been made."

"So, in this text, you were told where to pick up the girl?"

"Yeah, they gave me her name and a cover story. I was to pick her up and take her to her boyfriend. Once she got in the car, I gave her something to drink and started up I-25."

"Was the drink laced with something?"

"Not as far as I know."

"Is that what the toxicology report will say?" Thompson asked.

Stalin paled. "Ketamine."

"Nice," Kendall said.

He shrugged. "I don't like a lot of conversation while I drive."

"Why stop in the Springs overnight?"

"I had some other business there, and I was ahead of schedule to drop her off."

"And what was this business?"

Stalin wrapped his left hand around his right index finger and made an in-and-out motion.

"Adult?"

"He said he was."

The other agents in the room with Adam all groaned. "Who votes to let Thompson take him out back and beat the fuck out of him before his ride from Pueblo gets here?"

All hands went up in the air.

"Was this business conducted in your room?" Kendall asked.

Stalin nodded.

"With the girl there?"

Stalin shrugged. "She was out cold. I wasn't negatively influencing her or anything."

Thompson shifted, and Stalin scooted his chair back.

Kendall asked, "Where was the exchange location?"

"Cheyenne."

Another hour and a half up the road.

"Lucky we stopped you before you got into Wyoming. Did you know it's a federal offense to transport a kidnap victim across state lines?"

Kendall didn't wait for a response and instead pulled a printed picture of Frankie out of the file and slid it across the table. Adam sat up in his chair and leaned forward. His breathing picked up speed in time with his rapid heartbeat.

"Have you seen this girl?"

Stalin shook his head.

"Was part of the plan to pick up this girl on your way to Cheyenne and deliver her to your counterpart also?"

"No. I wasn't even supposed to stop at all. Not even for the night. I was supposed to drive straight to Cheyenne and stay the night there. Then give the girl—the other girl, not that one," he said, pointing at Frankie's picture. "The other one to the guy I was meeting."

Fuck!

Adam glanced at his watch. What a colossal waste of time when he had little to spare.

"I'm assuming you've missed your rendezvous time?" Kendall asked.

"Long passed."

"We checked your phone, Gary. All the text messages have been deleted. Now, that's not to say we can't get them, but it'll take time."

"Don't know what to tell you."

Thompson stepped forward. Stalin shrank back. "I'm going to need the address of the meeting place in Cheyenne," Thompson said.

Oh, yeah, Stalin is definitely pissing himself.

CHAPTER

15

Lori Arnold, Frankie's piano instructor, lived in a neigh-borhood not far from Mark and Poppy's home. It was a typical eighties two-car-garage split-level with a beige exterior and a zeroscaped front yard, artfully decorated with cacti and lava rocks of various colors. Many people in the state decided the hot Colorado summers with little rain made it hard to maintain a lush green yard without running the sprinklers every day, several times a day. That wasn't a good option where drought was imminent and the risk of devastating wildfires high.

Kendall and Adam walked up the front steps and onto the small landing. Apparently in an attempt to break up the desert theme the Arnolds had going on, they had chosen to paint the double front doors a warm orange clay color. The same color you'd find if you dug a foot down in the dirt.

Colorado was known for its colorfulness, yet the color scheme of most neighborhoods throughout the state was some variation on the muted and dull dry landscape of the eastern plains. Only in neighborhoods without HOAs would the houses be painted with any color. Or character. Which was a shame. Life was too short to be surrounded by beige.

Kendall pushed the doorbell button and rocked back on her heels.

The door swung open, revealing a woman in her late forties wearing a T-shirt covered by a light cardigan and jeans.

"Can I help you?" she asked.

"Hi," Kendall said, pulling her badge from her jacket pocket. "Are you Lori Arnold?"

"Yes." Her gaze flittered to Adam and then back to Kendall's badge. She wrapped her cardigan tighter around her, eyes widening slightly.

"I'm Kendall Beck with the FBI, and this is Adam Taylor from the Denver Police. We wondered if we could talk to you about one of your piano students?"

The woman visibly exhaled and her shoulders dropped, a small smile on her face, most likely from relief that it wasn't something more. Typical reaction when law enforcement showed up at anyone's doorstep—guilty or innocent. There was always a sense of impending doom.

"You must mean Frankie." She opened the door wider and stepped back, indicating with her arm for them to come inside. "Poppy called me this morning just frantic, asking if Frankie was here, and told me she was missing. I just can't believe it."

Mrs. Arnold moved into the living room adjacent to the door. A leather couch sat in front of an oversized picture window. A baby grand took up the rest of the space in the living room. A painting of the mountains, which could also be seen by looking out the window, covered one wall. "Please, have a seat. Can I get you some coffee, or water?"

"No, thank you," Kendall said, taking a seat next to Adam on the couch. Arnold pulled the piano bench out and sat on it. "When was the last time you saw Frankie?"

"Yesterday afternoon—well, evening, I guess. Her piano lesson is at five and ends at six."

"Did you notice if she was acting different? Did she seem upset?" Adam asked.

A small chuckle escaped Arnold's chest. "No more than usual when she's at her lesson. I don't think Frankie likes taking piano as much as she did when she first started about two or three years ago. But no, she didn't seem different than her normal preteen exasperated self. I'm used to it—see it all the time in my school students as well as my private ones. They hit an age and every-thing is the end of the world and annoying, and adults couldn't possibly understand the perils they face."

Kendall hadn't known Frankie long, but in the short time she had been exposed to Frankie and her friends, she had congratu-lated herself on not succumbing to the societal pressure of having kids. Preteen girls were hard enough to deal with at work; she didn't need to deal with them on her off hours. There might be murder involved, and Kendall liked her freedom too much.

"Has she ever talked to you about what's going on in her life? Complained about friends or family or any issues she was hav-ing?" Kendall asked.

Arnold's forehead wrinkled in contemplation. "No, but then I'm too old to understand her problems. You could ask my nephew; he sometimes talks to her while she waits for her mom to pick her up."

Finally, a glimmer of hope to move the investigation for-ward. Kids trusted other kids with what was going on in their lives. "And your nephew is?"

"Luke. Luke Mathis. He's my sister's son. They moved to Maryland a while back. Luke's been having some adjustment issues since moving there, and my sister thought it might be good for him to finish high school with his friends out here."

"How long has he been here?"

"Since the beginning of the year—start of the spring semester."

"What grade is he in?"

"Just finishing up his junior year."

"So that makes him . . . ?"

"Seventeen." Arnold smoothed out her barely shoulder-length hair. "Young enough that Frankie may talk to him about things."

"Is he around?"

"Uh, yeah." She got up and went to the stairs leading down just off the kitchen. "Luke?" she called out. When there was no response, she pulled her cell phone from her back pocket and smiled at them. "If he's gaming instead of doing homework, he'll have his headphones on and can't hear me. This is the only way to get him without having to go downstairs, which I avoid at all costs due to teenage boy smell trapped in the basement. I swear," she muttered almost to herself as she typed furiously on her phone, "I don't know what's worse—the smell of sweat or the overpowering body spray to cover the smell of sweat."

Kendall felt a little sick to her stomach at the thought.

Arnold slid back onto the piano bench, hands between her thighs, and glanced at the stairs. "He should be up in a minute."

Kendall smiled at the woman. "Do you think it's possible Frankie could've run away?"

Arnold's eyebrows knit together, and she frowned. "Like I said, I don't really know her that well, but she doesn't seem the type to run away. But then, I guess it's possible. Teenage girls sometimes feel overwhelmed with life, and any little thing can throw them off."

A door opened, and the sound of feet heavy on the stairs filled the air. A tall boy with longish brown hair and a touch of acne trudged into the room. He glanced at Kendall and Adam, then at his aunt.

"Luke, these two would like to talk to you about Frankie—I told you she was missing, remember? I thought, since you talk to her more than I do, you might know something that will help to find her."

Kendall and Adam stood. Kendall reached her hand toward the young man. "Hi, Luke. I'm Kendall, and this is Adam."

Luke shook her hand and then Adam's. "Are you guys cops or something?" he asked, not particularly nervous. More curious, straddling the line of wariness.

"I am," Adam said. "Kendall's an FBI agent."

"Sick," he said, looking at Kendall with a hint of respect.

"How well do you know Frankie?" Adam asked.

"Not well, really. We talk sometimes when she's waiting for her mom to pick her up and I'm skateboarding."

"Did you talk to her yesterday?" Kendall asked.

"Yeah."

"What did you talk about?"

Kendall sometimes hated questioning teenagers. Not having kids of her own, she wasn't sure if they were obtuse or just liked making adults pull teeth to get information from them.

"Not much, really."

Mrs. Arnold sighed heavily. "Luke, tell them what you talked about and stop being so difficult."

"Anything you can tell us—even if it might seem like nothing—could lead to something," Kendall said, trying to soften the blow but grateful Mrs. Arnold had stepped in and hammered the kid a bit.

Luke shrugged. "She talked about her hockey game mostly. I've never played, so I don't really get it, but I just let her talk."

"Did she say anything about having an issue with anyone on the team?" Adam asked.

"I think there was one kid she said was an asshole"—he quickly glanced at his aunt, a blush reddening his cheeks—"but that was a couple of weeks ago. Sort of was a joke to her, but she could've just been trying to play it off as nothing. I don't know."

"Anything else you remember about the conversation?" Kendall asked.

"The conversation? No. But when her mom pulled up, she got out and yelled at Frankie to get into the SUV, and then she told me to stay away from her daughter. She was really pissed. Slammed her door when she got back in and sped away."

Well, that was something Poppy hadn't told them about. A quick glance at Mrs. Arnold, eyebrows drawn together, told Kendall she hadn't been told about the incident either. "Why was she upset about you talking to Frankie?"

Luke shrugged again and stared at his feet.

"Was there anything she could have mistaken going on between you two?" Adam asked.

Luke's head shot up, and he glared at Adam. "No, and before you ask, there was nothing going on with me and Frankie. She would sit on the front steps now that it's warming up and watch me skate. Sometimes she would ask me questions about high school, or Maryland, and I would ask her about hockey, because that's all she seemed to care about. And that's it!"

Adam the overbearing, hostile inquisitor strikes again. Kendall was going to have to question people on her own if he couldn't rein in his impatience and pull his head out of his ass.

"Has Mrs. Taylor seen you talking to Frankie other times?" Kendall asked.

"Yeah, I guess once or twice."

"But this was the first time she got angry?"

"Yes."

Kendall softened her tone, again trying to repair any harm Adam's accusatory insertion had caused. "Why do you think she got angry all of a sudden?"

"No idea," he said, his voice clipped. "Go ask her what her problem is."

16

Wednesday afternoon
18:06:27 hours missing

ADAM HAD COMBINED the investigations into one war room, each at opposite ends of the space, avoiding needlessly occupying two different rooms. Plus he wanted to be in two places at once. This setup served that purpose well.

Luckily, Kendall and Jake were also involved in both cases. The newest member of the team was Officer Caleb Young, who Adam had requested be allowed to help him run down witness statements and do the general grunt work. Lou had been resistant at first but had given in when Adam reminded him that two of his team were deeply embroiled in locating his niece and Adam was virtually on his own with the double-murder/child-abduction investigation.

A bit of bullshit, but Lou had bought it, and Adam got his dedicated worker bee.

"I think we should start with what we know so far on the double homicide and get that out of the way before we move on to the other case." Adam was finding it more difficult with each passing hour to mention his niece by name in relation to the case. Time was going by too quickly, and he was desperate to slow it down and find Frankie alive. The alternative was too devastating to consider, so Adam blocked it from his mind and refused to allow it to take up space.

Saul cleared his throat as he pulled out his notebook. "The delivery truck driver Aaron Green's alibi checked out. He left prior to the shooting. According to company policy, drivers are required to check in with dispatch when they complete a delivery prior to going to their next drop off. Dispatch log shows him arriving at six thirty-eight and leaving at seven oh-three. This fits with what we believe is the time of the shootings, approximately seven ten. We also have his GPS log showing when he left the gas station, where he went after he left, and the time he arrived at the next convenience store. No way he could've been involved in the shootings or been a witness to anything that happened inside the store," Saul said. "He did, however, recall seeing a car pull in matching the alleged kidnapper's vehicle as he was pulling out. Couldn't ID from a photo lineup—says he didn't get a very good look at the guy—and was too busy watching for a break in traffic."

Adam crossed the delivery driver off his list of potential suspects who might have been involved in the robbery-gone-wrong. He usually loved being able to close in on suspects; however, the list was getting smaller, and soon they would be out of suspects to consider.

"Stock boy, eighteen-year-old Alex Martinez," Young said as Fletch circled the name on the whiteboard, "also had his alibi check out. As soon as the first shot was fired, he took off out the back door of the store, ran across the parking lot and into a Burger King, screaming that someone was shooting up the gas station. Surveillance from the bank, which covers the parking lot and is right next to the gas station, shows Martinez running past at seven oh-seven. BK security video shows Martinez entering the Burger King at seven oh-eight. He practically jumps behind the counter. Apparently scared the shit out of the breakfast patrons, who only heard that there was a shooting. Many of them crawled under their tables. The manager called the police. Nine-one-one recording matches Martinez's version of events."

"Have we found anyone who knows anything about our bad-guy kidnapper? What's his name again?" Adam asked, frustrated this case was taking a back seat to his niece's case. Which wasn't fair to the victims—especially Savannah. At any other time, this would've been his top priority. It should've been—except the case pulling him away was personal. And Adam could feel his professionalism slipping away.

Young lifted his hand slightly. "Darin Stevens. I located his mother, Rosie Stevens Henshaw. She lives in North Carolina, says she hasn't had contact with him since the day after he dropped out of high school about eight years ago at the age of sixteen. Trying to confirm that with other family, but it does appear that he showed up in Denver around that time—he was arrested for solicitation at the ripe old age of seventeen—got his driver's license at eighteen, and has only had a couple of minor drug infractions since. He's low-level enough that he isn't on drug squad's radar."

"Father?" Kendall asked.

"Darin Stevens Senior. In prison since Junior was five, doing life on a homicide conviction—some guy he caught in bed with Rosie when he came home from a week away long-haul driving. I spoke with Senior on the phone; he hasn't seen or heard from Junior since he was heading out of North Carolina without any idea where he was going. Told his father he would hitchhike until he found someplace he liked. Guess he liked the mountains."

"Lucky us," Jake said.

"Do we know where he was living?" Adam asked.

"The address on his driver's license is out of date. Landlord said he hasn't lived there in a couple of years. Drug squad is asking around to see if they can come up with some people who may know him."

Adam twisted in his chair, popping every vertebra in his back. The tension building in his body was excruciating. The more they investigated without turning anything significant up, the longer it took to close the case and the harder it was to focus on it instead of the case he really wanted to be paying attention to.

"Okay, let's try to follow up with family or friends of Mrs. Henshaw to corroborate her story. Check phone records to see if he's called her. Did he have a cell phone on him?"

"Yes. Waiting for records."

"Can IT not break into it?"

"It has a bullet hole through it."

"Well, fuck." Adam exhaled. "Let's keep on top of trying to get the cell records as soon as possible. Talk to Sheri Colburn and see if she can put this on the fast track. Let her know it's part of an investigation into a kidnapped child; that should motivate her." Adam clicked his pen a few times. "Best not to mention my name."

Young stared at Adam for a moment, then looked away. But Adam caught the shit-eating grin on the kid's face. Young was probably the only person in the building who hadn't heard the sonic boom that occurred every time Adam was in Sheri's presence following the breakup of their tumultuous romantic relationship. Sheri worked in IT forensics for the police department and was living proof of why you should never fish off the company pier. Most everyone on the force knew way too much about Adam's anatomy and inadequate sexual prowess.

"What do you think about enlisting the media's help to find out more about him?" Kendall asked.

"Not a bad idea," Adam said. And he meant it; he just hated asking the media for help. It felt like opening a door that couldn't be closed. "I'll talk to Lou about getting together a press conference." He pointed his pen at Kendall. "But if I have to go in front of the press, you have to be there too. It will carry more weight if the FBI is involved."

"Naturally," Jake said. Saul glanced across the table at him, a flat line where his mouth was. Fletch flipped Jake the bird. Kendall smiled and fist-bumped her partner.

Ah, camaraderie.

"Okay, let's move on to the other case," Adam said, pulling the file with Frankie's name out and opening it. "Any luck with the truck stop guy after Kendall and I left?"

Jake shook his head. "Unlikely it's part of the current case. We continued to question Gary Stalin, low-level dickhead, most likely part of an online predator setup down in Pueblo. Getting more popular these days, with kids having unfettered access to online forums at younger and younger ages. I made a call down to the FBI agency in Pueblo, and they're currently on their way to pick up both Stalin and Aleena and remove them from our hair and our jurisdiction."

"So why don't we think they're part of . . . *this* case?" Adam asked, tapping his finger on the file.

"Neither one was in the area when Frankie was taken. CCTV from the Home Depot parking lot shows Stalin pulling to the back of the lot and Aleena getting in the vehicle after the time Frankie went missing."

Damn. It had been a long shot, and Adam knew from Kendall's interrogation of Stalin that he was most likely not involved. But the clock was ticking, and Adam was no closer to finding his niece than he had been last night.

"On an unrelated note, but since all of you were involved in the Reaper case—"

That got Adam's attention. He glanced across the table at Kendall. Her face had paled. He knew she still carried around a massive load of guilt over the death of her friend at the hands of a madman who was after her. The resolution of that case had done nothing to heal anyone's hearts. In fact, it had done more harm than good, as far as Adam could see.

Except that a serial killer had been on the justice end of Kendall's bullet right through the heart.

"—a call came in from a detective in Asheville, North Carolina. He says he has a couple of cases with similarities to the Reaper. He put his case info into NCIC, and our case popped up."

"What the fuck? That dude's dead. No way he could be in fucking North Carolina," Fletch said.

"Slow your roll, Obediah," Saul said.

Adam lifted his head and stared at Saul for further explanation.

"His actual first name," Saul said.

"Man . . . Saul," Fletch muttered under his breath.

"How did I not know this?" Adam said. Saul shrugged.

"Oh, this is all sorts of gold," Kendall said.

Adam would have to thank Saul later for this gem.

"No," Fletch said, pointing his finger at each of them as if it were some type of threat. "No one but my mom calls me that."

"Whatever, Obediah," Jake said. "Best of luck getting that cat back in the bag."

"Fine, but it stays inside this room, agreed?" Fletch pleaded.

"Really depends on how much money you got on you, Obie," Kendall taunted.

Fletch ran his fingers through his hair. "Fuck me."

Adam didn't have the time or mental capacity to deal with someone else's serial killer. "Call Asheville back and let him know our guy was killed last year. Maybe he has a copycat," he said to Young, wanting this conversation to go away and not linger.

The last thing he needed was Kendall to lose focus and fall down the rabbit hole of massive guilt she'd been wallowing in the past few months. That wouldn't do anyone any good. Kendall was excellent at her job, and Adam wanted her giving full attention to Frankie's case, not reliving the case she labeled a failure.

A uniformed cop poked his head into the room. "Agent Beck, Savannah Hawley and her mother are in interview room three waiting for you."

Kendall closed her file folder, slid it into her bag, and grabbed a leather portfolio. "You're observing with Jake?" she asked, pointing to Adam.

"Yep, I'll be down as soon as I talk to Lou about the presser."

17

Wednesday afternoon
18:28:15 hours missing

T HE POLICE SOCIAL worker met Kendall as she came into the interview room. "I'll stay out of the way and will only interrupt if I see the child is in distress or think the question is inappropriate," she said.

Karen and Savannah Hawley were once again sitting on the couch in the interview room used for talking with young children. It was set up like a family room in a comfortable home, which put children more at ease. Along one wall was a framed mirror, through which Jake and Adam could observe. There were also cameras and recording devices set up in the room to capture every word. Every movement. The other interview rooms had the same cameras and recording devices but were intentionally stark white, with bright lighting and excessively uncomfortable chairs. That scene encouraged suspects—and witnesses—to give up information in a more timely fashion.

Karen began to rise, but Kendall stopped her. "Don't get up." She walked to the chair adjacent to the couch and reached her hand across the table toward the other woman. "Thank you so much for coming in today and talking to me again." She leaned in a little closer. "Hi, Savannah."

Savannah mumbled a "Hi" in return.

"Can we get either of you anything?" Kendall asked Karen. "Coffee, juice, water?"

"No," Karen said. "I think we're okay."

"Okay," Kendall said, opening her portfolio. "Savannah, thanks for coming back today to talk to me. It's not much fun to talk about this stuff, is it?"

Savannah shook her head.

"Well, what if I told you that once we get done here, you're going to get a tour of a real-life candy factory?" To Saul's credit, being a grandfather came with a wealth of ideas. It also helped that his son-in-law was the CFO of a family-owned candy company in Denver and had been able to get Savannah a private tour.

"Really?" Savannah asked, the first bit of joy Kendall had seen on the girl's face since she'd met her.

"Cross my heart," Kendall said, and she crossed her finger over heart for added emphasis. "So, can I ask you some more questions?"

"Okay," Savannah said, still smiling but less enthusiastic.

"You said that you got to the convenience store and the man driving the car took you out of the car and told you to stay near him. Is that correct?"

"Yes," Savannah said.

Kendall sometimes hated talking with kids. Yes, they were almost always truthful when they provided information, but getting that information out of them was an exercise in patience. It was typically the only time Kendall exhibited patience, but it took a toll on her. The faster she received information, the sooner she could act on it. And with cases involving child abductions, time was always of the essence and seemed to slip away faster than information came in.

"Can you tell me what happened when you went inside the store?"

"People got shot," Savannah said, tears instantly forming on the lower rim of her eyes.

"What happened when you first entered the store, before the people were shot? Did the man pick up any items off the shelves? Did it look as if he was going to buy anything?"

Savannah shook her head and wiped the tears from her cheeks. "No, he sort of looked around the store. Then he looked at his watch, I think, and said the f-word. When the lady at the cash register asked if she could help him, he pulled out a gun and told her to give him all the money in the cash register."

"And did she do that?" Kendall asked.

"I thought so, but then the guy let go of me and ran around the counter, and he was screaming at her."

"Do you know what he was saying to her?"

"Something about what the . . ." She glanced at her mother, then back to Kendall. "What was she doing. Then I heard the lady scream and a really loud explosion or something."

"What did you do when this happened?"

"I ducked and tried to get out of the way, so I hid in the corner. I was so scared. I didn't know what was going on."

"That's completely understandable. Anyone would've been scared. It was really smart of you to get out of the way, though." Kendall said, reaching over to rub Savannah's arm. "What happened after that?"

"A man was there—a different man—and he yelled at the guy and then shot him." Savannah's whole body shook with the memory.

"Where did the other man come from? Was he outside and then came in?"

Savannah shook her head again. "No, I don't think so, 'cause I was thinking I should try to go to the door and get out, but I was so scared. I couldn't move. I didn't see him come in, though."

Karen Hawley's chest rose and dropped in quick succession. Kendall was sure the woman was about to pull the plug on the interview at any moment. This must be excruciating for her, hearing the gruesome events her daughter had been through.

Kendall focused back on Savannah. The little girl looked at Kendall, her eyes pleading for them to be done.

Sometimes this job sucks.

"So, he was probably already inside the store when you came in?" Kendall asked.

Savannah nodded. So far this was matching the account the Good Samaritan, Melvin Craig, had given them.

"You said the other man yelled at the man who brought you to the store. Do you remember what he said to him?"

"He was screaming at him and saying, 'What are you doing? Why did you shoot her?' and stuff like that. Then the one guy told the other guy to, you know, 'f' off, and then he pointed the gun at the other guy and the other guy shot him."

Kendall needed to slow her down so everything was clear.

"Okay, so the guy at the back of the store shot the man you came with?"

"Uh-huh."

"Did the man at the back of the store have a gun with him? Did you see him take it out?"

Kendall already knew Craig had picked it up off the floor, but she wanted to reconfirm everything that took place in the store to the extent she could.

"No, he got it off the floor, but I didn't see it there when we came into the store."

"Okay, what happened after the man was shot?"

"The man grabbed me and ran out of the store with me."

"The man from the back of the store grabbed you?"

Savannah nodded.

"Did you see him drop the gun he had picked up?"

"No. When the mean man was shot, he fell next to me. His eyes were open, but there was a lot of blood. I didn't want to see him, so I closed my eyes. And I was screaming, and all I could hear was the gun going off in my head, so I covered my ears to get it to stop."

The girl was full-on sobbing, so Kendall took a break and let the girl snuggle into her mother and calm down a bit.

"How much longer do you foresee this interview going on, Agent Beck?" the social worker asked.

"I just have a few more questions—shouldn't take long."

The woman nodded and took her seat again.

Kendall wanted nothing more than to allow Savannah to get on with her life and try to banish the demons from her mind. But she needed a little more information before that could happen.

Savannah was tucked into her mother's side, but the sobbing had subsided, and she was breathing normally again.

"Savannah, I know this is so hard to talk about, and I promise I am almost done. But I just need to ask you a few more questions. But nothing about the shootings, okay? I need to know what happened when the man took you from the store. Do you remember that?"

"Yeah," she said, lifting her head and sitting up a little straighter. Her mother handed her a tissue, and the girl wiped her nose. "He picked me up and ran out of the store. And then he crossed the street and put me down. He grabbed my hand, and we sorta ran down the alley. And then he opened a gate, and we went behind this like little house thing—"

"Garage," Karen corrected her.

"Yeah, the garage, but it wasn't part of the house like ours is. It was at the back of the yard."

"Did the man say anything to you?"

Savannah took in a shuddering breath. "No, not to me. But he was saying something while we were running. I couldn't hear him, so I don't think he was talking to me. It was more like when my daddy talks to himself, kinda quiet."

"But you don't know what he was saying?"

"No. But when we got to the little—to the garage—he talked to someone on the phone."

That got Kendall's attention. Craig hadn't mentioned he'd called anyone. He'd told Kendall he had been in shock and that was why he hadn't moved when the police came and they'd had to force him to come out from behind the garage.

Who did he call?

"Do you remember what he said on the phone?"

"I think he asked someone to pick him up 'cause he couldn't get to his car. But he told the guy not to go to the store but go to some road, I think. He said we would meet him at the end of the alley."

"Okay, this is important, Savannah. Are you sure he said *we* would meet, or did he say *he* would meet?"

Savannah stared at the floor for a moment. "I think he said *we*, but I don't know for sure. I just remember wishing he would call my mom to come and get me, but I was too afraid to ask."

There was a knock on the door, and a woman came in with a large wooden case. Kendall nodded at her, and the woman took a seat next to the social worker.

"They talked to you about having Savannah work with the sketch artist to get an idea of what the man and woman who came to the house looking for the dog looked like, correct?" Kendall asked.

"Yes," Karen said.

Kendall nodded. "Savannah, thank you so much for being so brave and talking to me today. What you've told me will help so much to catch the people who took you. It will help to make sure they don't do this to anyone else, and that's a pretty big deal."

"You're welcome," Savannah said, but she was more interested in watching the sketch artist set up her things than talking to Kendall anymore.

Kendall walked to the door. The social worker stood, and Karen joined them. "I shouldn't need to question her again," Kendall said, "but if something develops, I may need to clarify information. I'll give you as much notice as I can, but things can sometimes move pretty quickly when we get a solid lead."

"I understand," Karen said. "Just let us know. I know it's difficult for Savannah, but I never want another mother to have to go through the hell I've been going through. And we both want to make sure no child has to endure what Savannah went through. I hate that she had to witness someone die, but I can't imagine what would've happened to her if the man who had her would've survived."

Kendall knew. Savannah would most likely have been passed off to another cog in the sex trafficking wheel and sold to the highest bidder, put on the sex market, and spent a short life servicing the sexual deviancies of adults.

The chances of recovery at that point were basically slim to none.

18

Wednesday evening
20:35:17 hours missing

ADAM OPENED THE front door of his brother's house without knocking. He knew his mom was there, along with Poppy's mother. No doubt both were in the kitchen making way too much food in order to keep themselves distracted from the realization that time was still passing even though it should've stopped the moment Frankie disappeared. Mark's truck wasn't in the driveway. He was probably diverting his attention from the helplessness of the situation with work at the fire station.

Adam and Kendall found Poppy in the living room, curled into a tight ball in one corner of the couch. Adam sat on the couch beside her while Kendall took the chair on the other side of the coffee table.

As soon as Poppy saw Adam, she sat up, her eyes wide with anticipation and wariness. "Did you find her?"

It nearly killed him not to be able to say yes and have Frankie run into her mother's arms. But that wasn't reality. And Adam needed to know why Poppy was keeping secrets from him.

"No," Adam said, and placed a hand on her knee. "But we need to ask you a few more questions. Do you want to do it here, or up in your office where there's more privacy?"

"Here is fine," she said, and seemed to fall back into the abyss she had just come out of.

"Poppy," Adam said, to pull her back to the present. "We spoke to Frankie's piano teacher and her nephew, Luke."

She wrapped her arms around her chest, a barrier created to separate her, but from what? Adam and Kendall? More questions?

To protect her from what was coming next. And that gave Adam pause. Why was she so anxious at the mention of the nephew?

"Luke told us there was an incident while picking up Frankie," Kendall said. "Can you tell us what that was about?"

Poppy stared into the nothingness between Adam and Kendall. Her body had stiffened and her arms wrapped tighter around her, so much so her knuckles were white from gripping her upper arms. "It was nothing. I asked him not to talk to Frankie."

"Why would that bother you so much?" Kendall asked.

"He's too old for her." The answer was flat, with no further explanation.

"Was she in a relationship with him?" Kendall pushed. "It would be weird for a seventeen-year-old boy to date a twelve-year-old."

Fire flamed in Poppy's eyes, and she glared at Kendall. "Look, I realize you don't have kids of your own, so you have no idea how quickly things can go badly between a girl Frankie's age, who's just starting to get interested in boys, and an older teenage boy who can manipulate her. It happens in the blink of an eye, and I won't have Frankie hurt by anyone if I can help it."

Whoa . . . Adam had never seen Poppy so quick to anger. It was a side she'd never let out before, and he wondered how well he knew his sister-in-law.

"According to Luke, nothing was going on. They would just talk while she was waiting for you to pick her up," Adam said.

Poppy snorted. "You're as naïve as she is, Adam." She nodded toward Kendall. "You have no idea the things boys can do and say to get what they want from a young girl. That is not going to happen to my daughter."

"How did Frankie feel about you yelling at Luke?" Kendall asked.

"I didn't yell at him," Poppy spat out.

"According to Luke, you ordered Frankie into the Explorer and then railed on him for talking to her. Why would he lie about that, Poppy?" Adam asked. He was about at the limit with his sister-in-law. This was a part of her he did not like. What the hell was going on with her? And why was she holding back information when her daughter was missing?

"Poppy," Kendall said in a soft voice, "how was Frankie when you got into the Explorer after your discussion with Luke?"

"She was mad," Poppy said, her gaze fixed out the front window.

"How mad?" Adam asked.

Poppy shrugged. "Mad enough."

Adam jumped to his feet, rage bursting like lava from his chest. "For fuck's sake, Poppy. Why the hell are you refusing to give me answers—straight answers? Your daughter is missing, and you're going to choose now to hold things back?" Running his fingers through his hair, he took a deep breath, knowing he needed to calm down.

Poppy's mother came into the room, wringing her hands on a dish towel. "Everything all right in here?"

Tears streamed down Poppy's face, but she didn't look at Adam or respond to her mother.

"Everything's fine," Kendall said, getting up and escorting Poppy's mother back to the kitchen. "Nothing to worry about. We just need some information from Poppy and we'll be out of here."

Adam dropped back onto the couch. "I need for you to be one hundred precent honest with me, Poppy, because I think you've been holding out on me, and for the life of me I can't figure out why. Did you and Frankie have words after you picked her up from her piano lesson?"

Poppy nodded. "Yes. She was furious with me. Yelled at me all the way to the rink. Said I was ruining her life, that Luke was her friend, and now he probably hated her because of me. I asked her what was going on with the two of them, and she screamed at me some more about how nothing was going on between them—and probably never would now because of me."

Adam grabbed a tissue from the box on the coffee table and handed it to Poppy.

"Thank you," she said, dabbing at the tears in her eyes. "I asked her what she meant by that, but she just said she hated me and then shut down and refused to talk to me. When we got to the rink, she got out and grabbed her bag from the back before I had an opportunity to turn off the car."

Poppy glanced at Adam. "That's the last time I talked to her, Adam. What if those are the last words she ever says to me?"

Adam scooted closer to his sister-in-law and put an arm around her shoulder, drawing her into him. He kissed the top of her head. "It won't be. But Poppy, you have to be straight with me about everything. If I don't have all the information, I can't do my job." He pulled away and looked her in the eyes. "If you feel weird telling me, tell Kendall. Okay? But no more keeping secrets. This is too important, and nothing—*nothing*—is worth keeping a secret about. Not when it comes to Frankie's safety."

Poppy nodded, but Adam wasn't sure he believed she wouldn't decide what was relevant to the investigation and what she could keep to herself. He wasn't even sure why she hadn't told them about the argument. It seemed like normal teenage stuff.

Which, he guessed, was why she hadn't thought it was important.

"Is there some reason you suspect more is going on between Luke and Frankie? Or that something could happen?" Kendall asked.

"No," Poppy said, and blew her nose. "I mean, I think she has a crush on him, and I don't want her, or him, to think anything can happen between them. Not ever."

Adam gave Poppy a hug, and he and Kendall said their goodbyes, promising to check in and update the family with any new leads.

Out on the front porch, Kendall turned to Adam. "So, in light of this new evidence, should we be reconsidering this as a runaway?"

Adam inhaled deeply and released it. "I don't know. I find it hard to believe Frankie would run away, but there are still too many questions. And something definitely seems off about Poppy."

"Maybe Frankie knows her mother is having an affair—"

"If she is," Adam interjected.

"Okay, but if she is and Frankie found out, and then on top of Poppy embarrassing her in front of a boy she may have a crush on—"

"—and Mark did say he thought Poppy and Frankie were having a tough go of it lately, whether it be preteen hormones or whatever—"

"—which doesn't matter, except that they're arguing more than usual, all of that could add up to Frankie just needing to get away from her mother."

Adam shook his head in disbelief at what was happening to his family.

"I find it hard to believe she would leave without talking to Mark. They're so close, Kendall. You've seen it. She's his mini-me. I can't imagine she would be gone for this long without talking to her dad."

"Well, it's still a possibility," Kendall said. "I think you should have Saul get someone to reinterview the parents, teammates, and friends. See if she's hiding out somewhere."

In a slew of dreadful potential outcomes, Adam couldn't help but pray this was the answer to his niece's disappearance.

CHAPTER

19

Wednesday evening
21:32:56 hours missing

T HE SUN SLIPPED over the western range, the blue sky dark-
ening with every passing minute. Soon the sunlight would
be replaced by the city lights twinkling with stars in the open
Colorado night sky. Kendall had been born and raised in Colorado, and except for the time she'd spent at Quantico when she
first entered the FBI, she had lived there all her life. Her father
still lived and worked the ranch outside Canon City, even after
the death of Kendall's mom a few years earlier.

The plan was for Kendall to interview Turner's aunt and
uncle, who conveniently lived next door to the coach—and then
wrap the day. It felt wrong for her to stop working when Frankie
was still out there somewhere, but she also knew that without
sleep, she would be worthless to the investigation. She would
miss something important. And Frankie slipping through her
fingers was just not an option.

Thankfully, Adam had given in and not come with her. It
helped that his boss was on his ass about why he hadn't spoken
with the cashier's boyfriend yet and he was in jeopardy of being
forced to take a leave of absence to "clear his head"—code for
pull his head out of his ass and do his job.

So that left making a visit to Geneva Schultz, Turner's maternal aunt, and her husband, Mitch Schultz. Kendall pulled into the driveway, which, unlike Turner's, was paved. A man was standing at the back of a pickup truck when she got out of her SUV. He stepped around the back end, a case of water bottles in his arms, and scrunched his eyebrows as he tried to place who she was.

"Can I help you?"

Kendall pulled her badge from her belt and held it up. "Are you Mitch Schultz?"

His head swiveled toward the front door, his tone wary. "What's this about?"

"I'm investigating a missing girl and wanted to talk to you and your wife about it, if possible."

"Don't know anything about a missing girl."

"She was a player on your nephew's team," Kendall explained.

Schultz physically exhaled through his entire body. "Oh, right, sorry. I did see that on the news." He shook his head. "Horrible thing. You haven't found her?"

"No, sir. Would it be possible to speak to you and your wife?"

"Sure, of course." The front door to the house was open but had a screen door. "Geneva?"

After a moment a woman with dark-blonde hair pulled back in a ponytail came to the door. She pushed the screen door open, her wary gaze on Kendall.

"This lady needs to talk to us about the girl from Jason's team who went missing."

Geneva stared at her husband for a moment, then her features relaxed, and she smiled. "Come on in," she said, looking back at Kendall, holding the screen door open.

"I'll just drop these in the garage and be right in," Schultz said, same wide smile across his face. He had done a one-eighty from when she first approached. But then again, no one liked FBI agents showing up unannounced at night.

Kendall walked up the cement path to the front porch and entered a small foyer. Whereas Turner's house was old and dilapidated, his aunt and uncle seemed to have done a great deal of work to theirs over the years. Wood floors, newer furniture, and a comfortable, homey feel made a stark contrast with the run-down flophouse atmosphere of Turner's house just a few hundred feet away.

"Please have a seat," Geneva Schultz said. She picked up a skein of yarn and some knitting needles from the couch and set them on the coffee table before sitting across from Kendall. "Jason told me one of his players had gone missing after the game the other night—it's really got him shook."

"What can you tell me about Jason?" Kendall took out her notepad and pen.

"Well, he's my sister's son."

"Do his parents live nearby?"

"No." She shook her head. "They're both dead. His father died when Jason was a teenager. And my sister passed away about three years ago. She had pneumonia and let it go . . . by the time she went to the hospital, she was in bad shape. Didn't last more than a day or so after. We—my husband and I—have taken him in, so to speak. He doesn't have any brothers or sisters, so we're his only family really."

"Do you have kids?"

"No." She looked up at her husband as he came into the room and took a seat next to her on the couch. Her eyes sparkled, and she smiled at him.

Mitch Schultz took his wife's hand in his and gave it a squeeze. "We were never blessed with kids. But we love them, and so it seemed obvious when Jason got out of school that he would come back here."

"It was lucky the house next to us was on the market," Geneva said. "It's not much, but it has potential."

"Yeah, good bones. Something he can fix up and make his own." Mitch looked around the living room. "Like we did. It may not be a mansion, but it is home."

"And we love it."

"It's lovely," Kendall said. "How long have you lived here?"

"Oh, jeez, what, thirty years?" Geneva asked her husband.

"Yeah, about that. Bought it when we were first married. Only the second house on this street." He looked up as if he was recalling a memory. "Yep, a lot of people have moved in and out of here over the years."

"I think we are the only original owners still here," Geneva added.

"And how long has Jason been living next door?" Kendall asked.

Mitch scratched his chin. "A couple years now."

"And do you see him often?"

"He comes over a couple of times a week for dinner." Geneva glanced at her husband for confirmation. "Less when he's coaching the rec team."

"Does he have people visit often?"

"I guess I've seen cars over there. I never pay much attention, so I really have no idea who they are or what they're doing over there."

"Does he have a girlfriend? Boyfriend?"

Mitch ruffled at the suggestion Jason might be gay. Not surprising. The idea wasn't welcomed by some of the older generations. Although people were starting to accept the concept of "love is love" more readily these days, there were still some holdouts—those people who said they were "okay with the gays" as long as it didn't touch their family. Kendall got the feeling Mitch and Geneva Schultz might fall into that category.

"He hasn't said anything about having a special someone in his life," Geneva said. "Certainly hasn't introduced us to anyone."

"So, the people he has over, would you say they're age appropriate for him? For instance, does he have any of the players over?"

"Like we said, we don't keep tabs on him—he's an adult, and we like to respect his privacy," Mitch said, suddenly gruff.

"But that said, we haven't seen anything that would be considered untoward. I know I've never seen any young people over there," Geneva added, softening the statement.

Kendall glanced around the room. On a table behind the couch were what appeared to be stacks of folded clothes. And by the look of the sizes and designs, the clothes were for children. "Do you have nieces or nephews who come over?"

Geneva followed Kendall's gaze. When she turned around, she had a smile on her face. "Oh, no, we don't. But we do babysit some of the children in the neighborhood."

"Sort of an in-home day care?" Kendall asked.

"No, nothing like that. Some of these families don't have the resources to pay for day care," Mitch said.

"And many have jobs that don't have regular hours, or they may get called in to work and don't have anyone to watch the children," Geneva said.

"So we help out by watching them."

"That's nice of you," Kendall said.

"It's neighborly. It's what we do here—look out for each other and pitch in where necessary."

"And the clothes?" Kendall pointed to the pile on the table.

"Well, like Mitch said, many of these people don't have a lot of money. So I sometimes find gently used clothes at the consignment shops around here and pick things up for the kids. It doesn't cost me much, and it helps out the families. It's our way of filling that void of not having kids—or grandkids—of our own."

"So, I know you said you don't really pay attention to what is happening at Jason's, but if you could think back over the last twenty-four hours. Do you recall seeing anything unusual at Jason's house? Any strange noises?"

"No," Mitch said.

"I know you're doing your job," Geneva said, "but really, you're wasting your time. Jason would never do anything to harm any of his players. He loves those kids—loves being their coach."

"Has he ever mentioned any of the players specifically? Discussed issues he's having with any of them or their parents?"

"Well"—Mitch drew the word out as he stroked the stubble along his jaw—"there are always parents who give him shit about how he's coaching. You know, 'Why isn't my kid playing more?' 'Why is that player getting special treatment?' You know, that kind of stuff. It's bound to happen. Hell, I probably did some of that when Jason was playing elite hockey before going to college. You want to make sure they're in front of the college scouts. That's how these kids get scholarships."

"And did Jason get a scholarship?"

"Full ride."

"To the University of Wisconsin." Geneva let out a heavy sigh. "Oh, he was so disappointed when the doctors said he should stop playing."

"And shared that with all the NHL scouts," Mitch spat. No mistaking how he felt about the situation.

"He was just heartbroken when he couldn't play in the NHL. It was a dream he and his dad had for him." She smiled, but there was no joy. "Along with Mitch," she added as an afterthought. "I'm just so happy he was able to get a coaching job. He's hoping he can make it to the NHL that way."

"What about Frankie Taylor? Did Jason ever mention anything about her?"

Geneva glanced at Mitch. "Doesn't sound familiar to me. Did he mention her to you, honey?"

"Nope. Never heard of her before seeing her on the news."

Mitch looked at his watch, the universal signal that Kendall had outstayed her welcome. She closed her notebook and fished a business card from her pocket. No use trying to bleed a turnip. It didn't appear the Schultzes were going to give up any useful information about Jason Turner.

She handed the business card to Geneva. "Thank you so much for your time. I appreciate you talking to me. If you think of anything at all, please give me a call."

CHAPTER

20

THE ELEVATOR IN Kendall's building jerked to a stop, the heavy metal gates sliding open. She put the key in the lock and walked into her new home. Except it didn't quite feel that way yet.

Would it ever?

Kendall had wanted nothing more than to come home and relax when she left the Schultz house. But now that she was there, alone, she wished she had gone with Adam to question the cashier's boyfriend about the murder.

Being alone was something she'd once cherished. Time to mull over the day, perhaps gain clarity in a complex investigation she was working, make a mental list of things to check out the next day at work.

And then Gwen died.

Kendall's life was now delineated between before Gwen was murdered and after. So many times Kendall had wished she had been the one to die instead. After all, Gwen would never have been a target if it hadn't been for Kendall. Amazingly horrific luck the man she was investigating for molesting his five-year-old daughter was the same man who had been responsible for torturing and killing so many women years earlier. The same man who had shot Kendall and left her for dead in the middle of the street when she had attempted to rescue one of his victims.

And even though Kendall had never gotten a look at his face all those years ago, had no idea or recollection of Scott Williams, Williams had remembered Kendall. And hadn't been about to take any chances that she recognized him. So he'd targeted her, but he'd ended up killing her best friend.

Kendall dumped her bag in the living room and flung her shoes from her feet. There were boxes everywhere. Tonight she should unpack one or two. Set up her home. Move on with life. Life after Gwen.

She sighed heavily, trudged to the cabinet, and pulled out a wineglass. Uncorking the bottle of wine—three-quarters of which Kendall had consumed the previous night—she emptied the remainder into her glass, nearly filling it to the rim.

She passed by the boxes without a second glance and went into her bedroom. A shower. That's what would help. Or maybe a bath in that giant, modern bathtub. She never took baths—was usually unable to sit still long enough to enjoy them.

Grabbing the remote from her bed, she switched on the TV for some noise. The news was on. Oh goody, she'd be able to see the press conference from earlier. Kendall knew the press had a job to do and they thought it was important—which, in cases like this, it was—but they often got in the way of investigations. And Kendall had a hard enough time at her job without inter-ference from an outside source who determined what the public needed to hear, investigation be damned.

Her cell phone rang, and she glanced at the caller ID. One letter popped up. Q. Short for Quentin, the other survivor of the three amigos.

"What up, wayward traveling man?" she asked after the call connected.

"Not much, hanging out in my hotel room."

"Is it super swank?"

"Hell yes." He had a fake accent Kendall could only assume was supposed to resemble a rich snob, which Q definitely was not. "I only stay at five-stars these days. It's really beneath me to mingle with the less economically successful."

"I hope you'll still associate with lowly me when you finally get back from your world tour." She slipped out of her slacks and blouse and sat on the edge of her bed. On the TV, she and Adam stood behind the lieutenant while he asked for assistance in getting information about the man killed at the gas station c-store. "Hey, do you have groupies yet?"

"Swarming around me like flies on account I'm so sweet."

"I thought flies were attracted to shit."

Q laughed. "What's going on there?"

Kendall hadn't told him about Frankie going missing. There hadn't been time, and she hadn't talked to him since before the hockey game.

"Where do I start?" she said. "There was a double homicide at a gas station convenience store, but amongst the dead bodies was a girl who'd been missing for a few weeks. So that was a happy ending." Q would know how monumental this was to her and the rest of the Crimes Against Children team. He had endured many horrific stories of girls found: alive, dead, and the worst ones—the ones who might have been better off dead.

Sounded harsh, and Kendall would never say it to anyone but her colleagues in the FBI office or to Adam or Q. But the truth was, when they recovered some girls, usually after a sting operation, the girls they found had already been missing for years, forced to get hooked on drugs so they'd be dependent on their abductor-pimps to get a hit. And the form of payment was degrading, humiliating, and tended to feed the desires of men with particularly disgusting sexual proclivities. The girls were shells of their former selves, and many of them went right back to the world they knew after being recovered. Some committed suicide. Even the ones who seemingly survived were never the same and found it hard to move on with life and put the past behind them.

It was devastating.

"Was she . . . okay?"

"Yeah," Kendall answered, knowing he was asking if Savannah had been raped or not. "Seems to have been found before things went too far into the shit."

There was a moment of silence. Kendall was bone weary. Not just from the physicality of the day—although she did have a sizable bruise on the side of her thigh, most likely from the dick-head she'd wrestled in the ditch—but also from the emotional fatigue that accompanied the disappearance of Adam's niece.

"So . . . what else?"

Q knew her so well. Too well, maybe. But he could always sense when she was holding back.

"Adam's niece is missing."

"Frankie?"

"Yeah." She let out a long sigh and fell back on her bed, her free arm over her eyes. "We all went to her hockey game, which is really the actual shit of it all—two law enforcement agents in the building, one who handles this crap every day—and she's swiped right under our noses. It would be embarrassing, but it's all too tragic."

"Jesus." Kendall could hear Q pop the cap off what she sus-pected was a beer. She sat up and took a deep swallow of her wine, letting it burn a path to her empty stomach and light her gut on fire. "How is Adam's family handling it?"

Kendall shrugged reflexively, even though he couldn't see her. "You know."

"Yeah," Q said, and she knew he did. "Do you need for me to come back? I could try to get a flight out in the morning."

"While I would love to have you here so I could cry on your shoulder about how revolting people are and how my life is one heinous day after another, there is really nothing you can do. I'm balls to the wall with these two investigations. I just got home, and I'm going to sleep soon so I can get in another fifteen- to eighteen-hour day tomorrow."

Q let out a sigh on the other end.

"I really do appreciate the offer. But you know how I get dur-ing an investigation, and right now I have two big ones on my plate and not enough hours in the day."

"It won't do either Frankie or Adam's family any good if you're run-down and not at your best. Order some food—some-thing substantial, not beige and deep-fried—before you pass out."

She smiled. This was why she loved this man so much. He was the brother she'd never had and always dreamed of. "I will. Thanks for taking care of me, even from afar."

"No worries," he said. "Tell Adam I'm sorry about his niece."

"I will. Good night, Q."

"Sleep tight, K."

She ended the call and lay back on her pillow, closed her eyes, and promptly fell asleep.

21

Wednesday night
23:29:17 hours missing

ADAM KNOCKED ON the front door of the house where the cashier, Ashley Collins, had lived with her baby and her boyfriend, Vincent Abuelo. It was getting late, but Adam couldn't help that. There was no telling what tomorrow would bring, and he might not have another chance to talk to Abuelo for a few days. The baby was probably down for the night, but it was still early enough that Mr. Abuelo likely wouldn't be in bed yet.

The door swung open. A young woman, probably midtwenties, long brown hair to match her long brown legs, stood before him. "Can I help you?"

Adam fumbled for his badge. It was kind of pathetic how easily a gorgeous woman could turn him into a blithering idiot these days. Adam chalked it up to not having had sex in so long he could easily become a monk. If guys had hymens, Adam's would've grown back by now. He wasn't even sure his dick actually worked anymore. Did you forget how to move if you went too long without sex? Or was it like riding a bike?

"Hello?" the woman asked.

Well, fuck.

"Sorry." He held up his badge. "I'm Detective Adam Taylor with the Denver Police Department. Does Mr. Vincent Abuelo live here?"

"Yeah, let me get him." She turned and left Adam standing in the open doorway for what seemed like a lifetime but was probably just enough time for Adam to pull his head out of his ass and remember he was investigating the murder of this man's girlfriend. The mother of his child.

Which brought up a question: Who was the young hottie who'd answered the door? Girlfriend? If so, was she living here?

A tall, equally good-looking man came to the door. "Yes?" he asked.

"Mr. Abuelo?"

"Yes, can I help you?"

"I'm Detective Adam Taylor. I'm investigating Ashley Collins' murder. Do you mind if I ask you a few questions?"

"Of course," Abuelo said. "Please, come in."

Adam followed him into the living room and took a seat on one of two recliners. Abuelo sat in the chair next to the one Adam had taken while the young woman sat on the couch.

"First, I'm very sorry for your loss. I understand you and Ms. Collins just had a baby?"

"Thank you, and yes, Alexandra. She's seven months old."

"Did Ms. Collins—do you mind if I call her Ashley?" The man shook his head, so Adam continued. "Did Ashley ever mention any problems she was having at work?"

"Well, it was a convenience store—I hated her working there, but I at least felt a little better about her being on the day shift—anyway, she always came home with stories. Mostly it was just about drunks coming in, chasing off homeless people trying to steal food—what you would expect."

"But nothing directly targeted at her?"

"You think this guy intentionally came in and shot her?" Abuelo leaned forward a bit, a scowl on his face. "I thought this was a robbery gone bad."

"And it does appear to be," Adam confirmed. "We're trying to cover all the bases before we close the case."

Abuelo sat back in his chair, but Adam could tell he wasn't completely convinced.

"Does the name Darin Stevens mean anything to you?"

Abuelo's eyebrows furrowed, and he frowned. "No, doesn't sound familiar."

"Ashley never mentioned him?"

The frown remained in place, but Abuelo cocked his head to the side, his gaze penetrating Adam. "Never heard the name before. How is he related to her murder?"

"He was the other victim," Adam said.

"Victim?" Abuelo's voice boomed. "The motherfucker killed Ashley. How is he the victim? How can you put him in the same category as her?" Tears flooded the man's eyes.

Adam softened his tone and paused for a moment. "I'm sorry. I understand where you're coming from, and I apologize. Simply stated, he is the other person who died in the store."

"And why do you think I know him? Do you think I had something to do with this?"

Maybe?

"No." Adam shook his head. "I'm trying to establish if Ashley ever said anything about this guy—perhaps he's a frequent customer she got to know or she had a problem with. We're trying to ascertain if this was planned or if it was random."

"No," Abuelo said, and shook his head. "Never heard of him."

"Mr. Abuelo, I know this is hard and the timing isn't good. There's nothing I would like more than to give you a few days to grieve. But I'm under the gun on this one, so I'm going to have to ask you some hard, potentially uncomfortable questions about Ashley. I know the first instinct is to protect her, but I really need for you to be straight with me."

Adam paused, unsure if he should divulge the next nugget of information. "Darin Stevens had a little girl with him when he entered the store. A girl who we have since learned was kidnapped a few weeks ago. So it is imperative I get all the information I can from you."

"Jesus," Abuelo said, raking his hand over his face. "How old was the girl?" No doubt he was thinking about what he'd be feeling if someone took his little girl, which was exactly why Adam had told him about Savannah.

"Ten years old."

Abuelo shook his head in disgust. "Ask me anything, Detective. I'll tell you what I know."

"How was your relationship with Ms. Collins lately?"

"Good. We were both tired all the time. Maybe we were a little more sensitive with each other than usual."

"What do you mean by *sensitive*?"

"It didn't take much for one of us to be pissed at the other, but it was just lack of sleep. People warned us that the last good sleep we would have was before Ashley gave birth, but you never realize how true it is until after you've spent most nights up trying to calm a colicky baby."

Adam didn't have firsthand experience, but he remembered Mark and Poppy walking around like zombies when Frankie had colic. He had made fun of his brother at the time, until his mother smacked him upside the head and he was forced to apologize.

"Did either of you step outside your relationship for emotional support?"

"Meaning what exactly, Detective?"

Adam glanced at the young woman sitting on the couch.

Abuelo's gaze followed Adam's to the couch. "Ah," he said, and pointed at the woman. "This is Victoria. Victoria Abuelo, my sister. She's here to help me with the baby."

Well, that made sense. And now Adam could see the family resemblance.

"Nice to meet you," Adam said, and turned his attention back to Vincent. "Sorry, but you didn't answer my question."

"No, Detective, neither one of us was cheating on the other. Our problems centered around a sixteen-pound being with the lungs of a Mack truck. Trust me, we were so tired that the thought of having to have sex with each other was as far from our minds as the moon is to the earth. Let alone having to sneak around to have it with someone else. Do you have kids?"

"Uh, no."

"Well, that's too bad. Because there is no way you will fully comprehend how debilitatingly exhausting having a baby can be."

After hearing all the stories about the hell that accompanied the first eighteen years of a child's life, Adam was sure he never wanted to find out. And he chalked up the *But it's all worth it* crap parents tried to peddle to pure bullshit. Misery loves company and all that, and parents needed other parents to commiserate with on a daily basis so they didn't go loony.

"Is it possible Ashley was working in conjunction with Darin Stevens in an attempt to make this look like a robbery?"

Abuelo chuckled, a look of disbelief on his face. "Why would she do that?"

"Well, one theory is that Stevens may have offered her a cut of the take if she went along with the robbery and just gave him the money from the cash register and then reported a robbery."

"I can't see that," Abuelo said, shaking his head. "There would be no reason to—we aren't rich, but we have enough. I make decent money. And Ashley just found out she got a scholarship for college, so she wasn't going to have to work anymore." Tears flooded his eyes, and he swiped them away. "She wanted to be a nurse."

And now that dream—hell, all the dreams she and Abuelo had for the future—were gone.

"What about the name Melvin Craig? Do you or Ashley know him?"

Abuelo inhaled deeply and released it. "No, never heard of him either."

"Was Ashley having any problems at work with her coworkers? Or maybe her boss?"

"Not really. They all seemed to get along pretty well. Ashley had a hard time saying anything bad about her boss. He gave her a job—trusted her with the cash register when no one else would give her a shot. So she was loyal to him."

"Well, she did call him a cheap mother . . ." Victoria interjected. "Sorry, cheapskate. He didn't want to do things like buy new refrigerators even though it was almost impossible to find parts for the dinosaurs they had in the store."

"Yeah, that's true," Vincent conceded. "That and the security system."

Well, this just got more interesting.

"What about the security system?" Adam asked.

"For starters, it was almost as old as the refrigerators. The guy who comes every other month to try to repair the damn thing told Ashley he didn't understand why the owner clung to that system. A new one would've been cheaper than constantly having the repair guy come out and fix it so often. He also told Ashley it was like the guy didn't want there to be better surveillance in the store."

"Did she say why her boss wouldn't repair those things?" Adam asked.

"No. Like I said, she was loyal. She rarely had anything negative to say about him. She just happened to tell me those things when they happened."

"Okay," Adam said, standing and putting his hand out to Abuelo. "Thanks so much for your time." He reached into his jacket pocket and pulled out a business card. "Anything you think of, no matter how insignificant, give me a call."

He left the small house and walked to his car, ruminating over what he'd learned. Why would a guy who ran a convenience store at a gas station in an area of town where businesses were often broken into and robbed not want to upgrade his security system? Was he really that cheap?

Or was he trying to avoid anything showing up on the surveillance he didn't want anyone—especially law enforcement—to see?

22

Wednesday night
24:16:59 hours missing

THE CONVENIENCE STORE was busy for just after eleven o'clock at night, but that didn't surprise Adam. All the night owls and tweekers, the people more comfortable moving about in the dark, were getting their daily supplies.

Six people were standing in line, waiting to be checked out. None of them looked to be in a hurry. Most stood, arms filled with bags of chips, candy, premade sandwiches, and beer. The breakfast of the night people. According to the schedule the owner had provided, Eddie Roberts was the man working tonight. The *beep, beep* of the scanner was almost in sync with Neil Diamond crooning about his sweet Caroline over the sound system. Adam headed for the coffee, even though he was sure he would regret it later that night when he was trying to sleep. Not because caffeine necessarily kept him awake—his system was too dependent on coffee for it to have any effect other than preventing headaches and jitters—but because at eleven o'clock at night the coffee was a type of sludge that had more in common with tar than a beverage. The beat cop filling his thirty-two-ounce Yeti didn't seem bothered by the thick liquid with the burnt aroma. Adam guessed he hadn't had a decent cup of coffee since being placed on the night roster.

The cop nodded at Adam as he strolled to the rolling hot dog machine and placed two large jalapeño sausages on buns before heading to the cash register. On his way, he snagged a bag of chips from an end-of-aisle display, gripping the bag between his teeth, since he had run out of hands to hold things with.

The other patrons gave the cop a wide berth, assuming he had telepathic powers and his Spidey-senses would be able to pick up on any crime the person had ever committed in their lives and arrest them on the spot.

Oh, but if it were that easy . . .

Adam settled on a bottle of Smart Water—he could use all the help he could get—and a bag of corn nuts. He only ever bought them when he was at a convenience store. Never thought about them otherwise. There was just something about the molar-cracking treat he couldn't pass up.

By the time Adam approached the cash register, the store seemed to clear out, and there was a lull in customers. He dropped his items on the counter, and pulled out his badge.

"Are you Eddie Roberts?"

The guy glanced around, and Adam wasn't sure if he was looking to see if anyone was listening or for the nearest exit. He hoped it was the former, because Adam was in no mood, or condition at this late hour, to chase him down.

"I'm just here to ask you some questions regarding Ashley Collins," Adam added quickly.

Roberts's face and shoulders slumped. "Poor Ash. I can't believe she's gone."

"How well did you know her?"

"Not super well," he said, placing Adam's items in a plastic bag. "I'd see her from time to time. I usually came in on my way to my day job."

"Which is what?"

"I work at the Amazon distribution warehouse, loading delivery trucks."

"What was your impression of her?"

"You mean, what did I think of her?"

Adam nodded.

"Super nice. Really hot. She was excited about going to college, always talking about how she never thought she was smart enough. Once she told me she didn't even know what college was until she was like eighteen or something."

Not surprising, given what Adam had learned about her childhood. Academics were most likely not a priority. Survival was.

"Did she ever mention any financial trouble she was having?"

Eddie wagged his head. "Nah, but then we weren't that kind of friends. I don't think she would've told me anything that personal."

"Is it possible she was working with the guy who was trying to rob the store?"

"No way." Eddie scrunched up his face. "Not Ash. She was one of those people that you looked at and thought, *What the hell are you doing working here?* She had her shit together. And she was all about trying to make sure her kid was proud of her." He shook his head in vehement protest of the allegation. "She wouldn't do anything to mess up her life."

Adam slid his credit card into the machine to pay. "What can you tell me about the security system here?"

Eddie snorted, placed Adam's receipt in the bag, and handed him his purchases. "That it sucks donkey balls. I don't even know why he has it. It's like it's just for show. Someone said he has it just to get a break on his insurance or something."

"I've heard he has some trouble getting repairs on it."

"Yeah, right. He's just too cheap to upgrade the system. Which is weird, since he has all new cameras and shit at his other store. But here, he just keeps the same crap. I think only a couple of cameras actually work. The rest he just keeps up as 'deterrence.'" Eddie used air quotes and wagged his head.

Interesting. Why would the owner upgrade the system at only one store? Was it to keep cameras from recording illegal activities here?

"Why do you think that is?"

Eddie opened a box of cigarettes and began restocking the supply behind the register. "Who knows?"

"I've heard the guy has come to repair the cameras but hasn't been able to do the work. Know anything about that?"

"Look, I like Mr. O—he's a really good guy and a great boss—but he is tight with money. If he thought the other place needed the upgraded security, who am I to question it?"

"Fair enough." Adam twisted the top off the water bottle and took a drink. "Know a guy named Darin Stevens?"

Eddie shook his head. "Doesn't sound familiar."

Adam pulled the picture up from Stevens's driver's license and turned the screen so Eddie could see. "Does he look familiar to you?"

Eddie pulled the phone closer and studied the picture. "Don't think so. But I see a lot of people every day. Unless he did something like start a fight or try to steal something recently, I doubt I'd remember."

"He was in here with a little girl the day Ashley was shot. Does that ring any bells?"

"No. I mean, I've seen a lot of young girls in the store when I come in during the day."

That piqued Adam's interest. "What's a lot?"

"I don't know, I guess once in a while. I hardly ever see them on the night shift."

"But enough so they stand out more?"

Eddie paused. "Yeah." He turned to face Adam and crossed his arms across his chest. "That and the dudes they're with . . . it just doesn't seem to fit."

"Meaning?" Adam asked.

"They're kind of sleazeballs, and the girls look normal. You know, like they come from good families and stuff. Dressed in nice—clean—clothes. Hair brushed. Things like that. "

"Do you know if the girls left with the men they came in with?"

Eddie shook his head. "Sorry, I didn't really pay much . . . oh, wait." He snapped his fingers and pointed at Adam. "There was one time I saw a guy with a girl when I came in to get coffee and something to eat on the way to my other job, and when I left, he and the girl were talking to another sleazeball. But I was in a hurry, so I didn't stick around to see what happened."

So, sordid men with young, healthy girls were frequenting this store. Alarm bells were going off in Adam's brain like fireworks on the Fourth of July. Something was amiss.

If Adam was correct—and he would run his theory past Kendall—the convenience store was being used as a cover for trafficking girls. The question was, how much did the owner know, and how deeply was he involved?

23

Thursday morning
31:13:12 hours missing

K ENDALL PULLED UP alongside the curb across the street
from the Farmers' house and caught Adam looking in the
windows of a Toyota RAV4 parked on the street. Sam Farmer
was the young man who had temporarily taken Frankie's place
on the first line during the hockey game the night she disappeared. And by all accounts, his father was the driving force
behind it.

"Anything interesting?" Kendall asked.

"Not really," Adam said. "A lot of fast-food trash but nothing
suspicious. Especially if this is the teenager's vehicle."

"Well, let's see what Mr. Farmer and Sam have to say."

They climbed the steps to the front porch. A deep, husky
bark sounded from inside when Kendall rang the doorbell. A
man yelled for the dog to quiet down. "Someone put this damn
dog out back."

A tall man with a chiseled jaw and rugged good looks, wearing sweatpants and a white T-shirt, opened the door. "Yeah?" he
said by way of greeting.

Like most insanely good-looking men, he had the personality
of a wet rag. Obviously, being attractive didn't always extend to
having a sparkling personality.

Kendall flashed her badge. "Special Agent Kendall Beck and Detective Adam Taylor, Denver PD. We'd like to ask you a few questions regarding the disappearance of Frankie Taylor."

Farmer exhaled and rolled his eyes. "I already told the police I didn't see her after the game." He retreated back inside the house, closing the door as he went.

Kendall put her hand out to stop it from closing any farther. "Yes, sir, I understand that, but we have some follow-up questions for you and your son."

"Sam's got school today," Farmer grumbled.

God, Kendall hated assholes first thing in the morning. And she'd only had one cup of coffee, so her patience hadn't fully awakened yet. Luckily, her smartassery was always ready to go.

"Okay, no problem," Kendall said sweetly. "We'll catch up with him there."

The statement worked. Farmer apparently didn't want the police talking to his son without him present. He backed up and opened the door wide again, yelling over his shoulder, "Sam, get your butt down here."

Farmer led them into a small sitting area with a settee and a leather armless chair. Everything in the room was white save the glass-and-chrome coffee table in the center. The house looked nicer than Kendall would've expected. Typically, the decor matched the occupants, and Farmer was far from well appointed and sophisticated.

A woman entered the room, her hair short but styled, wearing crop pants and a T-shirt depicting half the face of a woman on its left side. The graphic looked as if it had been created in a singular brushstroke. "Good morning," she said, looking at Kendall and Adam, then at her husband.

"Cops." More disdain from Mr. Farmer. "They want to ask Sam and I more questions about that Taylor girl from his hockey team."

Farmer's cell phone rang. He retrieved it from his pocket, glanced at the screen, and walked out of the room without a word.

"Oh," Mrs. Farmer said, her hand at her neck. "Such a tragedy. I heard that if they don't find a missing child in the first day or two, they probably never will."

Adam blanched, but to his credit held it together as he smiled at the woman and confirmed the statement. Kendall stood and moved nonchalantly around the room, pretending to be looking at family photos and the various pieces of art that graced the walls and glass bookcases. Oddly—or maybe not—the only books were turned so that the blank pages faced out. For some reason, this was all the craze in home decorating. Kendall didn't get it, but then, home decorating was not really her forte.

As she discreetly edged closer to the door, she could hear Farmer saying, "Yes, I have *it*." There was a pause, and then, "I can't talk. I have *company*."

Kendall returned to her seat as Farmer came back in, shoving his phone in his pocket, his face hard as stone.

Mrs. Farmer was still talking, but Kendall hadn't been paying attention. "I can't imagine what Poppy is going through. I should give her a call."

"Great," Farmer said, his teeth gritted. "And while you're doing that, tell Sam to move his ass."

Mrs. Farmer's gaze flared at her husband before turning back to Kendall and Adam. "Can I get you any coffee?"

"No, thank you, ma'am," Adam answered for both of them. He was going to owe Kendall a coffee when they got out of there. Possibly with a shot of vodka. Mr. Fabulous wasn't easy to take on the insubstantial caffeine intake she'd had so far this morning.

"I understand when the police first came to ask about Frankie, your vehicle wasn't here, is that correct?" Kendall asked Farmer, after his wife had left the room.

"Yeah, my son—older son, Jacob—he had it. Went to his girlfriend's house."

"And how old is Jacob?" Adam asked.

"Sixteen."

"Kind of young to be going out that late, isn't it? In the middle of a school week?" Kendall added.

Farmer remained standing, stance wide, arms across his chest, looking down his nose at Kendall. She knew it was supposed to be intimidating, but it almost made her laugh. "You raise your kids the way you want, and I'll raise mine the way I want."

Touché, Kendall supposed. Still, seemed awfully convenient the vehicle hadn't been here the very night the police were asking to check vehicles for a missing child.

"We'll need Jacob's girlfriend's contact information."

"They don't have anything to do with this." Farmer's voice boomed through the small living room.

Quick temper. Kendall would store that nugget of knowledge away. How had he handled it when his son was once again pulled from the first line? Had he flown into a rage? Acted on a whim? Perhaps seen an opportunity when Frankie was vulnerable and alone and grabbed her? That would certainly get her out of the way of his son getting more playing time, as Turner had stated was a prime goal of Farmer for his son.

Still too many questions without any answers.

A young boy sauntered into the room, backpack hanging off one shoulder. He wore a black T-shirt reading *In my defense, I was left unsupervised* in white ink. "Mom said you wanted to see me," he directed at his dad.

Farmer pointed at Kendall and Adam. "They have questions about Frankie Taylor."

"Are you Sam?" Kendall asked.

"Yeah," he said, and looked up at his father. "But I barely know Frankie."

"I understand you play hockey with her. Do you also go to the same school as her?" Kendall asked, before Farmer could intercede.

Sam sneered. There was zero doubt Sam was the miniature of his father. It was kind of sad; the world didn't need another asshole, especially in kid form. "Yeah, but we're not friends."

Kendall detected a slight snarl at the end of his statement. She had already been informed the Farmers were not Frankie fans, but Kendall would've thought they'd rein in the hate once they learned she was missing. Or maybe it didn't matter because they knew exactly where Frankie was.

"When was the last time you saw Frankie?" Adam asked.

"At the game."

"Did you see her after the game was over?"

Sam glanced at his father again. "No, not really."

"What does 'not really' mean?" Kendall asked.

Sam shifted his weight to his other foot and sighed, looking irritated. He was a carbon copy of his father, right down to the shitty attitude.

"Well, we all have to stick around to hear Coach tell us how well we played and when our next practice is, stuff like that. I saw her then. But I left as soon as Coach let us go."

"And you didn't see her after that?" Adam asked.

"Nuh-uh."

"Do you and Frankie get along?" Kendall asked.

Sam shrugged one shoulder. The backpack slid off and dropped to the floor at his feet. "Not really."

"And why is that?" Kendall asked, leaning forward with her hands on her knees, focusing only on Sam, hoping to block out anyone else in the room and keep his attention solely on her.

"Because she thinks she's a good hockey player and her parents forced Coach to let her on the team. And then Coach gave her my spot on the first line." His nostrils flared, and his eyes darkened. "But I *earned* that spot. Bobby Lister finally left the team—he was on the first line before me—and that spot was mine. Then Frankie comes along"—disdain dripped from his lips—"and Coach was all 'Let's give Frankie a shot at playing on the first line for a while,' and now she plays there all the time."

"Except for the last game. She didn't play the first period, right?" Kendall asked. "Do you know why she didn't play during the first period?"

"Nah," he said, but his gaze went to his shoes. He was lying. Or at least holding back information.

"Are you sure about that?" she prodded.

He shrugged again. "Might've heard something about Coach getting up in her face, but I don't know what about—didn't care as long as I got to play."

Nice. What a self-absorbed little fuck stain.

Sam snapped his fingers and pointed at Adam. "Hey, you're her uncle or something, right?"

Farmer's head snapped up. "Interview over. Sam has to get to school." He grasped the boy by his shoulder and turned him away from Kendall. Sam reached down and scooped up his backpack as he was hurried from the room.

Farmer pivoted toward Kendall after he had driven Sam from the room. "Now, if you don't mind, I need to get ready for work."

"Actually, I do mind, Mr. Farmer," Kendall said. "I'm investigating the disappearance of a young girl—a girl you and your family know. Who your son plays hockey with. And you can't spare me some time to see if you have information regarding what may have happened to her?"

Farmer's face reddened. "Look, Detective—"

"Special Agent."

"Whatever. Again, I don't know anything about what happened to Frankie. Sorry she's gone, but it has nothing to do with me or my family."

"And do you share your son's dislike of Frankie Taylor, *Drew*?" Kendall said as she rose. She was done with this asshole trying to bully her. This wasn't grade school, and they weren't on the playground. Kendall was well aware of the tactics men played to keep women in line. What he didn't know was that she wasn't easily threatened by men.

Farmer stuck his finger close to her face, but Kendall didn't flinch. "That girl, she came onto the team, and it was like some golden child had arrived. She took Sam's place on the line—a position he worked hard to get. He'd paid his dues playing on the second and third lines, and then Frankie comes in and snatches it away from him like she was owed something because she's a girl trying to play a boys' game."

"And that pissed you off, didn't it?" Kendall pushed.

"You're damn right it did." Spittle flew from Farmer's mouth. He was starting to resemble a rabid dog. "If Sam doesn't play on the first line, he won't be able to get onto any travel teams. If he doesn't get on travel teams, the big college recruiters won't give him a second glance. And then there goes his chance at scholarships—all because some woman couldn't give her husband a boy, so he had to try and turn his daughter into one."

Kendall felt Adam bristle behind her as he stood up. She only hoped he didn't knock this shit bag on his ass.

A flash of recognition crossed Farmer's face. He was losing his shit and straddling the line of assaulting a federal agent. He placed his hands on his hips, took a step back, and inhaled deeply. "Look, it would be one thing if she were a boy who came on the team and legitimately earned the spot on the first line over Sam. But she's a girl. And she's ruining Sam's chance at scholarships that she can't even get. That smells like bullshit to me. So yeah, *Special Agent*, I was just as upset as Sam. And while I hope nothing has happened to her, I hope she never comes back to the team."

Without another word, Farmer stormed out of the room. After a moment, Kendall heard a door slam in another part of the house.

"Guess he's done answering questions," she said.

"What a fucking asshole." Adam glanced at Kendall. "There are days I wish I wasn't a cop so I could knock the ever-loving shit out of people like him. Today is one of those days."

Kendall agreed and placed a business card on the table, sure Mrs. Farmer would be the one to pick it up. "Let's go."

When they got outside, she placed a call to Jake. "Get a tap on Drew Farmer's phone. And see if Brady will allow surveillance on the twatwaffle. He's up to something shady, and I can't shake the feeling he knows way more about what happened to Frankie than he's letting on."

THE CALL FROM Saul came just as Adam was climbing into Kendall's Range Rover after dropping his truck off at Mark's. It only made sense to use one vehicle. And control-freak Kendall insisted on driving. Apparently, Adam's driving "sucked ass," and there was a reference to driving like a grandma.

"Hey, Saul," Adam said, pressing the speakerphone button so Kendall could hear the conversation also. "Whatcha got for me?"

"A couple of things. First, Jake interviewed Frankie's best friend, and she was less than forthcoming. Jake got the feeling she might be more receptive to another female."

"Hi, Saul, it's Kendall. Have Jake set something up with her this afternoon, either at the PD or her school. I'll talk to her and see if she has anything of value."

"Got it," Saul said. "Next up, the IT geeks were able to pull the GPS from Poppy's Explorer. Looks like she's been heading over to the southeast side of the city a couple of times a week. Stays for about an hour and a half, two hours max, then goes home."

"Great," Adam said. "Text the coordinates to Kendall, and we'll see if we can figure out where she's going, and for what."

"We have a pool going back here on the where and the why, if you want to put a fiver in," Saul said.

Adam knew it was all in good fun; hell, he had started many a pool during an investigation. But this was different. This was his sister-in-law. Adam didn't feel much like participating, knowing how catastrophic the information they might uncover would be to his brother.

"I'll pass," Adam said, hoping his tone wasn't coming off too pissy. He didn't want the reputation that he was above a little harmless wager among investigators. It was still just a way for the other guys to detach, not get too personally invested so they could keep a clear head. And Frankie needed that more than making sure Adam wasn't offended.

"Kendall?" Saul asked.

"Yeah, I'll donate to the *seeing a friend* fund." Adam knew she didn't actually think Poppy was seeing a friend and lying to her husband about it. Like almost everyone else, she probably believed Poppy was cheating on her husband. But he appreciated her not jumping on that bandwagon for his sake.

"Okay," Saul said. "Fletch just forwarded everything the geeks found to Kendall's phone. Let me know if there are any issues."

"How did the other interviews go?" Adam asked.

"Nothing so far. Seems Frankie was popular and well liked by all. But we still have more to interview, so there may be something there yet."

"Thanks, Saul." Adam ended the call.

Kendall pulled into the drive-through lane at Starbucks and ordered two Venti black coffees and two cream cheese Danishes. While they waited for their order, she pulled up the text messages and added the coordinates to her GPS.

"Looks like your sister has been meeting someone at a strip mall in Cherry Hills," Kendall said. "Does she know anyone over there?"

"Not that I'm aware," Adam said, "but I don't know everyone she knows."

Once they got the coffees and breakfast treats, Kendall hopped onto the interstate and followed the GPS directions to the area Poppy had been frequenting lately. She pulled into the parking lot of a two-story strip mall. The bottom-floor units seem to be taken up by coffee shops and other boutique retail stores. The upper floor was all professional offices.

"Let's start on the bottom and see if anyone remembers her. Maybe she was meeting someone at the coffee shop. With any luck, they might still have security video of her last visit," Kendall said.

"Have to start somewhere," Adam said. He wished he hadn't eaten the Danish. It was sitting like a heavy rock in his gut. He wanted to vomit. The thought that he might get confirmation Poppy was cheating on his brother made him sick. And pissed him off.

How dare she throw away the life they had built? How dare she dishonor his brother, who'd worked so hard to give them a nice home, who'd loved her and Frankie more than anything in this world? If she didn't want to be with Mark, why not just divorce him? Why infidelity?

Was this why Frankie was gone? Had she found out and run away rather than face a life without one of her parents in the home? Frankie was so close to Mark, the perennial daddy's girl, it was inconceivable she wouldn't see him every day.

"Get out of your head, Adam," Kendall said. "Stop thinking the worst. There are a lot of reasons Poppy could be over here, and being secretive about it, that have nothing to do with cheating on Mark."

"Like what?" Adam asked. "And if it's all so innocent, why lie about it to us?"

"Maybe when she lied, she thought it wouldn't matter to the investigation. She may have thought Frankie would be home by the morning and she didn't need to say anything. It's not uncommon, and we hear it with nearly every investigation."

Adam scoffed. Yeah, Kendall could be right, but he knew deep in his bones Poppy was keeping a secret that could rip apart his family. He was struggling to keep his idealistic world from cracking in two, and to quash the desire to tear Poppy's heart out of her chest if he was correct.

Kendall whirled around, blocking him, to get him to stop moving. "We follow the evidence. We don't anticipate and make the evidence fit what we think we know. That doesn't help Frankie. This isn't a murder investigation where the fate of the victim is already determined. This is a missing child, and if we get this wrong, we never find her."

That hit Adam square in the chest, as if she had sunk a blade deep in his heart and was twisting it for good measure. He couldn't imagine life without Frankie. Kendall was right. He needed to stop expecting the worst and figuring out his next move without a shred of evidence to back him up.

He gave her a quick nod. She turned on her heel and started walking again.

Time to do some of that detective shit he was so good at and bring his niece home.

Through the coffee shop, a dry cleaner, a bath store, and two clothing boutiques, no one remembered seeing Poppy. They climbed the steps to the second floor. Door number one was an insurance agent. He didn't recognize Poppy from her picture and double-checked to make sure she wasn't a client. Adam didn't get a vibe of deceit from the guy, but he would keep him on the list for now. He was in his midforties and good-looking. Resembled Mark a bit.

Kendall pulled open the door for Henry Robinson, Attorney at Law. Comfortable chairs greeted clients, along with a young woman at a dark oak desk. "Can I help you?"

Adam pulled out his badge in sync with Kendall.

"Kendall Beck and Adam Taylor. I was wondering if you could tell me if this woman has been here?" Kendall flashed the picture of Poppy on her phone. "Her name is Poppy Taylor."

"Um, I'm not sure I'm allowed to give you that information." She stood from the desk and glanced down a short hallway behind her. "Can you hold on for just one moment?"

She didn't wait for an answer before ducking into what Adam assumed was an office. Before long, the receptionist came out with another woman much older than her on her heels.

"Can I help you?" the second woman asked.

Kendall went through the same introductions and asked the same question regarding Poppy.

"I'm sorry, but I can't tell you if she is a client. That information is confidential."

"Is Mr. Robinson in?" Adam asked.

"Yes." A sweet, completely fake, smile slid into place, as if it was an automatic response. "But he's very busy. You'll need to make an appointment."

"I understand," Kendall said. "But we're investigating a missing child—Mrs. Taylor's daughter—so we don't have time to make an appointment and come back. If we have to do that, it may be a homicide investigation."

Adam felt his blood run cold. He knew Kendall was trying to get a reaction from the woman, force her hand and get them in to see the attorney, but it hit Adam like an icy wind chilling him to the bone.

The woman's face blanched. "One moment, please," she mumbled and walked to the end of the hall, knocked on a door, and slipped into another office. After what felt like a thousand years, she stepped into the hallway and called for them.

A tall man in his sixties, maybe, who'd kept in shape, with dark hair and blue eyes, stood behind his desk and reached his hand out to Kendall. "Henry Robinson."

"Special Agent Kendall Beck," Kendall said, shaking his hand.

"Detective Adam Taylor, Denver PD."

Robinson was perhaps a little older than Adam imagined the man Poppy would be having an affair with was, but to each her own. And once again Adam was taken aback by how similar the man was to Mark in physique and looks.

Maybe Poppy had a type.

"What can I do for you?" Robinson asked, taking a seat in his high-backed leather desk chair.

Kendall and Adam sat in matching leather club chairs on the opposite side of the desk.

"We have reason to believe a woman by the name of Poppy Taylor has been coming here—quite frequently, in fact—over the past few weeks." Kendall flashed the picture of Poppy for Robinson to see.

"Perhaps you'd like to tell me why you're investigating Mrs. Taylor?" Robinson asked.

"What makes you think we're investigating her?" Kendall tossed back at him.

"Touché, Special Agent Beck." He rested his elbows on the arms of the chair and steepled his fingers in front of him. There was a glint in his eye. Adam had seen it in every lawyer he had ever met. They loved a challenge and appreciated anyone who was able to match wits with them. "*Are* you investigating Mrs. Taylor?"

Kendall leaned back in her seat and crossed her legs. "Right now, we're trying to ascertain her whereabouts for the past three to four weeks. We were led to understand she was coming here. Can you confirm this?"

"I assume you need this information as part of an investigation?"

"Assume away," Kendall said. Adam admired the way she could play people who thought they had the upper hand in a conversation. She was too good at her job.

And once again, he thanked the heavens for bringing her into his life. He had no doubt she would be the catalyst for Frankie coming home.

Robinson smiled and chuckled. "Okay, Agent Beck, I can confirm that Mrs. Taylor has come here on occasion."

"And why was she coming here?"

"You know I can't divulge that information."

"Are you having an affair with her?" Adam asked.

Robinson stilled. "No, Detective Taylor, I am not having an affair with her. I am a happily married man."

"But she is a client?"

"I cannot confirm or deny."

"Are you aware, Mr. Robinson, that Mrs. Taylor's daughter is missing?" Kendall asked.

That caught Robinson off guard. He stilled. His face paled. "What? No, I . . . when did this happen?"

"Two days ago," Kendall said. "So you can see why it's important that we understand Mrs. Taylor's whereabouts for the time leading up to the disappearance."

Robinson was still stuck on the circumstances of the actual disappearance, not Poppy's activities. "Did she run away? Or was she kidnapped?"

"Still undetermined," Kendall said. "Which is why we're trying to nail down Mrs. Taylor's actions."

"You can't possibly think Poppy had anything to do with her daughter's disappearance."

Poppy? First-name basis. Interesting.

So, maybe more than a client? But how much more?

"That's one possibility, but not one we believe will pan out. What we're really trying to determine is what she was doing over here and why, so we can determine if perhaps the reason will lead to someone following her. Making an example of her. Anything."

Robinson sat back in his chair, hand over his mouth, as he let out a long, heavy sigh. "Jesus," he muttered as he looked at the ceiling. "Look, I can't tell you why Poppy has been coming here. But I am ninety-nine percent sure it has absolutely nothing to do with the disappearance of her daughter."

"That's not good enough odds," Kendall said, letting out her own sigh, most likely for effect. "You see, I spend my days looking for missing children—it's *all* I do—and I'm pretty good at it. So I like to think I'm a better judge of whether someone might be involved in the disappearance of a child."

Robinson shook his head and stared out the window. Adam thought maybe he was considering giving them the information. He turned his gaze back to them. "I'm sorry, I can't ethically give you any more."

"Is Poppy planning on divorcing her husband?" Adam asked.

Robinson sat there, blank faced, revealing nothing. Adam thought maybe that said everything he needed to know.

Kendall handed the lawyer a business card. "If you determine there are things you can tell us, please give me a call."

Robinson picked up the card and tapped it on its edge a couple of times before placing it in his desk drawer.

"We'll see ourselves out." Kendall gave Adam a slight nudge on his shoulder to get him to move.

He wanted to strangle the lawyer. Or at the very least, sit there until Robinson finally gave up the answers. But Adam had to concede the man wasn't going to talk any further.

"Fuck," Adam cursed under his breath as soon as they stepped outside the law office. "That was a waste of time."

"Not really," Kendall said. "We know Poppy was coming here to see Robinson. And . . ." She pointed to the glass door. Under the firm name, it read, *Top Rated Family Law Firm in Denver since 1985*. "We also know he specializes in divorces."

CHAPTER

25

Thursday morning
34:31:58 hours missing

THE PICTURE OF Frankie taped to the whiteboard in the war room at the Denver Police Department barely resembled the girl Kendall knew. This was most likely a school picture, considering the standard blue background the photography companies used in virtually every school in America. Frankie had her hair down, brushed out so it was straight and shiny, and was wearing a pink shirt. Kendall had never seen her in anything but graphic T-shirts or sweatshirts with her hair pulled back in a ponytail.

The two sides of Frankie. It never ceased to amaze Kendall how often people had more than one side to their personalities. Not the dissociative split personalities, which Kendall wasn't even sure she bought as a real medical condition, but the various faces people put on depending who they were with and what they were doing. So many times she had interviewed people about a child molester who lived next door. The neighbors almost always said the same thing—the person was nice, quiet, and kept to themselves. No indication they were anything other than what they portrayed.

What was Poppy's truth? Kendall had always seen her as a dedicated wife and mother. In love with her family and her life. Hockey mom extraordinaire. But was it possible she was leading a double life? Was she having an affair with Robinson, despite his protestations? Was she planning on divorcing Mark and trying to get everything set up in advance of his being served papers?

Kendall sat straight up in her chair.

Oh, holy fuck . . .

Jake came in and sat down next to her. "Jesus, Kendall, see a ghost or something?"

"I just thought of something I hadn't considered before, and now I wish I could banish it back to where it came from."

Jake leaned forward and rested his arms on the table. "Well, you know that's impossible, so you better spill it."

"Adam and I found out Poppy has been seeing an attorney— a divorce attorney. So, I was thinking, what if she was trying to get things all set up for her new life without Mark before she asked him for a divorce?"

"Okay . . ."

"We know Frankie is a supreme daddy's girl." Kendall couldn't believe she hadn't considered this. "What if Poppy was afraid she would lose her daughter to her father in a custody battle?"

Jake's eyes widened. "No, you don't think—"

"She would fake a kidnapping in order to get Frankie away from Mark without a battle?" She shrugged one shoulder. "It's possible, right?"

"Yeah, but highly unlikely to be successful. Frankie isn't a baby or toddler who will eventually forget her father over time and distance. She's almost a teenager. She's not going to let her mother keep her from her dad."

True . . . but something was nagging at Kendall. Something that said it was still plausible.

"Maybe she tells Frankie some sort of lie about her father that would explain why she can't see him."

Jake looked skeptical. "Like what?"

Kendall didn't know. What would keep Frankie from her father?

She snapped her fingers. "What if she brainwashes Frankie into believing her father died? Maybe she convinces Frankie she wants only them to be together to grieve her father. And then she will convince her to move away—to another state, or maybe another country—because it's too hard to live in Colorado with all the memories of her dad."

Jake nodded. "Then she tells Mark she wants a divorce, leaves town, and he has no idea Frankie is with her. She'd need help from someone, though. Someone who could keep her secret life well hidden."

"Like an attorney? One she may be having an affair with?" Kendall quirked an eyebrow.

"Yeah, that would do it. But wouldn't Mark continue to search for Frankie even if Poppy isn't around?"

Kendall glanced at the door to make sure no one was coming in. She didn't need to make her theory public until it was no longer a theory. "Not if everyone is convinced Frankie is probably dead."

"You think she would do that to Mark? Let him think his daughter is dead?"

Kendall shrugged. "This whole theory rests on the assumption Poppy would lie about Mark's death to Frankie. It's not a stretch to think she wouldn't use the same lie on Mark."

Jake scrubbed his hand along his jaw. "This is some next-level diabolic shit, Kendall."

"Yeah." She looked up as Saul and Fletch came in and whispered, "Let's keep this between us for now."

"Who died?" Saul asked, tossing bags of chips and bottles of water into the center of the table.

"No one," Kendall said.

"You look like you've seen a ghost or something."

Kendall shook her head. "Nope, everything's fine here."

Saul quirked an eyebrow but didn't press the issue.

Adam came into the room, his officer-puppy Caleb Young on his heels. He glanced at the picture of his niece on the board as he took a seat across the table from Kendall. She couldn't imagine how he was able to get out of bed and function each day, let alone investigate two major cases.

Except that she did, and she knew movement in any shape or form was the only thing that kept the demons at bay. The dark devils who planted thoughts and scenarios and visions about what could be happening to a loved one who was missing. Kendall had gone through it with Gwen.

Now Adam was experiencing it for himself. And judging by the dark circles under his eyes, he wasn't getting much sleep at night, if any. The same demons she had battled were abusing him now. And there was very little she could do to help him.

Except find his niece. Alive and well and unharmed.

"Okay, let's start with the double homicide," Adam said, twisting the lid off a bottle of water and taking a drink.

"Still trying to track down the man Melvin Craig was supposed to meet that morning. No luck yet. I've left messages but haven't received a return call," Jake said, consulting his notes. "I did a quick Google search on the name Craig gave us but came up with several variations of Thomas Johnson in the area. I'm having the team back at our offices dig a little deeper into it and try to come up with something."

"Might be worth having a face-to-face with Mr. Craig," Adam said, making a note in his pad.

"And if you do," Kendall added, "ask him if he made a call after leaving the convenience store and running down the alley to hide. Savannah Hawley mentioned he called someone to pick either him up or *them*; she couldn't be positive which one. See if he has anything to say about that."

"What else?" Adam asked, glancing around the table.

"The presser resulted in some credible leads on Darin Stevens. We were able to come up with an address where he is— was—living. A CSU will be heading over this afternoon to work their forensic magic," Saul said. "Who would you like to go over and have a look around?"

"I'll do it," Adam said, with noticeable reluctance. "I need as many people as possible on the other case." And he needed to make sure Lou saw him working the double homicide, Kendall thought. "Where are we on the cell records for Stevens and Ashley Collins?"

"I'll check with Sheri," Fletch said, making a note.

"Also, find out what college Ashley was attending, or set on attending, not sure which. She apparently was in line to receive a scholarship that would allow her to quit her job. Let's see if that's true." Adam turned to Young. "The owner of the convenience store has another store. Find out what happened there a few months ago. They apparently received an insurance payout, which enabled them to buy a new security system."

"But not the other store?" Fletch asked.

"Not as far as Eddie the cashier is aware."

"I'll track down the insurance agent," Young said.

"That's all I have," Adam said. "Over to you, Kendall."

"Okay, let's keep working on questioning Frankie's friends, classmates, and teammates. Young Sam Farmer said he heard a rumor Coach Turner was yelling at Frankie before the game, but he didn't hear it himself. I want to know if anyone else remembers that and may have heard what the argument was about."

"The best friend didn't seem comfortable talking to a male, so I set up an interview at the middle school with Olivia Brown," Jake said to Kendall. "She's Frankie's best friend. A school counselor will meet you at the front office and get you set up in a room so you can have a conversation with her."

"Got it," Kendall said, making a notation in her notebook.

Jake continued, "The tap on Drew Farmer's phone has already hit pay dirt. He had a text conversation with someone discussing merchandise in exchange for cash only and has set up to meet at 'the usual place.'"

"Do we know who he was talking to?" Adam asked.

"Nope, and the phone came back as a burner."

"Do we have a tail on him?" Kendall asked.

"Yes," Jake confirmed. "They'll let me know when he makes a move."

Kendall nodded. "Saul, can you check court documents and see if anything comes up for Poppy Taylor?"

The room stilled for a moment, but Kendall went about gathering her things. It was barely a hunch she had, and she wasn't willing to let the team know what she was thinking unless there was something to talk about.

"Let's get back to it," she said, and walked out the door.

26

Thursday afternoon
37:04:13 hours missing

THE MANAGER OF the apartment building where Darin Stevens had lived turned the key in the lock and stepped back. Adam pushed open the door. The smell hit him like a gale-force wind—rotting food mixed with the overpowering aroma of sweat along with the pungent odor of cat urine—and knocked him back a couple of steps. One of the crime scene techs chuckled as he handed Adam a mask and some latex gloves.

"It's not the worst place I've had to work this week," the tech said as he passed through the door and into the apartment.

And Adam once again wondered why he had chosen this career. Wading through other people's shit—literally—was taking its toll. On top of only being half present as the crime scene techs collected evidence. He wanted—no, needed—to be working Frankie's case. The only thing providing him any solace was Kendall running the investigation. She was one of Adam's closest friends. She knew and loved Frankie. No one would work as hard to find Frankie and get her home safely. Adam had seen her dedication in action as she hunted down the man who had murdered her best friend a few months earlier. She had been relentless then, and Adam knew she would put the same effort into Frankie's case.

The crime scene unit worked methodically to bag the big items first: computers, tablets, and other electronics. They needed to find out why Stevens had Savannah. Why had the couple who had kidnapped her given her to Darin? What was he doing at the convenience store? If he had gone there specifically to rob the place, why not leave Savannah in the car?

Adam worked his way through the apartment, carefully avoiding the land mines left by a cat—yet to be located, which didn't bode well for the feline's current status—and avoiding the kitchen. He was sure it should be labeled a hazardous waste area, with any tech going in wearing a full hazmat suit. Adam didn't get paid enough to go in there and risk catching some deadly disease.

"Detective," one of the crime scene techs called to him. "You'll want to see these before I bag them." Adam avoided a pile of shit and stepped on a fast-food bag thrown on the floor. A loud screech startled him as a flash of orange bolted past him and out the door.

"Cat?" Adam asked.

"Yeah," the tech confirmed, nodding his head, his eyes still a bit wide. "Wasn't planning on finding it still breathing."

Adam slapped the tech on the back. "We saved a life today."

"Well, that's something, I guess." He handed a stack of pictures to Adam. The first was a young blonde girl, the next another girl of similar age but with darker hair. Adam quickly flipped through the stack of eight pictures, halting when he got to the last one.

Savannah Hawley.

"Mind if I keep these for a minute?" Adam asked.

The tech stared at him for a moment and finally nodded. "Don't go far. I'm not getting my ass in a wringer because you misplace some of those."

"Understood," Adam said, pulling his cell phone out of his jacket pocket. Kendall was probably in the middle of interviewing Frankie's best friend—best not to interrupt her. He opened his contacts and pressed Jake's name.

"Alexander."

"Jake, it's Adam. I'm at Darin Stevens' apartment, and the crime scene guy found a stack of pictures. They're all young girls—one of them is Savannah Hawley."

"Recognize any of the other ones?"

"No, but I'm not in the missing kid business. I thought I might take my own pictures of them on my cell phone and send them to you?"

"Yeah, do that," Jake said. Adam could hear a horn blast. Jake was in the car. "I'm heading back to my office. I'll circulate them and see if anyone recognizes them."

"Why do you think he had them?" Adam asked, but he was pretty sure he already knew the answer.

"I'm guessing the dickhead was part of a sex trafficking operation."

"Lovely."

"Hey, we saved one. Take your wins where you can."

"Let me know what you find out."

"Will do."

Adam ended the call and laid the pictures out on a sofa cushion. After he had taken each picture, he sent them to Jake before gathering them up and handing them off to the tech.

Adam wandered into the bedroom, which was only slightly better than the rest of the apartment, but not by much. How could people live this way? Adam wasn't a clean freak or anything, but he was seriously worried that he might need a tetanus shot after leaving the apartment. He wandered around the room, refusing to go anywhere near the bathroom. A relatively new fifty-five-inch flat-screen TV sat on top of a dresser. Next to the bed on a nightstand, the remote sat on top of a pile of magazines.

Adam didn't know anyone under the age of fifty who even received physical copies of magazines. Everything was on the fabulous whiz-bang Google devices attached to everyone's hands. Adam could only think of a few magazines a young stud like Stevens would have next to his bed. And they were most likely not for a bit of light reading before bedtime.

"Let's see what kind of kink you're into, Mr. Stevens." Adam picked up a few from the top of the pile. The first one he glanced at was an S&M special. Adam knew lots of people got into that sort of thing, but it all looked incredibly uncomfortable to him. With his luck, he'd put something on wrong, be unable to get out of it, and die in some rubber suit suspended from the ceiling.

Knowing the guys on the force, they would insist he be buried in the outfit with an open casket.

And that would be his legacy.

Adam tossed the magazine onto the bed and looked at the next one. His stomach roiled and vomit pushed up his throat. Child pornography. He could handle a lot of things in his business: death, mutilation—the depravity of humans was limitless. But he would take a decapitated body with entrails lying on the floor over seeing a child in one of these magazines.

He was just about to replace it on the pile before he tossed his cookies when he noticed writing on the back. In the only place where there was some white space, Stevens had penned a note.

One word.

Adam's head started spinning. His heart pounded in his chest. He couldn't breathe. He dropped the magazine on the bed and bent over, desperate to catch his breath.

Desperate to unsee what was written on the magazine.

A name.

Frankie.

And the bottom dropped out of Adam's world.

27

Thursday afternoon
37:05:43 hours missing

KATHARINE BATES MIDDLE School—named after the woman who wrote "America the Beautiful," not the scary actress in *Misery*—looked like every 1960s-style school in the country. Whenever Kendall entered a middle or high school, she was thrown back to cafeteria food and the excitement that came with Friday undercooked square pizza. Even though she knew it was disgusting, she still sort of craved a piece with a carton of chocolate milk.

She opened the door to the office and was met by the school resource officer. "Officer Buckley," he said, pulling his pants up by his belt. "But the kids just call me Buck."

Kendall doubted that. She had already come up with four alternatives, one that actually rhymed with Buck.

A thirtysomething woman in a white top, black skirt, and flat shoes nudged Buck out of the way with her elbow, lips pursed. Buck stepped back, red spots covering his face. The woman ignored him and smiled at Kendall. "Hi, you must be Agent Beck. I'm Heather Miller, Frankie's counselor. Why don't you follow me—we're set up in the conference room."

A young girl sat at the table wearing fashionably ripped jeans and a white shirt with a black-and-white drawing of a Boston terrier. Under the dog was the name *Mr. Phillip*. Kendall thought that was a pretty cool name for a dog and wondered if there was actually a black-and-white Boston terrier out there named Mr. Phillip. She hoped so.

"Agent Beck, this is Olivia Brown. She's best friends with Frankie."

"Cool shirt," Kendall said. "Is that your dog?"

Olivia looked down as if she had forgotten which top she had put on that morning. "Uh, no. I just thought it was a cute dog."

Kendall wondered if they made the shirt in her size. She pulled out a chair and sat across the round table from Olivia, pressed the button on her phone to begin recording, and slid it onto the table between them. Experience had taught her it was more important to watch how people reacted to questions than it was to note how they answered them. Children revealed a great deal of info without uttering a word. "How long have you and Frankie been friends?"

"Forever," Olivia said. "We met at day care before we started kindergarten."

"Wow, that is a long time. So, you two are pretty tight? Share lots of things, talk about everything, know each other's secrets?"

"Yeah." She nodded her head vigorously. "We're best friends for life."

"Did Frankie say anything to you the day she went missing?"

Olivia's face scrunched up. "Like what?"

"Like was she upset? Or talk about wanting to go away? Anything out of the ordinary?"

"No, not really. She was just normal, I guess."

"Okay." Kendall sharpened her tone just slightly. "I need for you to be honest with me, and I know I may be asking you to break a confidence, but do you think Frankie ran away?"

Olivia put a strand of hair behind her ear and then put her hand under her leg. "No, I don't think so." She glanced around the room and avoided looking at Kendall as she spoke. "I mean, she wouldn't have a reason to. She gets everything she wants, practically. She has a huge bedroom with her own bathroom. Doesn't have to share with her stupid little brother or anything. Why would she want to leave that?"

Kendall couldn't argue with the logic. Having a bathroom all to yourself as a teenager was a major bonus. And she gathered

Olivia was forced to share a bathroom with a younger sibling, since Frankie was an only child. But something in the way Olivia had seemed to tense up at the suggestion Frankie had run away was curious.

"Was Frankie having any issues with anyone at school?"

"Don't think so." A warm smile lit up her face. "We're both kinda popular and stuff, so everyone likes us. She gets along with all the boys because she plays hockey."

"I heard Sam Farmer isn't a big Frankie fan. Is that true?"

Olivia let out a *pfft* sound. "Sammy Farmer is a dork. No one likes him. All he does is talk shi . . . smack about Frankie."

"And how does Frankie feel about that?"

"Like we all do—we ignore the twerp. He thinks because his brother plays hockey in high school and is probably going to play for DU when he graduates that he's one of the popular kids."

"But he's not?"

"No way." She leaned in closer, more open and happily conspiratorial. "I mean, some of the boys let him hang around, but they usually talk about him behind his back and make fun of him and stuff."

A shiver ran down Kendall's spine. God, she was happy she wasn't in middle school. It was a minefield of confidence-shattering explosions if you took the wrong step.

"I've heard he believes Frankie stole his spot on the hockey team and he's pretty upset about it. Do you think he could've done something to Frankie? Hurt her in some way and is afraid to tell anyone?"

Olivia snorted out a laugh. "No way. I mean, he likes to think he's all tough, but he's a wimp. Frankie would beat the crap out of him and send him home crying." She nodded her head to make the point. "Sammy is scared of Frankie."

In Kendall's mind, that didn't eliminate the Farmers from the suspect list. If Mr. Farmer had thought Frankie was humiliating his son on and off the ice, he might have blown a fuse and done something to ensure his son had more scholarship opportunities. Farmer had already displayed a quick temper. And most people wouldn't believe parents would kill in order for their kids to gain better positions on teams, but it happened. Parents would do just about anything to give their kids a leg up—including paying someone to take entrance exams for higher scores or donating obscene amounts of money to ensure admission. Or killing a rival cheerleader. The world was a scary, unpredictable place. And parents were just as prone to overreact and do something stupid as kids were these days.

"What about boys?" Kendall asked. "Did Frankie have a boyfriend? Or girlfriend?"

Olivia shrugged and stared at the floor. Kendall was going to take that as a yes.

"Olivia, I can't help Frankie if I don't know what's going on with her. And that includes knowing about anybody she's involved with romantically."

Olivia leaned back in her chair and wrapped her arms around her midsection. "Well, there is one guy—I don't know his name. She says he's older, like high school, but she won't tell me anything else. I kinda don't believe her, though. I mean, where would she meet an older guy? And I'm her best friend. We talk about everything."

"So you think she's just making it up? Why would she do that?" Kendall wasn't convinced. She knew how Frankie could—and had—met a high school boy.

"Well, I've seen her talking to this boy in our grade—Dylan. He's nice but kind of a geek. I think she has a crush on him and is just embarrassed to say so."

Kendall wasn't sure she bought that either. She had the feeling Frankie was able to do what she wanted at the school and people would accept it. A trendsetter, so to speak. Someone kids would follow no matter what.

"Did she mention any problems she was having at home?" Kendall asked.

"Not really. I mean, she's super annoyed with her mom most of the time."

"Do you know why?"

Olivia shrugged. "Frankie says she's constantly on her case about stuff. Always asking Frankie if everything's okay and wanting to know about everything Frankie's doing." She rolled her eyes and added just the right amount of adolescent irritation to her tone. "I mean, all moms do it, right? My mom is a total pain in my ass." Olivia blushed deep red, remembering where she was, and glanced at the counselor. "Sorry, Ms. Miller."

Kendall didn't give a rat's ass if the girl cursed. She just needed to know what was going on in Frankie's life, and Olivia was her best chance at getting the truth. Parents rarely knew what the hell their kids were doing, no matter how strong the relationship.

"What about with her dad? Any problems with him?"

Olivia perked up, her eyes dancing in delight. "No way. Mr. Taylor's so cool. And he and Frankie are super tight."

Ahh, the girl crush on the older man. Kendall had been through it, probably at Olivia's age. Her best friend, Michelle—gawd, her dad was so cool. He would drive them around in his convertible and take them for ice cream. When Michelle's parents divorced, Kendall naturally had plans to marry him when she graduated from high school. Alas, he remarried when Kendall was in eighth grade, shattering her dreams.

"Okay, thanks, Olivia. I appreciate you talking to me."

Olivia got up from her chair and started to leave. "Frankie's gonna be okay, right? I mean, you're gonna find her soon?"

"That's the plan," Kendall said, not daring to make a promise she might not be able to keep. "I'll make you a deal, though. If I find her, I'll let you know. If you hear from her or hear anything about her, you let me know. Deal?"

"Deal."

Ms. Miller opened the door for Olivia. "Lunch period's just about to start. You can head to the cafeteria."

Olivia nodded and started out the door.

"Oh, hey, Olivia?" Kendall called after her.

The girl stopped and turned toward Kendall. "Yeah?"

"Just to circle back around to something we were talking about real quick. If Frankie were to run away, where would she go?"

Olivia's face went ashen. *Gotcha—you know something.* "I don't know," she stammered, her voice trembling.

Kendall watched her for a moment. Olivia shifted back and forth on her feet. "Okay, thanks," Kendall said.

Olivia licked her lips and walked out the door, her gate a little stiffer.

"Is there a way I can take a look in Frankie's locker?" Kendall asked Ms. Miller.

"Yeah, sure. Let me just see where it is and grab the custodian. He has all the keys to get into them."

While Kendall waited, she sent a text to Jake:

Get search warrant for Olivia Brown's house. Suspect she may be hiding something or someone.

Within about five minutes, Kendall was shuffling through papers and folders inside Frankie's locker. All the pictures taped to the inside of the door were of Frankie and Olivia being goofy for the camera. The one thing Kendall had hoped to find—a journal—was nowhere to be found. She was desperate to discover something that would point to what had happened or who might have taken Frankie. But there was no diary. No notes. No secret love letters.

Damn.

"Thanks," Kendall said, and closed the locker door. She and Ms. Miller walked down the wide hallway toward the front office.

"There is something that happened a couple of weeks ago. I don't think it has anything to do with Frankie's disappearance, but it was out of the norm for her."

Kendall's pulse sped up. "What happened?"

"Frankie was sent to the office for smarting off to one of her teachers. It was strange—I mean, not only had Frankie never done anything like that before, but it was to one of her favorite teachers."

"Was there any disciplinary action taken against her?"

"No, it was the first time, so she and I just had a chat about what was going on with her. I got the feeling there were some issues at home. Mainly with her mom. That's not at all unusual at this age. Mothers and daughters seem to turn into oil and water overnight."

"But Frankie didn't give any specifics about what was wrong or why she was acting out?"

With a head shake, Miller said, "No, and when I tried to get her to tell me what was happening, she said she was sorry she had talked back to her teacher and that it wouldn't happen again. When I checked back in with her last week to see how she was doing, she acted like she had no idea what I was talking about." Ms. Miller chuckled. "Girls and hormones. Difficult age to navigate."

Reason 753 why Kendall was not interested in having children. The teen years sucked for everyone on both sides. Kendall hadn't had much fun as a teenager and didn't want to experience it again as an adult.

"I don't suppose I could talk to Frankie's teacher?" Kendall asked.

Ms. Miller looked at her watch. "We can take a walk down to her classroom. The bell should be ringing soon, and then we can grab her."

As it turned out, Diana Curson, Frankie's science teacher, wasn't on cafeteria duty, so they were able to chat in the classroom after the students were dismissed.

"I understand there was an altercation involving Frankie in your class?" Kendall asked.

"Yeah, it was strange. I mean Frankie's involvement, at least." Mrs. Curson chuckled. "The boys have their own chairs with their names on them outside the principal's office."

Kendall smiled, but she was feeling the pressure of the minutes ticking away like a time bomb. She didn't want to be rude, but . . .

"Maybe start at the beginning."

"Well," Curson said on an exhale, "Frankie and a couple of boys in the class were having some kind of disagreement—never did find out what it was over. Anyway, I had told them to quiet down and work on the classwork I'd assigned." She shook her head and sighed. "The argument got louder, and before I knew it, Frankie was out of her desk and nose to nose with one of the boys. I told her to sit down, and she told me to 'f' off." She whispered this last part. "I told her to get out of my classroom and down to the office. Then I texted Ms. Miller and reported the incident."

Wow. Kendall never in a million years would've used language like that in front of an adult, let alone *at* one. And on top of it, a teacher? Her mother would've been mortified.

"Had Frankie had issues with these boys before?" Kendall asked.

"No, they were friends. Played hockey together."

Surprising. What had gotten Frankie so upset?

"And you didn't find out what they were arguing about?"

"Nope. They all said it was nothing and everything was fine."

Kendall wondered how true that was. More importantly, however, did the brouhaha with her teammates have anything to do with her disappearance?

"Can I get the names of the boys involved?" Kendall asked.

"Sure," Ms. Curson said, writing the names on a sticky note. Kendall would have to talk to them about the incident.

Returning to the office, Kendall handed the counselor a business card. "If you think of anything else, let me know."

As she crossed the parking lot, she pondered what she had learned from Olivia. Among the most interesting tidbits was that Frankie might have a boyfriend who was older and in high school. Could that be Luke Mathis? And if so, why hadn't he come clean about it? Did Poppy know more about their relationship than she was letting on? And if so, why wasn't *she* sharing?

Kendall slid behind the steering wheel. Her phone buzzed with an incoming call from Jake.

"Farmer's on the move."

CHAPTER

28

Thursday afternoon
39:09:56 hours missing

I T IS WELL-ESTABLISHED lore that when you're in a hurry and
breaking traffic laws left and right, every traffic cop will see it
and come after you. Such was the case for Kendall as she rushed
from the middle school to the 2nd Home Storage Facility.

She hit the hands-free on her steering wheel, glancing into
the rearview mirror. When the call connected, she yelled, "Saul!
I have two black-and-whites with flashers and sirens on my ass.
I'm not stopping for them, and I'd prefer not to be arrested in
front of Farmer, if I can help it."

"I'll take care of it."

By the time Kendall pulled into the storage facility, the cops
had peeled off and gone about their duties catching other people
in a hurry.

The storage facility consisted of one-story garage-style units.
Kendall passed the first three rows before she spotted the silver
RAV4.

Drew Farmer was just about to unlock the padlock as Kendall pulled up and blocked him in by parking perpendicular to
the front of his SUV.

Farmer's head jerked as she walked toward him. "What the
hell are you doing here?" he spat out at her.

"Weirdest thing. I was thinking I should stop by your house and check in when I happened to see you here."

"You saw that from the road?"

"I have excellent eyesight. Twenty/ten. Impressive, right?"

"What do you want?" he sneered.

"I have a few more questions regarding Frankie Taylor's disappearance."

He thrust his finger at her. "This is police harassment."

"I'm not the police."

An unmarked police car pulled in, and Jake landed at his bumper.

"What's all this?" Farmer waved a hand in the air. "Are you having me followed?"

Kendall shrugged. "I don't know what the police are doing—you'll have to ask them. The other guy, that's Jake; he's my partner." Kendall waved at Jake, who played along and waved back. "We were about to meet at Starbucks when I saw you."

"Thought your type all hung out at the donut shop," Farmer scoffed.

"Wrong stereotype. That's the police. I'm FBI. We drink designer coffee."

This was a fun sport. Kendall loved being able to practice her highly adept skills in sarcasm. Practice made perfect and all that, and Kendall had attained High Priestess of Smartassness.

Farmer's neck and face had a reddish-purplish tinge. "Yeah, well, I'm busy. If you want to ask me any questions, you can make an appointment."

Kendall looked around and spread her arms wide. "I don't see why that's necessary. We're both here; we can just get it out of the way now and go about our day."

He snorted and turned away from her. "I'm busy."

"I promise not to get in the way of whatever you're doing."

"I have nothing to say to you that I haven't already said."

"How do you know? I haven't even asked you a question yet." Kendall pointed toward the storage unit. "What's in there?"

"None of your business." Farmer took a step toward the driver's side door of the RAV4. "Now, if you will move your vehicle, I'd like to leave."

"Without going into your storage unit?" Kendall scrunched up her face in confusion. "Why would you want to leave? You just got here." She looked over her shoulder at Jake and the other officers, who were leaning against the hood of the unmarked car, enjoying the show. "If you need some help moving anything, we'd be happy to lend a hand."

"I don't need anything in there, and I don't need your help."

Time for fun and games was over.

"Why are you so eager to leave, Mr. Farmer? Is there something inside the storage unit you don't want us to see?"

"None. Of. Your. Business." He stepped closer. "Now get the fuck out of here before—"

Kendall planted her feet, chin raised. "Before what, Mr. Farmer?" No way was she going to let this asshat intimidate her.

The advance was quick. Farmer stopped just short of plowing into Kendall. But Kendall had braced for it, prepared for the impact. What she hadn't anticipated was his right hook slamming into her left jaw.

Pain radiated from her jaw up through her cheek, into her ear, and rattled her skull. Staggering back, she blocked the next swing from the left with her forearm. Farmer brought his right arm around for a second shot. Kendall grabbed his wrist and bent it back while twisting his arm around to his back. Farmer bent over at the waist to relieve some of the pressure. Kendall planted her foot along his side just below the ribs and kicked.

"Oof," Farmer groaned, and dropped to his knees. He rolled over and sprang to his feet. The muscular physique wasn't just for show. Farmer had some fight skills. He grabbed Kendall around the waist, lifted her off the ground, and dropped her to the ground. She landed on her back, the air pushed from her lungs.

Farmer stalked toward her, his foot primed to kick her in the kidneys. She grasped his boot with both hands and wrenched it 180 degrees. Farmer crashed to the ground. She released her grip. He rolled over and tried to sit up, but Kendall was on top of him before he could move, straddling his midsection. It was her turn to punch the fucker in the jaw, which she did, putting as much momentum behind her fist as she could.

Farmer's head snapped to the left, blood spurting from his nose. Her left hook sent his head jerking to the right. Blood gushed from his mouth. She hoped she'd knocked a few teeth out. His hands came up to cover his head or block another blow. He was screaming. Or crying. Kendall couldn't tell which. Didn't care. This was for every time a man decided to use his size to strong-arm a woman. For every woman unable to fight back.

And she wasn't even close to being finished with the asshole. She was just getting started. Red flooded her vision. She was in a dark tunnel, and the only thing in her sight was Farmer.

Arms wrapped around her waist. Her body was lifted off Farmer, and she was dragged backward. She struggled to get out of the constraint, but whoever was behind her was strong. And determined.

"Kendall, calm the fuck down." She recognized the voice. Adam. The anger dissipated to a simmer.

Farmer was on his feet, coming toward her. She squirmed against Adam's arms, ready to go after the fucker again, but Adam's hand was locked around her wrist. No way was Kendall was getting free.

Jake was on top of Farmer before he knew what was happening. He pushed Farmer back until he hit the wall of the storage unit. "Settle down, Mr. Farmer. You don't want to assault another agent. You're already in enough trouble."

"She beat me up," Farmer bellowed.

"She defended herself against an unprovoked attack," Jake corrected him.

Farmer turned his head to the side and spit. Blood and saliva splattered on the asphalt at his feet. "I'm filing a complaint. This is police brutality."

"We're the FBI, Mr. Farmer, not the police. Now turn around and put your hands behind your back."

"What for?"

"Makes it easier for me to get the handcuffs on you without further incidence."

"What? Why are you putting handcuffs on me?"

"Standard procedure when a person is being placed under arrest."

"What the fuck am I being arrested for? I was minding my own business and she attacked me."

"You assaulted a federal agent." And with that, Jake administered Miranda rights and assisted the cop in placing Farmer in the back of the police car.

Kendall wiped the blood from her mouth with the sleeve of her jacket.

Adam placed a finger under her chin, turned her head so he could see the left side of her face, and sucked air in through his teeth. "Swelling on your cheek. And you're going to have one hell of a shiner." He dropped his hand and stepped back. "I think you can kiss your bid for Miss America right out the window."

"Dammit," she muttered, checking her face in the side mirror of Farmer's SUV. "I really had a shot this year."

Jake walked up and stopped in front of her. Taking her in. "Well, you've looked worse."

"Thanks for the assist, partner," Kendall said.

Jake shrugged. "Looked like you had it under control."

Kendall dusted the dirt from her clothes. "Your 'damsel in distress' card should be revoked."

Jake looked around, one eyebrow quirked. "What damsel?"

Kendall grinned. "That was pretty good ass-kicking, huh?"

"Not bad."

"Fuck you, armchair quarterback. View good from the bleachers?"

Adam stared at them. The look on his face said he was sure they were both aliens from a less evolved planet.

"What do you think about breaking the lock and claiming exigent circumstances?" Kendall asked, ready to dig her bolt cutters out of the back of the Range Rover.

"With what for evidence?" Jake asked.

"Think we have enough for a search warrant?" Kendall asked Adam.

"It's going to be tough," he said. "Just because we think he's hiding something—or someone—in there isn't enough for any of the judges in our jurisdiction."

"I could run it by Brady," Jake said. "Since this is an investigation of a missing girl, I could probably bolster it enough to get a warrant on our end."

"Work your magic, partner."

It was an hour before the warrant arrived. By then, Saul and Fletch had arrived on the scene with coffee and a checked alibi for the man who'd fled from the gas station the morning of the double homicide.

"He said he heard a couple of pops but wasn't sure if they were gunshots until Craig and Savannah came out the door. One look at them and he took off. CCTV along the route to his house confirms it. We couldn't find any link between him and Stevens. Looks like he was just in the wrong place at the wrong time."

"And he did nothing to help Craig or Savannah?" Adam shook his head. "What is the world coming to when you save your own ass before a little girl?"

"Welcome to our fucked-up side of the investigation tracks," Jake said. "Need me to pull the bolt cutters from the Rover?"

Kendall pulled Farmer's set of keys from her pocket. She had cajoled them from the officer who had retrieved them from the ground after she and Farmer tussled. "I'm guessing one of these keys fits that lock."

Kendall removed the lock, the door clanging as it rolled up. She slid her hand along the interior wall, searching for a light switch.

Adam burst past her. "Frankie?"

Light flooded the unit. The three of them halted and stared. Rows of heavy metal racks were filled with computers of every type. Desktops, laptops, towers, monitors. They fanned out, looking behind the computers, opening up large boxes.

No little girls.

"I don't know whether to be upset or relieved Frankie's not here," Adam said.

"What the hell is Farmer doing with all these computers?" Kendall asked.

"Doesn't he work for a computer manufacturer?" Jake asked.

"Get the serial numbers off them and call the company he works for. Maybe they can shed some light on what these are doing here."

Fletch and Young went to work on gathering the numbers.

"What do you want us to do with Farmer?" Saul asked.

"Fuck, I was really hoping we would've found something," Kendall said.

"Bingo!" Fletch jogged over to them. "Just got off the phone with Farmer's employer. I gave them a few of the serial numbers, and they said these are computers that were returned to the company with one issue or another. They're supposed to be in a warehouse in Castle Rock."

"So what are they doing here?"

"My guess is Mr. Farmer is selling stolen property."

Kendall faced Saul. "Add possession of stolen property to the arrest and take him in."

29

Thursday evening
42:11:26 hours missing

ADAM SLID THE containers of Chinese food into the middle of the conference room. Groans of appreciation mixed with the aroma of ginger, garlic, and soy sauce. "I grabbed a bunch of different things," he said, tossing the paper plates, napkins, and plastic forks on the table. "If you don't like what's here, there's Snickers in the vending machine down the hall."

The ferocious rumble of Adam's stomach had prompted a stop at his favorite hole-in-the-wall Chinese place, and he'd ordered enough food for the entire team. They had all been working tirelessly to find his niece, and he needed them to continue. And to do that, they needed to be fed and caffeinated.

He dropped into his seat and opened the carton he had kept for himself. Kendall had a pile of chow mein noodles on her plate and an egg roll. He stabbed a piece of chicken and shoved it into his mouth.

Kendall peered over the edge of the container. "Whatcha got in there?"

"Sweet-and-sour chicken."

"You're not sharing?"

"Nope."

She reached her fork over. "Give me some."

He yanked the box away. "No. Eat your own food."

"You can't just keep it all to yourself."

"Of course I can. I bought all this food." He gestured toward the containers in the middle of the table. "Get some from there."

"It's all gone. Come on, Adam, don't be a dick. Give me a couple of pieces."

Adam rolled his eyes and tipped the box in her direction. "You're a real pain in the ass, Beck."

"I've heard."

Adam took another bite of chicken, chewed, and swallowed. "Okay, what do we have in the way of updates?"

Young raised his hand. Fletch forced it down. "This is not high school, man. Just talk."

"Sorry," Young murmured.

"Whatcha got?" Adam asked.

"I interviewed most of the employees of the convenience store," Young said. "None of them thought Ashley would have been involved with setting up a robbery. In fact, one of the guys—he apparently worked the shift after Ashley and would talk to her as they traded off—said Ashley was excited about not having to work there anymore because she was scared of someone coming in and robbing the store while she was working."

"Sounds like she was laying the groundwork for reasonable doubt before it happened," Saul said around a mouthful of beef broccoli.

"Maybe," Adam agreed.

"When I asked about how they liked working for Mr. Osborne," Young continued, "they all said he was a great boss. But digging into the statements made by Ashley's boyfriend about the security system, they clammed up."

"Perhaps they didn't know anything about it," Jake offered.

"Maybe, but as soon as I brought it up, they all seemed to get a bit squirrelly." He flipped the page and read from his notes. "The manager, Janet Gross, confirmed what Abuelo said about the security system, but in her version, she says Osborne is just cheap. He doesn't want to pay for a new system. I asked if anyone had it out for Ashley or Osborne, and she stated the employees are all very loyal to Osborne because he's just about the only person who would give them jobs, since most of them have juvie criminal records." He took a bite of moo shu pork.

"I'm just saying, if Osborne was into some illegal shit, who better to hire than people who skirt the line between legal and illegal activities?" He downed an entire bottle of water in one draw and launched the bottle across the room, where it hit the rim of the trash can before falling in.

"I also had a conversation with the insurance company. They referred me to Arlon Bell, who is investigating the insurance claims submitted by Osborne," Young said.

Kendall leaned over to Adam. "Are *you* doing any of the investigating on the double homicide?"

"I'm mentoring." Turning to Young, he asked, "Did you talk to Mr. Bell?"

"I did. Apparently, there was a flood at the other store Osborne owns a few months back. The insurance company paid out without question."

"Any idea what Osborne did with the money?" Saul asked.

"New coolers, new flooring, and a brand-new, state-of-the-art security system."

"So what prompted the investigation?" Adam asked. So far, he was massively impressed with the kid. Adam would love to take credit for Young's skills but thought they were more than likely born of a desire to move up.

"Osborne filed a claim following the shootings. He states the store sustained substantial damage as a result of the shootout."

"Shootout," Fletch snickered. "What are we, part of the Old West or something?"

"Yes," came the collective response.

"Did he list specific items damaged?" Saul asked.

"Coolers, beverages inside the coolers, cigarettes behind the counter, blood-covered food items, and—drum roll—five security cameras strategically placed around the store."

Everyone had most likely been involved in insurance fraud on a minor level, but this was taking it into a new realm.

"Mr. Bell said they became suspicious because it was the second claim in two months, so they flagged it for investigation."

"What story is Osborne giving him?" Adam asked.

"Bell hasn't talked to him yet. Osborne keeps putting him off."

So Mr. Osborne was being a little sketchy with his business. What else was he being sketchy with? Adam kept circling back to the statements about there being young girls at the store. Along with the lack of functioning security cameras, it added up to the possibility of criminal activity.

Adam tapped his pen against his lips. "Get Osborne in here for a talk. Invite Mr. Bell to observe—he may get the answers he needs. At the very least, he will be proximal to Osborne and can grab him for a chat when Osborne leaves the building."

Young's cell phone buzzed. He looked at the screen and stood up. "Phone records are in."

"Go," Adam said. "Don't dawdle on the way back."

Adam gathered up the dirty napkins and shoved them into the empty container. "Anything else?"

Saul swallowed and took a drink of water. "I called the school Ashley Collins was set to attend. Appears Ms. Collins was not being honest with her boyfriend and coworkers."

"Do tell."

"Not only did they *not* offer Ashley a scholarship, they didn't offer her admission into the school at all."

"Whoops," Fletch said, polishing off the egg rolls. The man was a human trash can.

"So, if she wasn't getting scholarship funds and was set to quit her job, how was she planning on getting money?" Adam pondered.

"Good question," Saul said.

"Methinks she had alternate means of funding," Jake offered.

"Less-than-legal ones, I'd wager," Fletch said. "Real question is—how much of this did baby daddy know?"

Adam made a note to call Abuelo and ask him that very question.

"Switching gears," Saul said. "I did a search of court documents relating to Poppy."

"Find anything?"

"Nothing recent. But there is a sealed juvenile record."

What the fuck? Adam had no idea she'd had juvie trouble.

"Any way to figure out what the charges were?" Kendall asked.

Law enforcement had means to pull strings and get all sorts of information on criminal records, even juvenile ones.

"If it were a criminal record, maybe. But this was in family court."

What would Poppy have been doing in family court that dictated a sealed record?

Young bounced back into the room. "More tea on Ashley Collins," he proclaimed, waving the text log over his head. The kid was enthusiastic. He handed the report to Adam.

"Care to share with the rest of the class?" Kendall asked.

Young beamed. "Seems Darin Stevens and Ashley Collins not only knew each other but are friends. And have been for a long time."

"And, according to the most recent text between them," Adam added, "Ashley owed Darin for something in their past."

"Well, that's an interesting turn of events," Fletch said.

Adam taped the log to the whiteboard. He now had something else to chat with Vincent Abuelo about.

"Where are we on questioning Frankie's teammates?" Kendall asked.

"They're still maintaining they don't know what the argument was about, don't know why Frankie may have been upset with the coach. Basically, the party line is they know nothing," Jake said.

"Someone knows something," Saul said.

Kendall retrieved the sticky note with the names of the boys Frankie had argued with in class and handed it to Saul. "See if you can find out what these boys were fighting with Frankie about a couple of weeks ago at school. It may shed some light on the discussion with Turner."

Saul read the note and nodded. "Get right on it."

"What about the goalie—what's her name?" Kendall asked.

Fletch shuffled through his notes. "Ruby Wilson."

"Let's talk to her; she may open up. If anyone is going to break the silence to help Frankie, it'll be the only other female on the team."

Fletch raised his fist in the air. "Girl power."

* * *

The war room had cleared once all the food was gone. Adam sat back in his chair, hands over his face, and took a deep breath.

Investigating a double homicide was exhausting on its own. And this one was a challenge.

But add in the stress and worry and fear of a missing loved one, and life became unbearable. He was so damn tired, but whenever he closed his eyes, he had horrible visions of Frankie. So he spent most of his time running through everything they knew while driving the streets of downtown Denver into the wee hours of the morning. After a while, fatigue muddled the brain to the extent that nothing made sense anymore.

He poured himself another cup of coffee from the pot in the corner. He had brought his coffeemaker from home, since he was spending most of his time here. Relaxing back in his chair, he took a sip from his cup and swiveled around in his chair. Frankie's picture up on the far board was starting to haunt him. It hurt too much to see her smile, knowing it might be the only way he would ever see it again.

Pulling out his phone, he dialed the number for Ashley Collins's boyfriend, Vincent Abuelo.

"This is Vincent," came the greeting when the call connected.

"Mr. Abuelo, this is Detective Adam Taylor. Do you remember me from last night?"

"Yeah, of course. What can I do for you?"

"Are you able to talk? I need to ask you some questions."

He heard a shuffle in the background and Abuelo whispering to someone, "Can you take her?" Then a door closing. "Sorry, needed to get the baby down for a nap."

"Is this a bad time?"

"Uh, no. It's fine. My sister has Alex, so I've got some time. What do you need to ask me?"

Adam pulled out a legal pad and wrote Abuelo's name at the top along with the date and time. "We've been hearing from some of Ashley's coworkers that—in their opinion—a disturbing number of girls are brought into the store with men, and that these girls don't look like they belong with these men. Did Ashley ever mention anything like that to you?"

There was a pause on the other end. "There was a couple of times she said she wondered what was going on—that there was a girl who came in who looked scared to death. Ash tried to talk to her, but the girl just stared at her and the man she was with yanked her away. She asked me what she should do, and I told her to see how often it was happening and let her boss know."

"Do you know if she talked to her boss about it?"

"I don't. She didn't bring it up, and I never asked."

"Are you aware that a young girl was at the store the morning Ashley was shot?" Adam asked, intentionally not reminding Abuelo that his girlfriend had been killed. As if the man could ever forget.

"I saw on the news, yeah. She had been kidnapped, right?"

"Yes."

"You know," Abuelo said, before Adam could ask a question, "I've been sitting here racking my brain, trying to figure out why Ashley would've gone for that gun. I mean, she knew better—we had talked about it a lot. If someone came in demanding all the money from the till, just give them the money. If they want to take every pack of cigarettes, help them bag them up. If they want your clothes, strip. Don't be a hero, just do what they ask and stay alive."

"And have you come up with an answer?" Adam asked. Sometimes it was good just to let people talk. You got information you never thought you needed.

"Not until just now when you mentioned the little girl. If Ashley was trying to protect the girl, she would have thrown caution to the wind. Being a mother changed her, in a good way. She was so careful with Alex, and she noticed other children more." He paused, and Adam thought he heard the man sniff. "Yeah, if she thought the man was hurting the child, she would've stepped in."

Adam hated to burst the man's bubble, but it had to be done.

"Would it surprise you to know Ashley knew the man who was attempting to rob the store? That she has known him for a while?"

"Really?" Abuelo inhaled. "I mean, she told me that someone from her past had come into the store, but she said she blew him off. She hated when people from her childhood came around her. It brought up too many bad memories with her mom."

"We have text messages between them within the past two weeks."

Bomb drop.

"She didn't tell you about that?" Adam asked.

"No."

Adam felt bad. He could only imagine the range of emotions Abuelo was feeling—anger, confusion, sadness, betrayal.

"So you have no idea what she might owe him?"

"No idea."

"Is it possible Ashley was involved in something with him? That whatever it was she was doing was to clear whatever debt she owed?"

"Ashley didn't need money. And if this asshole had threatened her, she would've told me. She was starting a new life, going to school, getting her nursing degree. We were going to get married and have more babies."

Abuelo was sobbing on the other end. Adam gave him a minute.

"I'm sorry," Abuelo said. "Sometimes it just hits me."

"No need to apologize. I'm sorry I have to ask these questions, but I need a better understanding of what happened in case there are others involved."

"I get it. But Ashley wasn't in that world anymore. She worked hard to be successful—she wanted to show her daughter what hard work could do. She was so excited when she got the scholarship. I'm telling you, she did not need the money."

Adam took a deep breath. There was no painless way to do this. Part of his job or not, it didn't make it any easier.

"Mr. Abuelo, there was no scholarship. We checked with the school. In fact, they state that her application for admission had been denied."

Bomb number two.

"I think we are done with this conversation," Abuelo said.

Then the line went dead.

CHAPTER

30

THE SHRILL OF her cell phone ringing over the speakers in
the Range Rover startled Kendall. Her heart raced. At some
point, she really needed to figure out why incoming calls were so
freaking loud.

She pressed the button to accept the call. "Beck."

"Hey, it's Thompson," came the deep baritone. She had been
working with the agent for years, and yet hearing him speak
always surprised her. "I'm sitting outside the Marriott, where our
favorite family law attorney has gone inside."

"Intriguing. Why would he need to go to a Marriott? Did he
have a fallout with the missus?"

"Could be, although I would've expected him to stay on his
side of town."

Kendall perked up even more. "Where are you?"

"Ten miles from the Taylors' home."

What the hell?

"But that's not the most interesting part of this story. Guess
who just showed up and went into the hotel?"

Oh no . . .

Kendall's skin was tingling. "Please tell me it's not Poppy
Taylor."

"You win a set of knives, Agent Beck."

"Fuck," she said, suddenly feeling heavy in every limb. "I'm on my way."

Kendall pulled into the parking spot directly behind Thompson, who sat in one of those standard nondescript black FBI Suburbans that stood out like a beacon in the ocean and screamed *undercover fed*. She slid into the passenger seat.

"Any action?" she asked.

"All quiet on the infidelity front."

That would be the preferable outcome of all this, as shitty as that sounded. But if her theory was correct, things were going to fall apart in spectacular fashion. It wouldn't be a matter of her marriage ending. Poppy's actions could be criminal.

"What happened there?" Thompson pointed at her face.

"Sucker punch."

"Taylor? Or suspect?"

Kendall gave him a sideways glance and chuckled. "Suspect."

"And how is he?"

"Possible broken nose. Failed to knock out any teeth, so a little sad about that."

"Yeah, teeth would've been good." Thompson sat up in his seat, lifting his camera to his eye. "Tallyho, here they come."

Poppy was first out the door. Fast on her heels was Robinson, who grasped her by the elbow and turned her around.

"Uh-oh, looks like a lover's spat," Thompson murmured over the *click, click, click* of the camera shutter.

The conversation seemed to go back and forth, Poppy throwing her arms in the air at one point. Robinson placed his hands on her upper arms, and Kendall feared she and Thompson were going to have to intercede and break up a domestic assault. After a moment, Robinson began rubbing Poppy's arms, and Kendall watched the woman visibly relax and fall against the attorney's chest. He wrapped his arms around her, stroking her hair.

Kendall's stomach clenched. She drew in a steadying breath at the sudden onset of nausea.

When they finally separated, Poppy kissed the man on the cheek and walked away. Soon her Explorer backed out of the parking spot and turned onto the street in the direction of her home.

"I'm going to see if I can get anyone to talk to me," Kendall said, slipping out of the vehicle. "You catch up to Poppy and see if she makes any other stops on her way home."

Kendall crossed the parking and walked through the lobby to the reservation desk. A chipper girl with a bob and a wide smile and a name tag that read *Fiona* looked up from the computer as Kendall approached. "Checking in?"

"No." Kendall pulled her badge out. "I'm wondering if you have a Henry Robinson staying here."

Fiona seemed to be unsure of what to do. She looked around to see if anyone else was there to deal with Kendall and the situation. Her standard refusal to give information about guests probably had never been addressed to a badge before.

"I promise, I'm not going to confront him. There will be no drama. I won't be here long. I just need to know if he's registered or not."

Fiona's fingers tapped on the keyboard. "Yes, Mr. Robinson is here for one night."

"Any idea if he's a regular here?"

"I'm not sure I have that information."

"Do you know what Mr. Robinson looks like?" Kendall asked. "Tall, older, still in decent shape."

"Yes, ma'am, I helped him when he checked in."

"He just met a woman here. Did you see them?"

"Yes, ma'am."

There was very little Kendall hated more than being called *ma'am*.

"Do you know where they were meeting?"

Fiona pointed across the lobby to the bar. "I saw them come out of there, but I don't know how long they were in there or if they went anywhere else in the hotel."

"Thanks, Fiona. You've been tremendously helpful."

Kendall entered the bar. There weren't many patrons in the cozy space. She sidled up to the bar and slid her badge onto the surface. "Hi," she said, as the bartender approached. "Are you the only one working the bar?"

"No, Carmen is the server." He pointed to a woman coming up behind Kendall with a tray of empty glasses. The bartender pointed at Kendall's badge but spoke to Carmen. "Visitor."

Carmen stared at Kendall for a moment. "Can I help you?"

"I hope so. I'm Kendall Beck." She picked up her badge and clipped it back on her belt. "I believe there was an older gentleman and a younger woman in here a few minutes ago. Did you serve them?"

Carmen nodded. "Uh-huh. Nice man. Good tipper."

Subtle.

Kendall fished into her pocket, found a twenty-dollar bill, and handed it to Carmen. The woman shoved the bill into the pocket of her apron. "What do you need to know?"

"Were they drinking?"

"He had a gin and tonic—two, actually, one before the woman showed up. She had water."

"Were you able to hear what they were talking about?"

"Just bits and pieces. When I dropped off the drinks, the guy was saying something like, 'Don't worry about the other issue, I'm on top of it, things are in motion.'"

"What did the woman say?"

Carmen emptied her tray and wiped it with a wet bar rag. "I couldn't hear her. She was talking softly, and I had no reason to linger."

"Okay, anything else?"

"I went back to check on them, and I heard the man ask where Frank was. That seemed to piss her off, because she stormed out in a huff."

"Did she say anything in response to his question?"

"Not that I heard. She bolted, and he went after her. Came back a few minutes later and apologized for taking off, and then tipped me and left."

"Where did he go?"

She pointed across the lobby. "Elevator."

Kendall thanked her and headed out to the lobby. What had Robinson meant by *things are in motion*? What things? And what was the other issue he'd referenced?

But the part that twisted like a knife in Kendall's heart was the question about Frankie. If Robinson was asking where she was, did that mean Kendall's theory was true? Poppy had staged a kidnapping and all of this was a ruse to get Frankie away from her father?

It still seemed impossible to believe. The person in Kendall's scheme was manipulative and selfish. And that was contrary to everything Poppy had shown herself to be. Could they really be the same person?

The elevator doors opened, and Robinson stepped out. Kendall slipped behind a column and prayed he hadn't seen her. Robinson made a beeline for a sitting area off to the side of the reception desk, a wide grin on his face. He wrapped his arms around a woman, bent his face down, and kissed her. Deeply. So passionately Kendall wondered if they were going to come up for air anytime soon.

Had Poppy come back?

If so, how had she explained her absence at home, especially if she planned on staying overnight with Robinson?

Robinson slid his arm around the woman's waist and walked beside her. Kendall got a good look at her. Young, pretty, and employed by the attorney as a receptionist. She had an overnight bag, which Robinson took from her and carried to the elevators. They never took their eyes off each other.

Kendall exhaled, warmth returning to her body. Robinson was having an affair, but it wasn't with Poppy.

And while that was the outcome Kendall had hoped for, it left more questions than answers.

31

Thursday night
44:11:29 hours missing

KENDALL WAS STILL reeling from the meeting between Robinson and Poppy and a little sick to her stomach over Robinson and his receptionist. But it was the conversation the server had overheard that concerned Kendall the most. On the one hand, if Poppy had Frankie, it was a good bet the child was safe. It would mean they only had to find her and get her home to her dad. But if not, they were back at square one with only theories and suppositions about what had happened to Adam's niece.

The ice rink was already buzzing with activity. In the lobby, little kids sat on the floor, parents unlacing skates and pulling them off. She hadn't even realized they made hockey skates that small. But they started them young these days. It was cool how many parents were getting their daughters involved in the sport. That hadn't been the case when Kendall was growing up. Once she'd gotten into third or fourth grade, there was no more youth hockey available for girls. The reason: not enough girls to make up a team, and not enough teams for girls to play against. Because God forbid girls play a boys' sport.

They might turn out like Frankie, be a badass, and show up the boys.

Skates against ice was a unique sound. Kendall loved it. She loved the cold air and the scraping sound of blades cutting into ice. The laughter and cheers and chatter of the players. There was just something magical about a hockey rink.

Ruby was sitting on the team bench, strapping on goalie pads.

"Hi," Kendall said, after she made her way across the ice and into the player box. "Ruby, right?"

Ruby nodded, but she had her gaze on the ice.

"Do you mind if I talk to you?" Kendall asked.

"I have practice." Her tone wasn't rude or dismissive, and Kendall wondered if she was nervous about talking to an FBI agent.

"I'll just ask questions while you get your gear on."

"Okay," Ruby said, keeping her head down.

"Did Frankie ever talk to you about issues she was having with Coach Turner?"

"No."

"How about any of the guys on the team?"

"No—well, Sam, but he's not really a problem. He's just a douchebag."

Everyone, apparently, seemed to have the same distaste for Sammy Farmer. That was about the only thing she could get these kids to open up about.

"So the two of you never discussed any problems that might have been affecting the team?"

Ruby looked up, and for a split second, she looked as if she was about to spill some tea—*thanks for that hip term, Officer Young*—but something over Kendall's shoulder caught the girl's eye, and she clamped her mouth shut. "I have to get warmed up."

"Okay." A hockey bag sat behind Ruby on the floor. "Is that your bag?"

"Yeah."

Kendall showed her a business card. "I'm going to put this in here. If you think of something or hear anything, will you let me know?"

Ruby shrugged and opened the gate to get out on the ice. "Sure."

Based on the information Kendall had so far, Frankie had engaged in a fight with her coach—allegedly—and a verbal altercation with a couple of her teammates before she went missing. Was it normal teenage angst? Or did it have something to do with her disappearance?

Kendall watched Ruby move the goal into place and begin roughing up the crease.

What was she going to have to do to get someone—anyone—on the team to tell her what the hell was going on?

32

Thursday night
44:12:12 hours missing

LYALL OSBORNE, THE owner of the convenience store, was less than cordial about being summoned to the police station to answer questions. Young had been the recipient of a verbal lashing—Osborne was a busy man, running two businesses, had already answered questions. So Adam geared up for some pushback from the man as he entered the interview room.

"Mr. Osborne," Adam greeted him, placing two bottles of water on the table. "Thanks so much for coming in."

"I'm very busy." Osborne wiped his nose with a handkerchief and shoved it into his pants pocket. "You have no idea how hard it is to run two businesses."

"Which is why I am very thankful you could come in today." Adam opened his file and took out his legal pad. "I just have a few questions, and then I can send you on your way."

Osborne nodded, but he was also frowning. Cooperative but pissy. This should be fun.

"I understand you had some issues over at your other store? Some flooding?" Adam asked.

"Yes, there was a water pipe that broke and caused a great deal of damage."

"And you filed a claim and received a payout from the insurance company?"

Osborne's eyebrows wrinkled. "Yes."

"And you made repairs with that?"

Osborne nodded. "Yes."

"I understand one of the things you bought for that store was a new security system."

"Yes, that's correct."

"How old was the security system that you replaced at the other store?"

Osborne stared at Adam for a moment, his eyes searching Adam's for something. Most likely curious about where Adam was going with this line of questioning. "I believe it was about five years old."

Adam pulled a receipt from his file. "I was able to obtain receipts from your security company. You are correct, the security system was only five years old. What I find interesting is the security system at the store where Ashley was killed—that system is fifteen years old. So I'm wondering why you upgraded a newer system rather than the one that only has two functioning cameras. And I use the term *functioning* loosely."

"What are you suggesting?" Osborne glanced around as if looking for an escape. "I . . . I . . . the system had been damaged in the flood."

"Okay," Adam said. "But why not take some of the money to upgrade the other system also?"

"There was no money left after I made all the repairs." Osborne placed his hand on his forehead. "I don't understand what's going on here," he said under his breath.

Adam pulled out the picture of Darin Stevens and slid it across the table in front of Osborne. "Do you know this man?"

Osborne glanced at the photo, his head shaking before he even looked at it. "No."

"What about the name Darin Stevens?"

"Doesn't sound familiar." A shaky hand reached out for a bottle of water. It took the man a bit to actually get the lid off.

"This man"—Adam pointed at the picture—"is Darin Stevens. He's the man who tried to rob your store and the one who shot and killed Ashley Collins."

Osborne closed his eyes.

"Did you know Darin Stevens was friends with Ashley?"

"I didn't know him, so how would I know they were friends?" Osborne sputtered.

"So Ashley didn't introduce you to her friend? Perhaps propose a business venture between the three of you?"

"No. No. I told you, I don't know that man." Osborne crossed his legs, then uncrossed them.

"Did you know Ashley planned on quitting her job?"

"Oh, yes." He nodded and seemed relieved he had an affirmative answer.

"How was she going to support herself?"

"She told me she had gotten a scholarship to go back to school and that was going to help with other expenses."

"Let's go back to the security company. Now, you told me that the security company was unable to repair your cameras. That they were supposed to come out but hadn't ever shown up to do the work. Do you recall telling me that?"

Osborne took a shaky breath. "Yes."

"Well, the security company says they made several attempts to repair the cameras, but when they arrived at the store, they were told you weren't there and they would have to come back. Can you explain that to me?"

"What? No. They are mistaken. I don't recall any time they have scheduled to repair the cameras."

Adam slid a printout the security company had emailed him. "If you'll take a look at that, you'll see the dates they were there and were told they wouldn't be able to do any work until you were there to sign off on any work done."

"But the manager would've been able to handle this." Osborne sat back in his chair, arms crossed defiantly across his chest. "They are wrong. This never happened."

"They claim they were specifically told *you* had to be present for the repairs."

"That's ridiculous. Why wouldn't I allow Janet to handle this? That's why she was promoted to manager."

Adam nodded. "Okay. Let's switch gears. Have you been made aware by your employees that they've noticed a lot of girls who are brought into the store? The statements we have say the employees were suspicious because the girls appeared to be scared and the men they were with were less than savory. Now, in that area of town, that's saying something."

The handkerchief reappeared and mopped Osborne's brow. "No one has ever brought that to my attention, I can assure you."

Adam sat back in his seat, his gaze on Osborne, and scratched along his jaw. It was a great way to get people talking. Just shut up and let them squirm. People hated silence, so they would invariably attempt to fill it. Sometimes with things they had no intention of sharing.

"I had no idea . . . I would've stepped in and tried to ascertain what was happening."

"Were you using your business to aid in the trafficking of girls by way of facilitating transfers of these girls from one person to another?"

Osborne froze. His eyes looked as if they might pop out of his head. His mouth opened and closed and opened again, but no words came out.

"Maybe you got in over your head and wanted out. But Darin Stevens wouldn't let you. Is that a possibility, Mr. Osborne?"

"God, no! I don't know where you're getting this from, but I would never . . ." He looked at Adam as if he had lost his mind.

"See, I can envision you trying to get out of a regrettable business deal and Ashley trying to escape a reminder of her past life just as she's turning a corner. The two of you concoct a plan whereby Ashley kills Stevens, claims Stevens was trying to rob the place, so she shot him. There are no working cameras in that part of the store, so no proof of what really happened."

A strangled laugh came from Osborne. "What would she gain by doing that?"

"A portion of the insurance payout. Enough to set her up for a while so she could quit her job and stay at home with her baby. As I understand it, you have submitted a claim with your insurance company due to substantial damages to the store from gunshots."

Osborne leaned forward, narrowed his eyes, his tone low and angry. "Am I under arrest?"

"No."

He pushed back his chair, the legs scraping against the linoleum, and stood. "Then I believe you have wasted enough of my time, Detective Taylor."

Adam watched the man walk out of the room. The interesting part of all of this was that Osborne hadn't answered the last question. Hadn't denied it.

Was that because Adam had hit the nail on the head? Had Osborne and Ashley planned to kill Stevens? If so, how had it gone so wrong?

CHAPTER

33

"QUEUE IT UP," Adam told Fletch as he came into the war room.

Saul followed him in. "What have we got?"

Fletch hit a button on his laptop that projected onto a white wall. "The IT geeks were going through the video from the c-store."

"And they found something from the day of the murders?" Saul asked. "Figured that was a lost cause."

"Oh, it was," Fletch said.

"Then why the hell are we watching it?" Adam asked, frustration rankling him at the thought of wasting any more time.

"Because of what they found on the tape two weeks earlier."

The interior of the convenience store appeared on the makeshift screen. A woman was standing in front of the coolers with the door open. A rolling cart filled with drinks sat behind her.

"That's Ashley Collins," Fletch said.

As she restocked the coolers, a man came into view.

Fletch pointed to the man. "And that's Darin Stevens."

"Well, I'll be," Saul said.

The two seem to be having a discussion. Without audio, though, it was impossible to understand the context.

Kendall breezed through the doorway, looking as if she could drop at any minute. It was the harried look all of them had. But none of them would be willing to give up just to get some rest. Not when there was work to be done.

She slid into a seat next to Adam. "What's this?"

"Video from the c-store two weeks before the murders. Stevens and Ashley are talking to each other."

"What about?"

"No clue."

After a few minutes, Ashley and Stevens embraced.

"That doesn't look like a woman who's trying to escape her past," Kendall said.

Young rushed into the room and dropped documents in front of Kendall. Adam rolled his chair closer to her to read over her shoulder.

"What's this?" Kendall asked.

"Text messages from Frankie's phone."

"And who is she texting?"

Young smiled like a little kid anxious to reveal a secret. "Luke Mathis." The piano teacher's nephew who'd sworn he barely knew Frankie.

"What?" Adam snatched the document from Kendall. "So the little shit lied to us. He never mentioned they were texting."

"What are they texting about?" Saul asked.

Adam looked through the messages. They were . . . boring. Frankie asked a lot of questions about what Luke liked to do for fun, suggested places he should go, and sometimes implied they should go together.

"Mathis avoids making plans with her." Adam read the texts from Luke a second time. "He's very interested in her family and how they live, though. A few questions about Mark. But the majority are about Poppy."

"And here's why," Kendall said, and began reading from another document. "Poppy's text messages. Incoming: *I just want to see you again.* Poppy's response: *No, I shouldn't have met you last time. It was a mistake.*"

"Who was she texting?" Adam asked, the hairs on the back of his neck on end.

"Luke Mathis."

34

Thursday night
46:34:29 hours missing

"WHERE THE HELL are we going?" Adam asked.
Kendall swung into the driveway of a two-story brick house.

"I got a phone call right before we left from Ruby Wilson's mom."

"The goalie?" Adam asked.

"Yep." Kendall hit the button, and the SUV's engine shut off. "Apparently, after our little non-information-sharing discussion this evening at the rink, she went home and talked to her mom. Mrs. Wilson called me and asked if I could stop by their house. Ruby has been upset about Frankie, and her mother thinks there may be something Ruby is afraid to talk about in front of her teammates."

"Should I stay out here?" Adam asked. "I don't want her to feel pressured or uncomfortable."

Kendall knew he was feeling the same sense of urgency she was. As if they weren't getting any closer to finding Frankie than the night she disappeared. They were willing to do anything for one scrap of evidence that would lead them . . . somewhere. Chasing their tails around was making them irritable and dizzy.

"Come in," Kendall said. "I'm pretty sure she was just nervous around the team. If it looks like she's distressed with you there, we can accommodate then."

Mrs. Wilson answered the door and led them into the kitchen, where Ruby was sitting at the high bar counter. Her eyes were red and rimmed with tears.

"Hey, Ruby," Kendall said, taking a seat next to her and rubbing her back. "What's the matter, sweetie?"

After choking back a sob, she looked up at Kendall, her lower lip trembling. "I lied to you—at the rink—I'm so sorry."

"That's okay; I'm glad you want to talk to me now. What did you want to tell me?"

Ruby wiped her nose on the sleeve of her sweatshirt—the same hoodie Frankie wore with the team logo on the front. She glanced at Adam, who was lingering in the doorway. "I'm really sorry about Frankie."

"Are you and Frankie friends?" Kendall asked.

"Not really."

Mrs. Wilson said, "They're friendly, but they don't attend the same school. Ruby goes to a private school." She mouthed the word *bullying* while Ruby wasn't looking. "Ruby, honey, tell them what you told me."

Ruby blew her bangs from her eyes. "Frankie found out some of the boys on the team are buying pot . . . from Coach Turner."

Shocking . . . yet it had been right in front of Kendall's face the whole time. Why hadn't she suspected that after visiting Turner's home? He'd been nervous about something.

"And Frankie found about this?"

"Yeah. She was really upset. She told me she got into trouble at school because she got into a fight with them over it. Told them they had to stop or she would tell on them. She said they acted like they couldn't get into trouble for it."

The day she'd told her teacher to fuck off, no doubt.

"Is that why you didn't want to talk to me at practice? You were afraid the boys would get mad at you?"

"I don't care what they would they do. They're idiots."

"So why hold this information back?"

She reached across the island and held her mother's hand. "Mick."

Kendall glanced at Mrs. Wilson, who said, "The rink manager."

Kendall nodded, placing the name.

"Anyway," Ruby continued, "he told me to keep my mouth shut about things I didn't understand. That he knew people who could make sure I never spoke again. And then he asked me if I had ever had my jaw broken, and did I know how much it hurt and how long it took to heal." Tears streamed down her face.

Mrs. Wilson's nostrils flared and her eyes turned cold, her expression tight.

Heat flushed through Kendall's body. Mick was going to pay dearly for scaring this girl.

"Ruby, I need for you to know this—Mick will never be able to hurt you. Adam and I are going to make sure he will never come near you again. But I need you to tell me what was going on to make him threaten you."

"I overheard some of the guys on the team talking about how Mick can help them bulk up. They thought Frankie and I were dumb, like we couldn't figure out what they were talking about. But I knew Mick was selling them steroids."

"Did Frankie know about this?" Adam asked.

"I'm not sure. We only ever talked about the pot. But she could have. I was going to talk to her at the next practice, but then she . . ."

Kendall squeezed Ruby's hand. "Ruby, can I tell you something? You're an incredibly brave girl. Telling us about Coach Turner and Mick is going to stop them from hurting anyone else. But beyond that, you have given us a lead to hopefully find Frankie. And no one has been able to do that yet. So not only are you brave, you're also a hero."

35

Thursday night
49:00:56 hours missing

AFTER THE BOMBSHELL from Ruby, Kendall had dropped Adam off. He knew he should've gone home and gotten some sleep, but he was too wired. The coach and the rink manager were selling drugs to kids. *Kids.* It was one thing to make a profit off adults who knew better and still put that shit in their bodies. But to pad your bank account by selling drugs—and highly dangerous ones like steroids—to juveniles who couldn't possibly understand the ramifications of their actions? Disgusting. Kids believed they were invincible.

But it was the thought that Frankie might have approached the coach and Mick about their side action that terrified Adam. Had they done something to her to keep her quiet? And if so, what?

Adam didn't really want to go down that road.

Perhaps they'd threatened her like Mick had threatened Ruby. If Frankie had voiced her concerns about what they were doing and jeopardized their business, what would she have done upon receiving threats? Adam would like to think she would've come to him, or her father. But she hadn't let them know what she'd found out. Instead, it appeared she might have taken things into her own hands and confronted them.

Adam had resisted the idea that Frankie had run away, because he just couldn't believe she would leave her family to worry about her. But if Mick and Turner had threatened her—or threatened her family—maybe she'd thought it would be better to leave and lie low for a while. Let things cool off. She was still a little girl—only twelve years old. Was it possible she didn't know what the best course of action was and had just acted impulsively?

If so and if she didn't trust anyone, or didn't want to get her friends in trouble for trying to hide her, was she on the streets? Trying to survive without any money?

Adam swung his vehicle around and headed downtown. There were certain places in the city where kids congregated when they ran away. It was always interesting to Adam how kids always seemed to find each other. There was a sense of safety in numbers. Unfortunately, Adam knew this was rarely the truth. Desperation made people do things they otherwise wouldn't. And predators were in every nook, cranny, and dark alley, just waiting for prey they could intimidate and control for their own gain.

Frankie might have thought she was leaving one volatile situation and walked straight into hell, thinking she would find a safe place.

Adam pulled along the curb on Colfax Avenue, pressed the key fob to lock the doors, and started walking the streets. It was a different world after midnight, so many young kids trying to sell themselves for a quick hit of whatever drug du jour they were hooked on. The homeless were curled into tight corners and doorways, trying to make themselves invisible and avoid having what little they had left taken from them. In this world, it was best not to attract too much attention.

Adam pulled up the picture of Frankie on his phone. He approached a group of teenagers huddled together. When he approached, two took off. He quickly turned his phone toward the remaining kids. "Have you seen this girl around?"

All of them shook their heads no and quickly disbanded.

Adam worked his way down the south side of the street before crossing over and making his way back to his truck on the north side. It was an exercise in futility. He looked too much like a cop. And as soon as they saw him coming, they hightailed it away from him. The few who would talk to him, mostly because he had caught them off guard, all denied seeing Frankie.

"Hey!"

Adam turned to see who had called out. An older man with long gray hair and about a week's worth of stubble was motioning for Adam to come closer. His left hand gripped a paper bag–wrapped bottle. Adam took a few steps towards the man, a sense of safety along with a powerful smell of urine forcing him to stand a few feet away.

"You that fella asking about a girl?" the man asked.

"Yeah, you know something?" Adam asked.

"Maybe. What's she look like?"

Adam hesitated and then took a few steps forward, the phone extended as much as possible in front of the man's face.

He drew a crooked, arthritic hand down along his jaw and made a *tsk* sound.

"She does look kinda familiar," he said slowly, and then looked up at Adam. "But it's so hard to tell. Lots of girls end up down here. After a while they sort of all blend together, you know?"

"Yes," Adam said, pushing the picture a little closer, "but you think you may have seen her?"

"Well," he drew out, "maybe. It's hard to see in this light. And my eyes aren't what they used to be." He looked around, his gaze landing on a 7-Eleven on the corner. "If I could be in the light, I might be able to see her picture better."

Adam nodded, and they sauntered down the sidewalk. The door beeped as they entered. The cashier looked up at them and immediately shook his head. "No, no, no." He pointed at the old man. "I told you to stay out of here."

"I'm with him," the old man said, grasping the sleeve of Adam's shirt.

"You steal, so you can't come in here," the cashier stated.

Adam pulled his arm from the old man's hold. "I'll make sure he doesn't take anything without it being paid for."

The cashier stared at Adam, then narrowed his eyes. "Fine. But I'm watching you." His gaze swung back and forth between the two men. "Both of you."

"Understood," Adam said. He turned to the old man and held his phone up. "Take a look again."

The man grabbed his stomach with both hands, his face crumpled in what Adam guessed was supposed to indicate pain. "Oh, I'm just so hungry. I haven't had anything to eat in days. Maybe if you could get me a sandwich, I could concentrate better?"

Adam knew the ruse. And at that point he was willing to buy the guy a three-course meal in exchange for information about his niece.

He exhaled through his nose and urged the man toward the mini deli/hot food area of the store. The man grabbed two sandwiches, a regular-sized bag of potato chips, and a box of Oreos. He unloaded them on the counter, put up a finger for Adam to wait before paying, and headed to the back of the store. When he returned, he had two large beers, one in each hand. "Something to wash it down."

"Right," Adam said. He plugged his credit card into the machine and waited for the cashier to give him the receipt and bag up the food. Adam grabbed the bag before the old man could snag it and leave. Once they were outside the store, Adam said, "Okay, you get all this when you tell me what you know about this girl."

The old man squinted his eyes and stared at the photo. "Yeah," he drew out, "I've seen her around."

"Recently?" Adam asked.

"Days kind of run together, but I'm pretty sure I saw her today. You can tell the new ones—they have wide eyes and look like they're about to piss themselves. She walked past a few times."

A rush of warmth coursed through Adam. Finally, a lead on where Frankie could be. "Where did she go? Did you see? Which way was she headed?"

"Uhhh, I think it was down towards the zoo." He glanced up at Adam, his eyes wide.

"Are you sure?" Adam asked.

"Uh-huh." He nodded, his eyes going to the bag of food. His tongue darted out, and he licked his lips.

Adam tightened his grip on the bag. "Was she with anyone?"

The old man wagged his head, but didn't take his gaze off the bag. "No, no, she was alone. Can't say as she's still alone. They usually meet someone who is willing to help them learn the streets." He pointed to the bag. "I told you what you wanted to know. Can I have that now?"

Adam handed him the bag. The old man didn't wait for Adam to say anything, just took off to his roost in front of some abandoned storefront. Adam turned and started down the street toward the zoo.

A car door opened, and a man stepped out in front of Adam. Fed.

"You're Adam Taylor?" the man asked.

"Yeah," Adam said. "And you are?"

"Calvin Charles." He put his hand out. "I work with Kendall. My partner and I are assigned to checking all the popular teen runaway haunts to see if we can catch sight of your niece."

A woman got out from the driver's side and joined them on the sidewalk. "Callie," she said, and shook Adam's hand. "We saw you talking to the old man."

"How much did he take you for?" Charles asked.

"About thirty dollars."

"Wow, not bad. We didn't cut him off until he had taken us for damn near fifty bucks' worth of stuff," Charles said with a laugh. "Did he tell you he'd seen your niece?"

"Yeah," Adam said. "Said he had seen her earlier today walking down towards the zoo."

"Huh," Callie said. "He told us he had seen her last week going down the alley."

"Which is a neat trick," added Charles, "seeing as she's only been missing for two days."

"So, are you saying he's lying?" Adam asked, ready to turn around and take back all the shit he had bought for the old man.

"No telling. He's been on the streets for a while. I think he sees a great many things, and probably only half of them are actually real," Callie said.

Charles placed his hands on his hips. "I showed him a picture of my wife when she was young, and he told me he had seen her also."

"Damn." Adam had been sure the old man had seen Frankie and he was one step closer to finding her since she'd gone missing. Disappointment weighed on him like a wet blanket.

"We have some pretty good contacts down here," Callie said. "If your niece is down here, we'll find her."

Adam nodded and thanked them. Sliding behind the steering wheel of his truck, he released a long, heavy sigh. He trusted the agents to work hard to find Frankie. This was what they did every day. Find missing kids.

But Adam hoped that if Frankie was living on the streets, the agents would locate her before she got in over her head and was lost to them forever.

CHAPTER

36

Friday morning
58:06:29 hours missing

KENDALL PULLED TO a stop in front of Lori Arnold's house. Adam's hand had been poised next to the door handle for the last three miles. As soon as she put the SUV in park, Adam unlocked his seat belt and pulled on the door handle. Kendall grabbed his arm and pulled him back against the seat. He looked like shit. Dark circles sat beneath his eyes, and he had a somewhat haggard appearance. All of this was taking a toll on him. Discovering Poppy had lied about knowing Luke Mathis and there was some sort of relationship between the two had pushed Adam to the edge. Rage simmered just below the surface. It wouldn't take much for him to blow.

"You cannot go in there half-cocked, Adam. We need to get Luke to talk to us, not shut down and refuse to give us anything."

"The little shit is going to tell us what he knows and come clean, or I'll haul his ass into the station and throw his scrawny little butt in a holding cell until his lips loosen up."

"This is why I think it's a bad idea for you to go in there."

"So your plan is to go in there with kid gloves on? We did that last time and he lied out his ass, and probably laughed at how gullible we were."

Okay, he's dangerously close to stepping over the line now.

"I'm sorry, do you think I'm new? Do you think I'm green and have no idea how to talk to a teenage boy in order to get information? Have you forgotten what I do for a living?"

Adam sat back in the seat and scrubbed the growth along his jaw. Sucking in a deep breath, Kendall tried to remember this was her friend. A friend whose niece was missing. A friend who might have found out his sister-in-law was not only cheating on his brother—but with a boy who was underage.

That was a lot to deal with.

"I just need for you to let me handle this, Adam. I really do know what I'm doing, and I would never do anything to jeopardize this case. Can you trust me?"

Adam moved his hand to his forehead and closed his eyes. "You're the only person I trust, Kendall."

"Okay, then let me do the talking. You've already put him on the defensive, and he's not a big Adam Taylor fan. I have a rapport with him. Let me lean on that. And Adam?"

"Yeah?"

"If he confirms he's having a romantic relationship with Poppy, I'm going to have to arrest her. Immediately."

"Yeah. I know." He let out a long heavy sigh. "What the hell is happening to my family?"

Kendall wished she had an answer that would help release all the tension and give him some hope. Instead, she opened her door, walked up the front walkway, and rang the doorbell.

Mrs. Arnold answered the door and stared at them quizzically. "Agent Beck."

"Good morning, Mrs. Arnold. Sorry to disturb you, but we have a few more questions regarding Frankie."

Arnold wrapped her arms around her body but didn't invite them in. "Oh, uh, I'm sorry, Agent Beck, but I have a student. I'll be done in about thirty minutes, if you'd like to come back."

Time was of the essence, and waiting was not an option. The clock was ticking, and they needed answers. Now. "We need to talk to Luke, and no, we can't come back."

Mrs. Arnold stared for a moment, her face going pale. "What's happened?"

"I really can't say until we talk with your nephew. Is he here?"

"Yes," she said, opening the door wider. "Come in."

They followed her to the dining room. "Have a seat. I'll get Luke."

This time Mrs. Arnold went down the stairs, opened the door to the basement, and called for Luke to come up. Kendall could hear murmuring as Luke reached his aunt at the top of the stairs but couldn't make out what was being said.

Luke came into the room, wiping sleep from his eyes. "What's up?"

"That's a good question," Kendall said. "What is up, Luke?"

Adam pushed the chair out with his foot from under the table. "Have a seat." The young man dropped into the chair with a thud and immediately slouched into it.

"When we were here the other day asking about your relationship with Frankie, you weren't completely honest with us." Kendall pulled out the text message log from Frankie's phone. "You neglected to tell us you had been texting each other."

"She texted me." Luke rolled his eyes and pushed the document back toward Kendall. "I never initiated shit with her."

"You seemed very interested in her family, though. Care to talk about that?"

Luke shrugged. "What else was I supposed to talk to her about? I mean, she was always texting me. I knew she had a crush on me, and I didn't want to be a dick and ignore her, but I wasn't going to lead her on, either. I thought asking about her family was safe."

"And it didn't have anything to do with the relationship you have with her mother?"

"What?" Mrs. Arnold gasped as she entered the room. The front door closed, and Kendall assumed her student had been dismissed. "What are you saying?"

Luke's head dropped.

Kendall picked up the text log. "*I just want to see to you again.* That was from you to Mrs. Taylor. She responds, *No, I shouldn't have met you the last time. It was a mistake.* Then you say, *I just want to talk to you. That's it. Nothing more, I promise.* And she ends the discussion with *Stop contacting me. And stop using Frankie to try and get closer to me.*" Kendall paused, placing the text log back into the file before speaking again. "Can you talk to me about the nature of your relationship with Mrs. Taylor?"

Arms across his chest, eyes down, defiance pulsed through the vein in his neck. "No."

"Luke!" Mrs. Arnold hollered. "Answer Agent Beck's question."

"No," Luke said to his aunt, then turned to face Kendall. "I won't talk to you about Poppy."

The use of her first name made it intimate. Kendall's skin crawled, and she had to physically stop herself from shuddering. She really hadn't believed it could be true.

She leaned forward and softened her tone. "If she's threatening you in any way, telling you not to talk to us, we can help. What she's doing is wrong, Luke, and she knows it."

Luke dropped his head back and chuckled. "You don't know what you're talking about. There is nothing wrong with our relationship. If you want to know more about it, you'll have to ask her. It's not my story to tell."

Kendall was stunned. She hadn't expected this. She'd figured that as soon as he was confronted with the text messages, he would crack.

"Is that all you needed to talk to me about? I have to get ready for school."

Kendall pulled her head out of her ass and focused on what needed to be done. It was disconcerting that a smartass seventeen-year-old had stumped her.

"No," Kendall said. "That's not all."

A loud crash came from the basement.

"What in the world?" Mrs. Arnold's head snapped around toward the stairs to the basement. Luke was on his feet and headed across the kitchen to the stairs.

Kendall grabbed him and held him back. "Stay here."

"Please, just let me go down there—" Luke begged.

"Sit down," Mrs. Arnold commanded with her high school teacher voice, and Kendall almost took a seat.

Adam and Kendall slowly crept down the stairs to the basement.

"What do you think?" Adam asked.

"I think we keep guns holstered but at the ready."

"What are we thinking this is?"

Kendall wasn't thinking it was an *it* at all, but a *who*. But sharing that with Adam would be a mistake. He was too reactionary when it came to Frankie. If he convinced himself she was here, he would throw caution to the wind and get them both in hot water.

Most of the basement looked like it was Luke's personal space. One side had a large desk with three computer monitors on it. Q had a similar setup—a gamer's paradise, complete with gaming chair and an oversized bean bag chair.

On the other side of the basement was a queen-sized bed. Piles of clothes littered the floor. Rope lights ran along the ceiling and floor providing a blue hue to the room.

"How does he see in here?" Adam asked.

"I think that's the point."

A pile of clothes in the corner to the right of Kendall shifted. Kendall gave a short, low whistle to get Adam's attention and pointed to the pile. He pulled his gun from the holster but kept the muzzle down. Kendall grabbed a handful of clothes, yanked them from the pile, and tossed them behind her.

A yelp came from the pile. A girl was crouched in the corner.

"Up," Kendall said. "Let me see your hands."

The girl stood, hands on her head. "Please don't hurt me."

"Who are you?" Adam asked.

"Luke's friend."

"Why are you hiding?" Kendall asked.

"I . . . I'm not supposed to be here. Mrs. A doesn't think it's appropriate for Luke to be alone down here with a girl. If she finds me, Luke will get grounded again."

Adam holstered his gun. His face was pained, and Kendall knew he had hoped it was Frankie hiding under the pile.

Kendall had too.

"Let's go." Adam pointed to the stairs.

"Please," the girl said, her voice a high-pitched squeal. "Can't I just stay down here?"

"No," Adam said. He gestured toward the stairs and followed the girl up.

A frame on the bedside table caught Kendall's eye. She picked it up and studied the photo—a young girl sitting in a field, sunglasses covering most of her face. But it was her small smile that made Kendall wonder what the girl in the picture was thinking. She replaced the frame and climbed the stairs.

By the time Kendall returned to the dining room, tears were streaming down the face of the girl from the basement. Lori Arnold looked as if her head were about to explode.

Adam was showing Luke's friend a picture of Frankie, but the girl shook her head.

"I don't think we need to keep her, do you?" Kendall asked Adam.

"No."

"Didi," Mrs. Arnold said, "go home. And expect me to call your mother later."

Didi was up and out the door in two seconds flat.

Adam sat in the chair vacated by Didi—right next to Luke. He rubbed the bridge of his nose and let out a long sigh. "Okay, I'm tired of playing games, Luke. I'm going to ask you questions, and you're going to answer them."

Luke nodded, his head down.

"Did Frankie ever talk to you about having any issues with anyone on her team?" Adam asked.

"Yeah, there was some twerp—I think she said she took his spot and he was pissed about it and would wank about it, but she usually made it a joke. I don't think she was all that bothered by him. At least that's how it came across to me."

"What about her coach?"

Luke sat back in his chair and blew his long bangs from his eyes. "Yeah, she said she had found out some stuff about him."

"Did she say what it was?"

"Apparently, he was selling weed to some of the kids on the team. It really upset her. She said she was going to tell him she knew and if he didn't stop, she would rat him out to her cop uncle." He glanced at Adam. "I told her she should probably stay out of it."

"And you didn't think this was important information to pass yesterday when we questioned you?"

"I guess, looking back on it now, I should've said something. But I figured she was just pissed at her mom and making her pay for yelling at me by running off to one of her friends or something."

Adam tossed his business card on the table in front of the kid and stood up. "If you hear from her at all, your next move better be to call me. Are we clear?"

Luke nodded. "Crystal."

Adam stormed out of the house. Kendall gathered up the text logs and shoved them into her portfolio. Mrs. Arnold walked her to the door.

"We'll be talking to Poppy," Kendall said. "Depending on what she says, we may be arresting her. If that happens, Luke will need to come in and make a statement."

"Should I get him an attorney?"

"That's up to you," Kendall said, placing a hand on the woman's arm. "But in the eyes of the law, Luke did nothing wrong."

Mrs. Arnold squeezed Kendall's hand and nodded, a tight smile on her lips. "Thank you, Agent Beck."

Kendall nodded and started down the steps but turned back. "If I could make one suggestion? I would monitor his phone. Chances are good he's giving Poppy a heads-up that we know what's going on. If she responds—"

"I'll take his phone and let you know if she attempts to contact him."

Friday morning
60:02:58 hours missing

KENDALL PULLED INTO Mark and Poppy's driveway and glanced at herself in the rearview mirror.

"Jesus, why didn't you tell me my hair was a mess?" she asked, pulling a hairband from the center console, smoothing back her hair, and securing it in a ponytail.

"Your hair's a mess." Adam had his nose in his phone. It had blown up with messages. A few were voice mails from Mark wanting an update, his tone becoming more angry with each message. Adam felt bad. He had sent a few texts back with little to no substance, letting Mark know they were running down leads, nothing new to share, and various other brush-offs. He was horrified that he had no real leads and hated to hear the disappointment, stress, and hopelessness in his brother's voice. There was only so much Adam could load onto his own shoulders, and talking to Mark was one burden he had decided to dump. It was probably a shit thing to do, and he was sure Mark was close to hunting Adam down and forcing a conversation—right after he beat Adam to a pulp—but Adam needed to use every ounce of energy he had to figure out what he was missing in this case. Besides, he needed to find out what his sister-in-law was doing before he talked to Mark.

How the hell am I going to tell him about Poppy and Luke?

There was a very real chance that Mark might shoot the messenger when he found out about Poppy's infidelity.

Adam glanced at the call log. "Looks like someone tipped Poppy off that we know some stuff about her. I have five missed calls and a text message to call her as soon as I get this." Adam's stomach clenched, followed by a wave of nausea. This job was going to give him ulcers—if it hadn't already.

"Well, let's go see what she has to say, then," Kendall said.

Adam didn't bother knocking on the front door. What was the point? And really, he didn't have the time or the temperament to be polite. He stalked into the living room, ready for a fight.

Poppy was pacing, chewing on a fingernail, and looked harried. Adam might've felt bad for her in another time, under other circumstances. But this Poppy—he had very little sympathy for whoever this person was at the moment.

Scowl on her face. Eyes on fire. She dropped her hands to her sides and marched toward them, pointing to the stairs. How could such a slender woman stomp that heavily? He and Kendall followed her into her office. She made a show of forcefully shutting the door.

Adam would've laughed if he didn't want to kick her ass.

"What the hell are you doing talking to my lawyer?" she snapped, taking a challenging step closer to him.

Adam met the challenge and took a step toward her. "Why are you lying to me about where you've been?"

"Going to see Henry has nothing to do with Frankie."

Henry? First-name basis on her side also? Seemed to be more than a business relationship.

"See, you saying that, on top of keeping this 'nothing' to yourself, only makes me think it has a great deal to do with Frankie."

"Adam, I promise you, if it had anything to do with Frankie, I would've told you. It just . . . doesn't."

"Then why keep it from me, Poppy?" Heat flushed through his body. "If it is truly nothing, then you just wasted a shit ton of my time while I chased down a discrepancy in your story. And that blows my mind. Your daughter is missing, and you think you get to decide what we know? Let me clue you in—we get to know everything. It's how we find Frankie."

He took another step closer, forcing Poppy to back up. It was a low blow, using his height and weight advantage to intimidate her, but there was only so much Adam could take with a severe lack of sleep and enough stress to fell an elephant. And she was trampling his last nerve. "But I think it is something, Poppy. I think it's a huge something. I think you're planning on divorcing Mark. What I couldn't figure out until today was why. I thought maybe it was because you were having an affair with *Henry*."

Poppy rolled her eyes. "I'm not having an affair with Henry."

"I know—it's even worse than that. See, I figured out your secret."

Red flushed Poppy's throat and face. Her eyes widened, tears flooding them.

"I'm sickened by this, Poppy. I never in a million years would've thought you capable of this kind of thing."

"I know—I'm so sorry." Her hand covered her mouth. "I never meant for anyone to find out."

I'll bet you didn't.

"Well, you should've covered your ass better, I guess. I've seen the text messages." He rubbed his eyes. Exhaustion was setting in. "I know all about Luke."

Poppy fell back into her chair. "Oh God." She looked up at Adam. The stench of fear permeated the room. "You can't tell Mark. Please, Adam. He can't know about Luke. It will kill him."

"He's going to find out, Poppy." She couldn't possibly think he could cover this up? "I can't just sweep this under the rug. It's too big. Too many people know about it now."

Sobs racked Poppy's body. Adam placed a hand at his side and pulled his other hand down his face. *What a fucking shit day.* He was beat. Heartbroken. And pissed.

"How could you do this, Poppy? Help me understand, because I can't for the life of me figure this out. You have a great life, a husband who adores you, the most amazing kid—"

Poppy dragged in a ragged breath, her body trembling. "No one was supposed to find out. Not ever. I had it covered—I took care of everything. It was supposed to be a secret forever. No one was supposed to be hurt by what I allowed to happen."

Out of the corner of his eye, Adam caught Kendall typing away on her phone.

"For fuck's sake," Adam said. "How *did* this happen? How could you do this to Mark? To Frankie?" This was straight out of a nightmare. "Is that what you and Frankie were arguing about? Did Frankie find out the truth about you and Luke? Did she run away because of you?"

"Don't say that, Adam." A sob burst from Poppy's chest. "Oh God, Frankie can't know—it would destroy her."

"Maybe you should've thought of that before you started having sex with a minor."

The air stilled. Poppy froze. Her eyes widened. She opened her mouth, but no words came out as she sat up straight in her chair. "What?"

She didn't really believe this sweet, innocent act was going to sway him, did she?

"Jesus, Adam, what are you talking about?" Poppy swiped the tears from her face, a look of utter disbelief and confusion etched into her facial features.

"I'm saying it's pretty clear from the text messages that there is something going on between you and Luke Mathis."

"And your first conclusion was that I must be sleeping with a seventeen-year-old boy? Is that really what you think of me?"

He drew in a slow, steady breath and tried to call up the professionalism he usually exhibited when questioning a suspect.

"Not in the beginning—but then I didn't think you would lie to me. Keep information to yourself during an investigation into your daughter's disappearance. An investigation where every minute counts."

Poppy clenched her fists and groaned. "I am not having an affair with Luke Mathis."

"Then why are you texting a seventeen-year-old boy you claim to not know?"

"Because he's her son," Kendall said.

Poppy's shoulders dropped.

Kendall took a step toward them. "Robinson isn't your divorce attorney. He's your adoption attorney."

Adam looked over his shoulder at Kendall, his mind racing to understand what she'd just said.

Poppy choked back a sob.

"Luke is your son, isn't he?" Kendall prodded.

Poppy deflated, fell back into her chair, and slowly nodded.

"You must've been quite young when you had him," Kendall said.

"Fifteen."

Now it was Adam's turn to stumble back and sit on the couch. The room was spinning. Poppy's confession had sucked all the air out of the room, and Adam couldn't breathe. "Wait, slow down. Luke Mathis is your son? How?" Adam forced out. "When did this happen?"

"When I was a freshman in high school."

"Does Mark know?" he asked.

"No, and he can't find out."

"You can't keep this from him, Poppy." Why hadn't she told him? His chest tightened. Christ, was he having a heart attack? Why had Poppy decided to lie to Mark all these years?

Kendall put her hand up in front of his face and mouthed *Breathe* to him before turning back to Poppy. "What happened?"

Poppy pulled a couple of tissues from the box on her desk and wiped the tears from her eyes. "I was seeing a boy. He was a senior, and my parents didn't approve of the relationship. So, one night, I snuck out, and we ended up in his basement. I thought we were just going to watch movies, but we started making out. Just kissing at first. Then it started to go farther. I was scared—I wasn't ready to have sex. I told him I wasn't ready.

"He said that was bullshit and I knew it—knew what we were going to do that night. He told me I had agreed to this when I decided to go with him to his house." She drew in a ragged breath and closed her eyes. "He got on top of me and held me down, and told me not to worry because he was really good with virgins." A sob broke free. Her head came up, and she looked at Adam. "I tried to push him off, Adam, I really did. But I couldn't move. I was afraid to scream, because I didn't want his parents to find me there and tell my parents."

Tears streamed down her face. "I begged for him to stop. I kept telling him no, but he had this look in his eyes. I knew he was going to do what he wanted whether I wanted to or not. So, after a while, I stopped fighting and just let it happen." Her shoulders quaked with sorrow.

"When he was done, we got dressed and he drove me home. He actually thanked me for letting him be my first. I snuck back into my house and spent the rest of the night vomiting. The next day he broke up with me. A month later, I found out I was pregnant."

She dropped her head to her hands. Her body shook with sobs. And probably shame. But Adam knew he should shoulder all the shame. He had jumped to the most disgusting conclusion when he should've known better.

He crossed the room, dropped to his knees, and gathered his sister-in-law in his arms. "I'm so sorry, Poppy."

Poppy wrapped her arms around his neck and cried into his shoulder. They stayed that way until Poppy's breathing leveled out.

"Do you think you can go on?" Kendall asked.

Poppy nodded and blew her nose. "I'll try." She gave a weak smile to Adam. "Once my parents found out, I was sent to live with my aunt until I gave birth. It's ironic, huh? I was sent to live with my aunt to deal with my problems, and Luke was sent to his aunt for the same reason."

Adam smiled at her. The tightness in his chest loosened, and it no longer hurt to breathe.

"Anyway, there was never any discussion about keeping the baby. My parents insisted I give it up for adoption. And to be honest, I was okay with it. The baby was just a reminder of how stupid I had been, and gullible, and I just wanted it gone." She shook her head and scowled. "Sounds horrible now."

"Sounds perfectly understandable," Kendall said.

"We insisted on a closed adoption. I never wanted him to know who I was. Never wanted any contact with him."

Adam pulled a chair closer and sat next to Poppy, holding her hand in both of his. She was cold and still shaking.

"Sort of a coincidence that you would end up taking Frankie to the adopted mother's sister for piano lessons," Kendall remarked.

"Actually not. I had met her and her sister—Luke's mom—a couple of days before I gave birth. They would sit with me while I was having contractions. Lori told me she was a piano teacher. So, when I decided to get Frankie lessons, she was the only teacher I knew."

"How soon after Frankie started going did you meet Luke?"

"Beginning of the year. As soon as I walked in the door, I knew it was him."

"When did you find out he knew you were his mother?"

"I was early picking Frankie up one day, so I was sitting in the SUV waiting for her. He came up and knocked on the window. We talked about Maryland and how much he hated it there. Then he asked why I was called Poppy and not Caraleena."

"And who is Caraleena?" Kendall asked.

"My first name. My middle name is Poppy. It was a concession between my mother and father. He wanted me to have his grandmother's name, but my mom wanted something fun. So, they named me after Great-Grandma Cara but called me Poppy."

"It must've been a shock when he said that."

"It was. I told him I had to run an errand and drove off. I waited until Frankie texted me to pick her up to go back. After that I avoided him."

"He has a picture of you," Kendall said. Adam stared at her. Why hadn't she told him? "It's framed and sitting by his bed. You're wearing big sunglasses."

"In the field behind my parents' house. I had forgotten I gave that to them."

"So why were you going to see your lawyer?" Adam asked.

"To see if there was some way to get Luke to leave me alone. He got my cell phone number—probably from the intake form I filled out for Lori—and started calling me. I finally met with him one time just to get him to leave me alone. He said he wanted to get to know me. To be a part of my life."

She turned in her seat to face Adam. "I couldn't do that. I couldn't risk Mark and the rest of the family finding out what I had done. No one would look at me the same way."

Adam's heart broke. "Poppy, we would've understood. Mark loves you—he would never turn his back on you because you'd been raped. Even if it hadn't been rape, he would've understood. He's not naïve—he had sex in high school too."

"Do you think Frankie found out Luke is your son?" Kendall asked.

Poppy shook her head. "I don't think so. If she knew, she would've asked me about it. She's not one to suffer in silence lately, especially when it comes to me."

"Was she upset enough about what she might perceive as you interfering in her relationship with Luke to run away?"

"What relationship?"

"Frankie has been texting Luke."

Her hand flew to her mouth. "Oh no. Oh God, this is bad. But I don't think she would run away. She would never be able to be away from Mark for this long."

A knock drew all eyes to the door. Mark opened it and stepped inside. "Everything okay in here?"

His gaze landed on his wife. His face paled. He dropped to his knees in front of her and grasped her around her upper arms. "What's wrong? What's happened?" He looked up at Adam. "Did you find Frankie?"

"No." Adam looked at Poppy. "You have to tell him." He squeezed his brother's shoulder as he passed him and joined Kendall in the hallway.

"Interesting turn of events," Kendall said as the door closed behind them with a soft click.

"Understatement of the century." Adam ran his hand through his hair, relief flooding his body. "But better than I was expecting."

"I almost feel bad for thinking the worst of Poppy, but she didn't help herself by not coming clean with the truth earlier. Unfortunately, I don't think we can rule out that Frankie didn't discover the information somehow and run away."

"I agree. If she had a crush on Luke and then found out he was her half brother, it could've been too much for her to handle and she could have bolted for a while."

"The only problem is, unless someone is hiding her—and we've checked all her friends' homes—she has nowhere to go."

Adam didn't want to think about Frankie being somewhere alone, scared. *Please don't let her be on the streets.*

"What's the plan now?" Kendall asked.

"I think we should visit our drug-dealing rink manager and see what he has to say."

"Let's do it," Kendall said as she swung her key ring around her finger and headed out the front door.

Adam took a final glance up the stairs. No yelling. Nothing being thrown at walls. No sounds of glass breaking. Adam knew

Mark would never hold anything like giving up a child due to a teenage pregnancy—especially one caused by rape—against Poppy. But trust between them had taken a major blow. Adam prayed they could work it out.

They were going to need to lean on each other to get through this—especially if Frankie never came home.

38

Friday afternoon
61:25:48 hours missing

THE BRIGHT SUN had warmed up the morning, but now that early afternoon had rolled around, there was enough of a chill that Adam pulled his light jacket on. Living in Colorado meant wearing layers—there was no telling what the weather would do, and Mother Nature often liked to show the weather-guessers who was in charge.

The front lobby of the arena was dark, the place eerily quiet. When there wasn't the hustle and bustle of hot, sweaty bodies milling about, the arena was downright frosty.

Adam and Kendall walked up the ramp toward the rink and stopped to survey the area. Only a few of the lights were on over the slick, shiny ice rink. There was a sinister stillness. It reminded Adam of four-thirty morning practices before school started. The first blades hitting the ice felt as if they were waking the dead.

In front of the skate rental, Mick the manager stood talking to a man in a leather jacket. They seemed to be having a cordial conversation, totally oblivious to the new onlookers. So comfortable in the belief they were alone that Mick handed the man a fat wad of bills. The man flipped through the stack, ensuring he wasn't getting ripped off, and slid the cash inside his jacket. A large manila shipping envelope was tucked under his arm. He passed it over to Mick. Mick glanced inside and shook hands with Leather Jacket.

Adam glanced at Kendall. Had they actually witnessed a drug deal go down?

Well, that would make having enough to arrest Mick a lot easier than relying solely on the word of two teenagers' hearsay evidence.

Mick caught sight of Adam and Kendall and took off running to the locker rooms.

"Mick," Adam called to Kendall as he darted into the locker room.

"Dammit," he heard Kendall say before she started yelling at Leather Jacket. "Hands up, on your knees! Don't you dare run, motherfucker."

The locker room door slammed closed behind him with a clang. No doubt Mick was trying to dump whatever illicit drug he had just procured down the toilet. Adam had to get to him before he was able to dispose of it. No drugs, no drug charge.

There were eight stalls, four on each side. He pushed open the first door on the left, figuring Mick would go for the quickest and easiest. Empty. He crossed to the other side. Empty. Next stall. Empty. Crossing again, he flung open the door and whacked Mick as he was reaching for the flushing handle.

Mick's body toppled forward. He placed his hands against the wall and steadied himself. Adam grabbed him by the collar of his shirt and dragged him out of the stall. Gun out of the holster, he aimed it at Mick.

"Don't move, asshole. I'm having a really bad day, and I will not have an ounce of remorse about shooting you in the back if you try to run."

Now here was the dilemma: Adam could jeopardize the drugs dissolving in the toilet water or release Mick. Should he rescue the drugs from their watery grave or risk Mick running as soon as the gun was no longer aimed at his head?

Adam had to hope Kendall had secured her guy and would be able to snag Mick if he got out of the locker room.

"Stay put." He holstered his gun, let go of Mick, and swung the stall door open. A large ziplock bag was floating on the top like a big white turd.

Fucking idiot thought he could flush an entire bag down the toilet.

Criminals were not the brightest bulbs in the pack. Adam had learned that fact many years ago, but Mick was definitely a few filaments short of a working bulb.

As expected, Mick was no longer patiently waiting for Adam to rescue his drugs and arrest him. "For fuck's sake," Adam muttered. The door flew open with a metallic bang against the wall. Damn, he was angry, and ready to pounce on Mick as soon as he caught sight of the asshat.

He looked around the rink.

No Kendall.

No Mick.

The heavy glass doors at the front of the building closed with a loud clang.

"Fuck!"

Adam dropped the drug bag along the exterior of the rink boards and took off toward the front lobby after Mick. The parking lot was empty except for Kendall's Range Rover. There was no place for Mick to hide. And if his size was any indication—short legs, rotund middle—he wouldn't have the stamina to actually make it through the park and onto the busy road to flag down a ride without having a heart attack. Adam could've sat back and watched Mick drop from exhaustion halfway across the park.

But Adam was pissed: at Mick, at Poppy, at the person who had taken Frankie, maybe at Frankie too, if she had run away.

Mostly at himself. He should've found Frankie by now. The fact that he wasn't even close to figuring out what had happened to her made him feel like an utter failure.

Adam burst into a run, adrenaline and anger propelling him across the parking lot. Mick was within his grasp. Adam reached for the collar of Mick's coat.

But Mick surprised him. Bent over, pivoted, and flung his arms around to get out of Adam's clutches. The man was wily for his age and size. Mick got his bearings and took off running again. Adam was in full sprint and gaining. One step. Two more steps, and he launched himself on top of Mick. Both men tumbled to the ground.

Mick emitted a loud *oof* as he hit the hard ground, rolled onto his side, and tried to stand up. Adam pulled his gun out of the holster with one hand and pushed himself off the ground with the other.

Aiming the gun at Mick, he attempted to catch his breath. "Didn't I tell you that if you ran, I would shoot you, Mick?"

Mick's answer was loud wheezing as he tried to inhale. "I think . . . you broke . . . my ribs."

"I'd apologize, but I'm not sorry."

"I'm going to . . . sue you . . . and the police," he said between gasps.

"Great idea. Except you were buying a substantial amount of drugs with the intent to sell to minors. That won't help your case much."

"You don't know that . . . you don't know what I was doing."

Adam wondered if he should just shoot Mick.

"Do you think I was there by accident, Mick? Or do you think I had some intel regarding what you've been up to? Now put your arms behind your back, dickhead."

Mick squirmed and squealed as Adam yanked his arms back.

"By the way, you're under arrest," Adam said as he tightened the handcuffs around Mick's wrists.

Kendall came out of the front doors: clothes a mess, escorting Leather Jacket in handcuffs, and holding up the abandoned bag of drugs.

"Want to tell me what's in the bag?" Adam asked Mick.

"Don't know what you're talking about."

"Of course not." Adam smacked him on the back of the head and called for a patrol car to pick up their alleged drug dealers.

Kendall met him halfway across the parking lot, one hand tucking her shirt in as she approached. "Well, that was fun."

"Yeah, and here I was worried I wouldn't get a workout in today."

"What are we doing now?"

"I'll grab a ride back to the station with the black-and-white and grab my truck. It's probably a good idea if we divide and conquer." Adam walked with Kendall toward her SUV. "I need to talk to our Good Samaritan about who he was supposed to be meeting. He gave us a couple of numbers, but one is out of service, and the other goes to a voice mail no one answers."

"Why not just call him?"

"I want to talk to him face-to-face. See how he reacts when I question him about why we can't corroborate his story. Also, he's not returning my calls."

"Rude." Kendall opened the driver's side door and slid onto the seat. "I guess I'll head over to Jason Turner's and question him about his extracurricular business. I can't tell if he's working with Mick or not, but it seems like a coincidence they're both selling drugs to players. CSU should be on their way to search the house, so I'll see what they come up with too."

Adam grasped the door and steadied himself. Jesus, was he that out of shape? "If Frankie threatened Turner and Mick found out, either one of them could've grabbed her."

Kendall nodded. "Check in with any news."

CHAPTER

39

Friday afternoon
63:03:52 hours missing

IT HAD BEEN a long day. So much had happened, yet nothing
had been solved, except two more drug dealers were going to
be off the street and unable to put children in danger any longer.
That was good news.

But they were still no closer to finding Frankie and bringing
her home than they had been that morning. Kendall couldn't
dwell on that. It would zap what remaining energy she had. And
that wouldn't help anyone.

She was worried about Adam. If the day had been exhausting for her, it had to have been a living hell for him. He swung
back and forth like a pendulum; one minute it appeared he was
holding it all together, then he'd swing the other way and he'd
look like a man treading water who was about to slip below the
surface and drown.

So many secrets had been uncovered. So many emotions
pulling and tearing everyone apart. And there was still so much
work to do. She was going to have to make sure she took Adam
out for a drink, or five, when this was over.

But right now, she had a hockey coach to apprehend.

CSU hadn't arrived at Jason Turner's house yet. The cops
with the search warrant weren't there either. Saul had called and

let her know they were on the way. So Kendall decided to find the coach and make sure he wasn't going to get in the way. If he had a heads-up there was going to be a search of his house, he might try to get rid of the drugs. If he had Frankie there, things could get ugly if he tried to get rid of *that* evidence as well.

No way was that happening.

No answer to the knocks on the door at Jason's house. His Jeep was in the driveway, so chances were good he was there. She stepped off the cement slab porch and looked in the front living room window through a gap in the curtains. TV was on.

Where the hell is he?

She glanced across the lawn to the neighboring house. Could he be visiting his sister?

It was apparent by the state of the house and yard that Turner wasn't anywhere near Homeowner of the Year. In fact, he did the bare mins when it came to upkeep. No grass to speak of in the front yard, only hard-packed dirt. The yard was clear of weeds, but Kendall doubted he had much to do with that. Every few feet there was a block of broken concrete or an empty beer can.

The current color of the house was dirt. Two of the windows had rotted wood shutters, barely hanging on. One decent windstorm would surely knock them off completely. Which, at this stage, might improve the exterior.

As Kendall got to the corner of the house, the sweet smell of marijuana greeted her. A wisp of smoke, nearly dissipated, wafted along the breeze from the backyard.

Bingo.

Jason Turner, joint dangling from his lip, counting a large stack of bills, sat at a large wooden picnic table. Kendall was too far away to make out the denominations of the bills, but there were a lot of them.

And they say crime doesn't pay.

The tabletop was filled with small baggies—most had pills. Some contained weed and gummy bears. A veritable smorgasbord of drugs.

"What do we have here?" Kendall asked. "Something for everyone, I see."

Jason jolted, the money flying into the air, fluttering like feathers in the wind. He caught himself before he fell off the edge of the bench and onto the ground. Hopefully, the hockey coach wasn't going to bolt, thinking he could outrun her because she was just a woman. Kendall had taken down bigger men than Jason. But she crossed her fingers the cops were close by. Having someone bringing up the rear in case shit went south was never a bad idea.

"Hey, you can't just come onto my property." His voice had an adolescent squeak, and he cleared his throat. "You're trespassing."

Everyone fancied themselves an expert on the law whenever law enforcement was around.

"I came by to talk to you. I knocked on the door, but there was no answer. Then I saw smoke. I feared you might be in danger and in need of assistance, so I thought I should investigate. And look what I found—you and all this stuff just sitting out here in plain sight."

"What do you want?" Turner grumbled.

"Yeah, I think we're going to have that discussion down at the police station."

Jason continued to pick up the money—Kendall could now see it was mostly twenties—off the ground.

"Looks like possession of a few controlled substances with intent to sell." Kendall *tsk*ed, picking up a bag of pills and tossing it in the air, catching it in her other hand. "Adderall or Molly?" She shook her head. "Now, I'm not a cop, but I'm pretty sure there's enough here for a felony conviction—even under the new less-stringent drug laws in our beautiful state."

His face paled, his eyes like saucers. "This isn't mine—I'm holding it for a friend."

"Not a very nice friend, leaving you to hold the bag, so to speak."

Turner shrugged.

"Oddly, I don't believe you, Jason. I think all of this belongs to you, and I think you've been dealing to minors. That's not good." She shook her head and frowned. "Not good at all."

Two uniformed police officers came around the corner. She held up her badge for them to see. "Come on over and join us." She looked across the table at Jason. "I'm going to need you to stand up, turn around, and drop to your knees with your fingers laced behind your head."

Jason threw the money he had been collecting onto the table. "Fuck."

"Indeed." She rounded the table and stood in front of him as one of the uniforms secured handcuffs around Turner's wrists. "Jason Turner, you are under arrest for possession of a controlled substance with intent to sell." She gave him the rest of the Miranda warning as the cops lifted Turner to his feet.

"Now, you're going to take a ride with these fine men in their car. I will meet you at the police station. I suggest you think about how you want things to go and what you want your future to look like. Helpful alleged drug dealers are more apt to get a sweet deal in exchange for information than ones who are less than forthcoming."

Turner was just about to round the corner of the house when Kendall called out to him. "Oh, Jason?" He stopped and looked over his shoulder at her. "Thought you should know—we are conducting a search of your house."

His knees buckled, and his face went as white as the little pills he was peddling to kids. And, in the midst of all the crappiness of the past couple of days, that made Kendall's heart flutter with a little bit of happiness.

40

Friday afternoon
63:04:27 hours missing

THERE WAS A certain unpleasant odor locked into the hallways of older apartment buildings. A mix of dirt, dust, mildew, trash, and every meal ever made over the many years people had resided there. And mandatory inadequate lighting. It was akin to walking into a cave, not sure what was around you or if what you stepped on was something alive or dead. There was very little about the building where Melvin Craig lived that said *Welcome home.*

Adam knocked on the door to apartment 2C. When Craig cracked the door open, he didn't look happy to see Adam. Something in his eyes. Or maybe it was his scowl. Adam wasn't sure which, but then he didn't really care if the Good Samaritan was miffed to find the police on his doorstep.

"Mr. Craig, I think your phone is having technical issues," Adam said with a smile. "That's the only reason I can think of for you not returning my calls."

"How about I'm busy? What can I do for you, Detective?"

"Well, you could invite me in so I don't have to have this conversation out here in the hallway . . . where your neighbors might overhear." Adam raised his voice to make a point. "You know how nosy neighbors can be, especially when a police officer is at your door."

"Fine," Craig said, and stepped back to let Adam in. "What is it you need to know?"

Adam walked into the living room. A massaging recliner was the only furniture in the room. The TV—an eighty-five incher, if Adam was correct—was mounted to the wall. Just beyond was a door to the kitchen. A round dining table with four mismatched chairs encircled it. It was apparent Craig never ate at the table, instead using it for paper collection.

"I need to know why the man you said you were meeting is also not returning my calls. The personal cell phone number you provided is out of order—"

"I told you I don't normally talk to him on the phone."

"—and the other number goes straight to voice mail. I've left a few messages, informing Mr. Johnson that it is imperative I speak with him. Yet I have yet to hear from him."

Craig stood with his arms across his chest and stared at Adam, an air of intentional uncooperativeness on his blank face.

"When was the last time you spoke with Mr. Johnson?" Adam asked.

"I guess it was the night before he was supposed to meet me."

"You haven't spoken to him since?"

"No, I've been preoccupied. The press has been hounding me—wanting to interview me. This is the first day I've had any peace."

"Not enjoying your fifteen minutes of fame?"

"Never asked for it, not interested in having it."

"But you're a hero, Mr. Craig. You rescued a missing girl and took out the bad guy." Adam stood next to the table and surveyed the apartment. It wasn't bad, just old. The property management company had done some updates, but it still looked like an apartment from the fifties. "Some cops never accomplish that in their entire career."

"Yippee for me." He twirled his finger in the air.

"I gotta say, I find it more than curious you haven't called Mr. Johnson to find out why he never showed up. Or tell him how important it is that he call me and confirm he was meeting you the day of the shooting."

Craig shrugged one shoulder and put his hand out, palm up. "Like I said, I've been busy."

"Right," Adam said. "Avoiding the press. It can be a full-time job, I understand."

Sometimes the games they had to play to get people to talk were a challenge. He wished he could forgo the diversion and get to the heart of what was going on with Craig, but it didn't appear the man was interested in providing information without the sport.

"Are you aware the number you gave me as Mr. Johnson's work phone is a pay-as-you-go phone?"

Craig swallowed. He shifted from one foot to another and looked down at his feet. "No, I had no idea. Maybe he was just scamming me or something."

"Why would he do that?"

"I don't know. You'd have to ask him."

"Ah, but if I could." Adam inhaled deeply and forced out a cough. "Excuse me. Spring allergies." He coughed again, adding more hacking. "Could I have a glass of water?"

Craig expelled a deep, irritated sigh, and the famous scowl returned. "Fine, but then you need to leave. I don't know how else to get in contact with Johnson."

The wonderful thing about surprise visits was that no one knew you were coming. Therefore, they couldn't clean up. Or put things away they wouldn't want others to see. Like a table brimming with documents and bills. And handwritten notes on torn pieces of paper. All left out in plain sight.

And that was the best work-around for obtaining information without a warrant. The plain-sight exception to search and seizure. Adam loved it. Used it whenever he could.

Taking full advantage of Craig being in the other room, Adam quickly surveyed what was on the table. Bills. Junk mail. All tossed on the table. Next to Adam's hand was a piece of paper that looked as if it had been torn from a notepad. On it was a date, address, and phone number.

Adam glanced behind him while pulling out his cell phone. Craig was no doubt trying to find a clean glass. Or dissolving rat poison in Adam's water. Adam opened the camera app and took a picture of the note, sliding the phone in his pocket as Craig returned and handed him the water.

"Thanks." No way was Adam drinking it. "How long have you lived here?" He asked, looking around the apartment as if he was interested in moving there himself. He was not.

"A while."

"I guess in your line of work, you don't spend a lot of time at home. Always on the road—driving here and there all over the city."

Ah, small talk. Sometimes it worked, sometimes . . .

The arms went across the chest again, the scowl returned. The lines in Craig forehead seemed to deepen and he looked angry. "Is this really what you came over to talk about?"

"No, just curious."

"Then I'm going to have to ask you to leave."

Adam placed the glass of water on the table and glanced around the place one final time before he walked toward the door. "I won't take up any more of your time." He turned the knob and opened the front door. Turning back, he said, "If you do happen to hear from Mr. Johnson, please let me know. I actually do need to speak with him so we can put this case to bed. My boss insists on dotting all the *i*'s and crossing all the *t*'s."

Craig's shoulders dropped, and the twitching muscle in his neck disappeared. "I'll do that," he said, his voice less antagonistic. He actually put his hand out for Adam to shake. "Have a good day, Detective."

"You too, Mr. Craig."

Adam slid behind the wheel of his truck and texted the picture he had taken to Fletch, then pressed the speed dial on his phone. No telling what he had found or if it had anything to do with the homicide investigation. But it was worth a shot.

"What's up, boss?" Fletch asked.

"I just texted you a picture. I need to confirm the address listed is for the gas station where the double homicide occurred. And I need to know who the number belongs to. Can you get me that information as soon as possible?"

"Uh, yeah, hold on." There was silence on the line. "Yes, the address is for the gas station. Let me send the number down to the forensic geeks and see if they can work their IT magic."

"Thanks." Adam hung up.

If Craig had another number for Johnson, why wouldn't he give it to Adam? The easy answer was Mr. Johnson's business was less than legal and Craig didn't want to get wrapped up in it. Or be found out to have been part of it.

This double homicide investigation was different from most Adam worked on. In this case, the shooters were already known. It was the whys that were plaguing him.

Why had Stevens decided to rob the store that morning? Had he planned it? With Ashley? And why had Ashley pulled the gun out? But the most perplexing question was, how had Stevens ended up with a missing girl? And where was he taking her?

His phone rang. Fletch. "Yeah?"

"The number belongs to none other than our resident deceased bad guy—Darin Stevens."

What. The. Fuck.

"Get a black-and-white over to Melvin Craig's apartment now," Adam said. "And get a holding cell ready for him."

CHAPTER

41

Friday afternoon
65:34:26 hours missing

MAKING A SUSPECT sit in an interrogation room and wait was a highly effective law enforcement tool. And one of Kendall's favorites. It allowed the anticipation of the suspect to build to a fever pitch, which in turn loosened tongues.

Jason Turner sat in the interrogation room, head down, foot bouncing a million miles a minute. He'd been waiting for about thirty minutes for Kendall to come in. Not an exorbitant amount of time, but enough for anxiety to build and desperation to set in. She needed him talkative. If he knew anything about Frankie's disappearance, he needed to give it up. Now.

As soon as she opened the door, his head shot up. His eyes were red and puffy, but it appeared he had stopped crying. For now, anyway. Kendall took a perverse pleasure in reducing grown men to tears and groveling. Extra points if they actually peed themselves. She considered it a perk of the job.

"Well, this is quite the shit show you've gotten yourself into, Jason." She tossed a file folder on the table, sat down, and slowly opened the folder and looked through it. She glanced up at him and smiled. "You're like the Walmart of controlled substances." She read from the paper in her hand. "Ecstasy, Rohypnol, Adderall, and over twelve pounds of marijuana. And, with the statements I have from the players on your teams, it seems you're selling a majority of these drugs to minors."

Kendall shook her head. "You are aware each of these offenses carries a minimum eight-year prison sentence, up to thirty-two years. For each offense, Jason." She sat back in her chair, arms across her chest , and shook her head. "What the hell were you thinking, man? Selling to kids?"

Jason's body shook, and the waterworks started again.

"That's"—she started ticking off on her fingers and threw her hands in the air—"life. In prison. With big hairy men named Butch and Dick." She leaned across the table as if sharing a secret. "And someone with your good looks is going to be very popular."

He gulped in air, sobs choking him.

Kendall had no sympathy. He knew what he'd been doing. And he knew what he was doing was illegal. "These kids, they looked up to you. Trusted you. Wanted to be like you. And you turn them on to drugs?"

"I'm sorry."

"That's not good enough." She slammed her fist on the metal table, the sound reverberating in the small space.

Turner jumped up, knocking his chair over, and backed into the wall. Eyes wide, face pale. She was sure he was on the brink of pissing himself.

"What if one of these kids had died of an overdose from the drugs you sold them? Would the additional income have been worth it? Or do you just assume that these kids—some of them not even teenagers yet—know the risks when they take this shit?"

The sobs grew louder. His mouth was agape, and a long string of spit hit the floor at his feet.

She was disgusted. He wasn't sorry he had put these kids' lives in danger. He was sorry he'd gotten caught. Selfish little prick.

"Sit down," she said.

He righted the chair and did what he was told without question.

"Now, we're going to talk about the night Frankie went missing, but this time you're going to be completely honest with me. No more bullshit, Jason, or I will literally nail your balls to the wall."

She was only half kidding.

"I know Frankie had an argument with you the night she disappeared. And I know she was confronting you about selling drugs. Did she threaten to tell the police?"

Turner was staring at his feet, tears dripping onto the floor.

"Hey!" His head snapped up. "This is the time you need to answer me, Jason. Because I already know Frankie intended to confront you about the drugs. And if we don't find her, I'm going to assume you killed her to keep her mouth shut."

His head wagged from side to side. "I didn't touch her, I swear. I didn't do anything to her."

"You better start talking. What happened that night?"

He sucked in a deep breath. "She came up to me before the game started, during warm-ups. I had been talking to one of my players from the Elite team."

"And by talking, you mean selling him drugs."

He didn't confirm. He didn't need to; it was written all over his face. "She told me she knew what I was doing. Then skated away. The look of disappointment in her face, it was horrible."

"So horrible you decided to sit her on the bench the first period?"

He nodded. "But the others were wondering why I was allowing them to get their asses kicked, so I put her back in. After the game, she told me what I was doing was wrong. I told her she didn't know what she was talking about and walked out the door to the back parking lot. She followed me out, yelling at me about how she was going to tell her uncle and he was going to arrest me. It freaked me out, so I decided to go home and stash everything just in case."

"That's why you were so nervous when Detective Taylor and I showed up at your door."

"Yeah. I didn't think you would get there that fast. I thought I had some time to get things out of the house before anyone came asking questions."

"And you thought you'd get high while you were at it?"

"I needed to calm my nerves. She shook me up. I mean, I don't sell to *all* the kids on her team, only like two, and it's only weed. But I'm pretty sure most of them know about it. I was shocked Frankie was gonna turn me in."

"Only weed? To twelve-year-olds? You do understand you are in a position of authority, correct?" Kendall took a deep breath and held it, counting to ten before slowly releasing it. She needed to get her blood pressure under control. She was disturbingly close to launching herself across the table and choking this shithead until his head popped off.

"What happened to Frankie after she followed you outside?"

"I don't know. I was freaked out. I got in the Jeep and took off."

"Where was Frankie when you left?"

"Last I saw, she had gone around the side of the building to go to the front of the rink."

"Why not go back in the door you had come out of?"

"It locks."

"The only way she could've gotten in was back around the front?"

"Yeah."

"But you didn't make sure, at ten o'clock at night, that she made it back to the front?"

"She threatened to turn me in to the cops—I was scared. I wasn't thinking about her safety."

"Just your own." *Asshat.* "Tell me about Mick. Did Frankie know he was selling steroids?"

"I don't know. She didn't say anything about him."

"Did you warn him that she might turn him in also?"

"Didn't need to. He was standing behind her while she was talking to me."

"Close enough to overhear the conversation?"

Turner nodded.

Fuck.

Kendall got up and left the room. Jake and Fletch met her at the door. "Where's dickhead number two?"

Fletch pointed down the hall. "This way."

"Has anyone been in to talk to him?"

"Not yet. We were waiting to hear from you how to handle it."

"I've got this."

Mick Donahue was sitting in the chair, no longer the kind older gentleman who managed the rink with an intense love for youth hockey. Comfortably sitting back in the chair, one foot propped on the opposite knee, arms crossed over his chest. Shit-eating grin on his face. Arrogance and condescension flowed from his pores, stinking up the room.

Without greeting, Kendall sat in the chair. "Where is Frankie Taylor?"

Donahue spread his arms wide. "No idea."

"I think you're lying to me."

"I don't give a shit."

"When was the last time you saw her—the truth this time."

He exhaled through his nose. "She was following that dipshit Turner out the door to the back lot."

"Did you follow them?"

"Why would I?"

"Because you had just overheard a conversation between her and Turner about how she was going to report the drug activity at the rink to her uncle, the Denver Police detective." Kendall leaned closer, her arms resting on the table. "Here's what I think happened. I think you did follow them out. I think when Turner walked away from her, you grabbed her and forced her into your car and hid when her father and uncle came outside. What I want to know now is what you did with her."

Kendall knew it wasn't true—she had been speaking with Mick in the lobby at the time. But it might encourage him to rat out Turner to save his ass. The possibility still existed that he and Turner were working together to get rid of Frankie.

"Great story, but that's all it is, something you've made up. I don't know how many ways I can tell you I had nothing to do with her disappearance."

"This is your chance to get in front of this. Your house is being searched as we speak. If they turn up any evidence to the contrary—if I find out you're lying to me and you've done some-thing to Frankie and are continuing to keep it from me—I will make sure you never see the outside of a prison cell."

"Are you threatening me, Agent Beck?"

"Warning you."

"What you should be doing is talking to that waste of space Turner. He's the one who's reactionary. He was the last one to see her. Seems pretty clear he's the one with the answers you need. Now, I think I'm done talking to you and would like a lawyer."

Kendall got up and left the room. Jake and Adam were in a cubicle observing the interrogation on a computer screen. The PD had converted the observation rooms to interrogation rooms and added CCTV, allowing observation on a large monitor.

"Anything turn up on the search of dickhead Good Samaritan's house?" Kendall asked.

"Nothing there. They've got the car and are going over it, but it could be a while before anything comes from the DNA swabs."

"Jake, see if we can send them to Quantico and get them fast-tracked," Kendall said. "They may do it with a missing kid involved."

"What's the next step?" Jake asked.

She pointed to the monitor showing Jason Turner. "See if I can get him to squeal."

"I'm going to have a chat with our Good Sam and see if I can't wrap that case up. Or at least get a little closer," Adam said. "Meet you on the flip side."

Kendall returned to the interrogation room and placed a bottle of water on the table in front of Jason Turner. He grabbed it, twisted off the cap, and downed half the bottle before taking a breath.

"I'm ready to talk," he said.

"What would you like to talk about?"

"First, I want to make a deal. I want immunity."

Kendall stood and walked toward the door, her hand on the doorknob. "Let me know when you want to be serious."

"Wait, don't you want to know what I know?"

"Yes, but there is no way the DA is going to give you total immunity. Now, if your information is good and leads us to Frankie, there's a better-than-average chance he could help you out. Drop some charges down to misdemeanors. But that would all depend on what you give us."

Turner considered what she had said, a grim smile across his face. "Okay, but if I tell you what you want to know, you'll talk to the DA?"

"You have my word."

"Okay." He took a deep, dramatic breath. "I don't know where Frankie is, but I have a good idea who took her."

Now we're getting somewhere.

"Go on."

"My uncle."

That was unexpected. Kendall's heart was beating, and there was a rhythmic thrumming in her head. "And what makes you say that?"

"Let's just say, there are weird things going on at his house."

"You mean the house he shares with your aunt?"

"Yeah, but I don't think she's really involved. I think he forces her to be quiet and go along with it."

Kendall hadn't really gotten *controlled and manipulated spouse* from the woman she'd met with Wednesday night. "Okay, what weird things are going on in the house?"

"They always have a lot of young girls there."

Kendall shrugged one shoulder. "According to them, they babysit all the kids in the neighborhood."

Turner shook his head so hard she feared it might come off and hit her. "No, that's not true. No one likes them. People avoid them. I don't think anyone talks to them, let alone allows them to watch their children. Mitch is a son of a bitch and not the most neighborly."

"So why are all the girls there, then?"

"I'm not sure. They're only around for a few days, I think. I hardly ever see the same ones twice. I asked Aunt Geneva about them once, and Mitch punched me in the gut and told me never to ask about them again or he'd 'take care of me.' We've never really gotten along, so I'm pretty sure he's just looking for a reason to kill me."

Kendall could give a rat's ass. He was making her skin crawl. "And why do you think Frankie is there?"

"Well, she's missing. And they have been really interested in the case. Always have the news on, glued to the TV whenever they talk about it. I mean, it sort of fits, right?"

Kendall wasn't in the mood to answer questions. "What do they do with the girls while they're there?"

He shrugged. "Got me. I only ever see them coming or going."

"You never see them outside, or watching TV?"

"No, it's like they show up and disappear inside the house. Then in a couple of days, this guy shows up and takes them away."

"The house isn't that big. Where could they disappear to?"

"Who knows? It's not like I go rummaging through their house looking for them."

"Okay." Kendall wanted to beat the ever-loving shit out of this man for not doing something to help these kids. "What guy takes them from the house?"

"I don't know, some creepy-looking dude."

"Never been introduced?"

"No, I tend to mind my own business when I'm at my aunt's place. Safer that way."

"And you don't know what happens to the girls after they leave?"

"No."

Why did shitbags like this exist?

"And you've never found this behavior disturbing? You never wondered why they had girls coming in and out of their house?"

"I mean, I wondered what was going on—and I did try to ask that one time—but it wasn't my business."

"Then whose business was it? Can you really not imagine a scenario that would explain why girls are being shuffled through your aunt's house? Never thought this was weird behavior and perhaps you should let the police know?"

"Never really thought about it."

Right. Because he didn't want to put much thought into it for fear he might figure out his aunt and uncle were probably dealing in child trafficking.

"Anything else you'd like to add?"

"No."

Kendall got up to leave. She had work to do and alleged child traffickers to question.

"Hey, can I ask you a question?" he called after her.

"What?"

"Can I get like a burger and fries and a Coke?"

Kendall pulled open the door and walked out.

CHAPTER

42

MELVIN CRAIG HAD been sitting in an interview room, stewing, for forty-five minutes. No doubt he was going to be in a foul mood—people typically were when they were arrested.

Adam's phone rang, and he thought about ignoring it and letting it go to voice mail. But it could be something about his niece, so he pulled it from his pocket and checked the screen.

ME. Fran. He touched the screen to answer. "Hey, Doc, what do you have for me?"

"I finished the autopsies on both of the victims in the convenience store murders. I've confirmed Darin Stevens was killed by a single shot to the chest, the bullet piercing his heart, died instantly. But Ashley Collins is a different story."

"Why?"

"She was shot in the side, the chest, and then the head. As I said at the scene, the side injury was a through-and-through and was not the cause of death. The injury to the chest was also not the fatal shot. The bullet didn't hit her heart; it only went into the lung. No guarantee she wouldn't have eventually died by basically drowning in her own blood. But I'm convinced the shot to the head is the one that killed her. I'm also confident it was the final shot fired, based on how much blood was present in the lungs, which was a large amount. If the head shot had been first, all the blood would've been around her head at the crime scene, and a minimal amount in her chest cavity. As it was, and in comparison to the amount in the chest, there wasn't much at the scene."

"Okay, thanks, Doc. Can you send the report over to me?"

"I'm not done."

Adam perked up. "I'm all ears."

"Ashley Collins' body had two different rounds in her. The shots to the side and chest were not the same caliber as the shot to the head. I could tell when I removed the bullets during autopsy. I had ballistics do me a favor—they just sent over their findings. The bullet from the head matched the bullet found in Darin Stevens chest."

Adam's brain froze. *Motherfucker.*

"I'm going to assume by your silence that this is just as interesting to you as it was to me."

"Bombshell-quality shit here, Doc."

So the Good Samaritan wasn't such a hero after all.

"Is there more news?"

"No, that's all the magic I have for you today, Detective."

"Thanks, Fran. I appreciate you letting me know."

"Go forth and exact justice, my friend."

Adam hit the end button and just stood there, paralyzed. There had been a chance to save Ashley Collins, but after killing Stevens, Craig had made sure Ashley didn't survive by putting a bullet in her brain.

Adam took a deep, cleansing breath, tried to push aside the desire to punch Craig in the face, and opened the door to the interview room.

"I demand to be let go," Craig yelled as soon as Adam entered the room.

"Well, that's not going to happen, Mr. Craig, so I suggest you lower your voice and settle in. We have a lot to go over."

"You haven't got dick."

"I know that the person you were meeting that morning at the convenience store was Darin Stevens."

"Not true," Craig said, leaning back in his seat. "I'd never seen him before that morning."

Adam pulled up the photo on his phone and turned it around for Craig to see. "If you didn't know Darin Stevens, why is his phone number on a piece of paper with the date of the shooting, the time you were meeting him, and the address of the convenience store?"

"Hey, you can't come into my place and take pictures. That's an invasion of my privacy. That's an illegal search."

"You left it out in plain sight where I, or anyone else, could see it. I thought the phone number was to the business associate you were going to meet that morning." Adam rubbed his chin. "I guess that was true. You just left out the part where Darin Stevens was your business associate. Right now, as we sit here, I have you for the murder of Darin Stevens as well as child trafficking." It was a bit of a stretch. Craig hadn't actually done anything with Savannah except remove her from the store.

A jury might believe he was trying to keep her from seeing too much.

But he was a cog in the wheel. If Stevens had been there to do a drop, the evidence was pointing to Craig as the receiver.

Adam thought it best to keep the information regarding the death of Ashley Collins to himself. He could pull that rabbit out of the hat later, if Craig didn't want to cough up information.

"Look, Mr. Craig, I don't know how involved in this you are. But I can tell you, it's in your best interest to get out in front of this. All the best deals go to the person who talks first. And at this rate, you are looking at up to forty-eight years for the child trafficking and mandatory life for first-degree murder."

Adam intentionally blew a long, slow stream of air from his lungs while shaking his head. "I don't know, but if I were in your position, I might want to see what kind of deal I could get—and the only way to do that is to show good faith. Good faith is telling me what you know about this trafficking organization Stevens was involved in."

Craig stared at Adam, his teeth grinding together. After a moment he grimaced and said, "I don't know anything. I was asked to meet Darin at the convenience store to pick up his niece and take her to her father. That's all I had to do."

"And you were going to do this out of the goodness of your heart?"

"He said he'd pay me three hundred and fifty dollars."

"Fuck. Where were you taking her, the moon?"

"Airport."

"And you didn't find that strange?"

"He said he was desperate. He had another job and couldn't take her. So he asked me."

"So you two were friends?"

"That shitbag? Hell no."

"But he trusted you with his 'niece.'" Adam used air quotes. "A guy he's not friends with, according to you. Had you done jobs like this for him before—with other nieces?"

"One other time."

Adam stared at the man for a moment. What a piece of shit.

"How did you get paid—the first time?"

"Money was in an envelope with instructions on where to go and who to meet at the airport."

Interesting. There had been no money in an envelope at the crime scene or in Stevens's car. So how was Craig going to get paid?

"And you had money in hand when you did this? You got the girl and the money at the same time?"

"Usually."

"Usually? You just said this only happened one other time. How many times have you done this, Melvin?"

Craig chewed his bottom lip. "Ahh, fuck." He glanced up at Adam. "I tell you what you want to know, I get a deal."

"I can't promise you that, but I've been around long enough—the DA is very agreeable if the information passed helps save a life. If children are involved, even more agreeable."

"Okay." Craig took a deep inhale and scrubbed the growth on his jaw, weighing his options. The view had to look pretty bleak from his side. "There's a couple, older; they have a scam where they find a young girl and approach her. The kid usually always goes along with them because they look like kindly grandparents."

So far, this was matching Savannah's statement.

"They get them back to their house and hold them there, put their pics on some website for men who are looking for . . . that kind of thing."

That kind of thing? Adam wanted to puke. How Kendall hadn't lost her mind dealing with this type of scum was beyond him.

"Anyway, as I understand it, it never takes longer than forty-eight hours to find an interested party. Then they have a network of people they work with—couriers, like me."

Couriers? These were little girls, not business documents. Adam was a hairsbreadth away from pounding this guy into the next world.

"They like to break up the transportation of them—the girls—so if one person is identified with the girl, it doesn't lead back to the rest of the organization."

"So, what? Someone picks them up, meets you, and you take them to the airport?"

"Yeah. Darin usually is the one that gets them from the house. Then I drop them to our guy at the airport, who can get them through security without raising any red flags and with another person who gets them on the plane. They usually fly to a major hub, like Chicago or Atlanta, and then from there, the kid is put on another plane that takes them to whoever has, you know—"

"Bought them?"

"Yeah."

"Who do they have at the airport to get them through security?"

"They have airline employees that can get them through as unaccompanied minors. Then they turn them over to flight attendants who are also on the payroll. They make sure the kids are given a drink that knocks them out so they can't talk to anyone."

"Do you have names of the employees? The airlines they work for?"

"No, I just know how it all works. I never get any farther than picking the kid up and dropping them at the airport."

"Who told you? Darin?"

Craig sat back and stared at the ceiling for a moment and took a few deep breaths. "I know the couple who run the org from this end."

"Names."

"Mitch and Geneva Schultz."

43

Friday evening
66:15:29 hours missing

KENDALL WAS JOGGING down the hall to where Adam was interviewing his double homicide murder suspect. Before she got there, the door flew open and Adam dashed out into the hall, eyes wide.

"Fletch," he yelled.

Fletch came around the corner. "Yeah?"

"Get someone to sit on this asshole."

Kendall stopped in front of him. "Adam, we have to go. I may have a lead on where Frankie is."

"Shit!" He glanced back at the interview room. "Dickhead just dropped the names of the grandparents who kidnapped Savannah and are running a sex trafficking ring."

He looked torn, his eyes questioning her about what he should do. She knew he was desperate to find his niece, but he was a cop. And he had a job to do. And bringing down sex traffickers was a top priority, in Kendall's opinion.

"You have to go after them, Adam."

His face fell, and she knew he'd been hoping she would give him permission to put that investigation on hold. "If he tips them off, they could leave the area and we'll never find them. You have to stop them before they take another child."

He raked his hand down his face. "Yeah, I know."

"You can trust me. If Frankie is there, I will find her. If she's been there and gone, I'll spend all night tracking her down. I promise. Go get your bad guys."

"At least I know where I'm going."

"What do you mean?"

"Been there before—next door, at least—day before yesterday."

Kendall's heart kicked into high gear. "Where?"

"Mitch and Geneva Schultz."

Kendall felt all the blood drain from her face and pool in her gut. She wanted to vomit. She wanted this to be a mistake.

She wanted not to tell Adam she was going to the same place.

"You can ride with me," she said.

"What?"

"Jason Turner believes his aunt and uncle have Frankie."

Adam fell against the wall, his hand over his mouth.

Kendall caught him before he hit the floor. They'd both known this was a possibility—that Frankie had been taken by some sexual deviant—but they hadn't voiced it.

Because they were desperate to cling to hope that Frankie was a runaway and they would find her. Or she would get cold, or lonely, or scared, or just plain bored, and come home on her own. If Turner was right, that hope, the dream of finding Frankie unharmed—hell, of finding her at all—was quickly diminishing.

"Adam, look at me. This is just a girl who needs our help, like any other girl who needs our help. This is your job. Don't you dare fall apart on me now. We have work to do. And we have to get moving before the Schultzes are tipped off."

CHAPTER

44

THE MAKESHIFT MOBILE command center was a block away and around the corner from the Schultz residence. Close enough to keep tabs on the couple. Out of sight enough that they couldn't see what was coming for them. The SWAT team had also cleared the neighborhood without creating a fuss. No one was going to get caught in the cross fire if things went sideways.

Adam had been amazed at how quickly Kendall was able to mobilize a team to raid the house. Yeah, this was what her team did, but he'd had no idea people were basically on standby in case they got information that required immediate action.

Computer screens filled the inside of the truck. Two guys were running everything electronic. A map of the area was up on one screen. A recent floor plan of the house was up on another. Apparently, the Schultzes had done some renovations recently and had needed to submit a blueprint of the floor plan to the county, among other documentation.

Kendall motioned for Adam to step outside the vehicle with her. "We're getting ready to go in. I need to know that you've got your head on straight and not jammed up your ass. We go in and get the Schultzes, then we search the house. You need to convince me that I should allow you to go in with us."

"I'm good." And he was. The drive over had allowed him to think about everything. He knew what he had to do, and he knew what he couldn't do. Removing Frankie from the equation was critical to his being able to function. This was a raid on a suspected child sex trafficking operation. He had gotten to the place where he wasn't thinking about anyone in particular, only what had to be done to ensure the Schultzes were convicted and out of business. With any luck, they'd be able to bring down the entire infrastructure.

Kendall looked him in the eye and then nodded, apparently satisfied he was in the correct headspace. "You and I are on the team breaching the front door. We have people in position who can see into a good portion of the house. We'll know where they are when we go in and should be able to get the Schultzes without incident. That's the hope, anyway."

Adam tightened up his tactical vest and secured his weapon.

A guy in black from head to toe, carrying an assault rifle, came up behind them. "Let's saddle up. We're a go," he told Kendall.

Ten SWAT team members in full gear, all carrying M4 rifles, walked heel to toe, making barely any sound, as they approached the house. They walked single file, careful to avoid being seen by anyone looking out the side window of the house. Kendall and Adam followed close behind them. Adam had been trained in SWAT tactics, but it wasn't something he did often. It was a little trial by fire–esque, but he knew the men and women in front of him, along with the team at the back of the house, were professionals and knew exactly what they were doing. They also trained for all sorts of scenarios and had a plan for every possible contingency.

They stopped at the side of the house, all lined up against the exterior wall. The lead agent pulled the search warrant out and notified the agents at the back that they were executing. Once again in a semi-single-file line, they turned the corner, and the team split into two lines behind the two agents at the front. The agents brought up their rifles, aiming them at the door. Kendall and Adam held their Glocks against their chests, cocked and ready to go.

One agent pounded on the front door. "FBI executing a search warrant. Open the door now." A few seconds passed. Adam looked behind him, making sure neither of the Schultzes had found a way out the SWAT team didn't know about.

Again the agent pounded on the door. "FBI executing a search warrant. Open the door, or we will be forced to break it down."

This time the door opened. Geneva Schultz was in a sweatshirt with a cat on it, her hair in a tight bun, hand at her throat. "I'm so sorry. What is going on?" Her voice was as sweet as molasses.

The agent with the search warrant held it in front of her face. "We have a warrant to search the property. We will need you to come out of the house until we're done."

"I don't understand," Geneva said. "Why do you need to search the house?"

"Ma'am, where is your husband?"

"He's not here," she said, but she had made the mistake of pausing before she answered. It was enough to let everyone know she was lying.

The agents pulled her out of the house and forced her down the driveway. One of the agents guarded her. The rest of the team moved inside.

Kendall and Adam waited just inside the door until they heard the all clear. The team moved in. The search of each room was like a choreographed dance. After each room was entered, there would be an announcement that the room was clear.

The lead agent came back to the front. "All clear," he said into his voice-activated comms, letting the team in the backyard know what was going on. To Adam and Kendall he said, "No sign of the old man."

"Might want to let the agents outside know to keep a watch out for him in case he comes rolling in and gets spooked seeing agents in his front yard."

"Copy," he said. "We'll start collecting evidence and getting it out to the van. What do you want to do with Mrs. Schultz?"

"Just hold her there until the search is done." Kendall glanced around the room. "Between Turner's statement and Craig's, there's bound to be evidence to cover probable cause for her arrest."

Kendall walked into the kitchen. Adam followed, his heart heavy. He'd thought Frankie would be here. He felt she was here. But it had been wishful thinking. As it stood, there was no concrete evidence she had ever been in the house. After all, according to what Turner had told Kendall, it was all supposition on his part. He had never actually seen Frankie here.

"Let's take a walk through the house," Kendall said. "You might see something the agents passed over because they didn't think it was relevant. You know Frankie—if she's been here, maybe she left you a clue."

Hope flooded Adam. Kendall was right. When Frankie was little, she would beg Adam to read "Hansel and Gretel" to her. She loved how the kids outsmarted the witch and were able to find their way home. She would tell Adam all the time that if she was ever lost, look for the bread crumbs and that's where she'd be. He knew she wouldn't give up until she was found.

They entered the first room. There was a dirty mattress on the floor, a half-empty water bottle next to it.

Kendall pulled out her cell phone. "Jake, get pictures of the Schultzes in front of Savannah and see if she recognizes them. It may be me, but they resemble the sketches. But I'd like to get a positive ID." She looked up at Adam. "No," she said, "no sign of Frankie, but we've just entered the house."

She ended the call and returned her cell to her pocket.

Adam pointed at the mattress. "I'm betting we find more DNA on that than just Savannah's."

"Yeah, it could answer questions on a lot of open cases of missing girls."

Adam opened the closet. Stacks of water bottles from a discount warehouse filled the space. Jesus, that was a lot of water. Which meant a lot of girls kidnapped and processed through here were on their way to a world of drugs, sex, power, and control.

Adam's gut twisted in a knot.

They exited the room and walked down to another bedroom, this one across from the Schultzes' room. To Adam's surprise, an actual bed was pushed against one wall. It would've been impossible for anyone to sleep on it. Stacks of magazines, newspapers, and boxes were piled on top.

The only other piece of furniture was a large freestanding wardrobe. Kendall opened it. Empty.

"Weird," he said. "You'd think they'd put all the shit on the bed in there so they could use the bed."

"Providing comfort isn't part of the operation. These girls—once taken—are no longer little girls. They're inventory to be sold on the internet, just like any other product."

Something didn't feel right to Adam. Why have an empty wardrobe? It didn't make sense. Everyone had stuff they dumped in them—clothes, extra blankets, odds and ends. Why have one if not to use it?

Adam walked around it. "Where's the closet?"

"What?" Kendall asked.

"The closet? This is a bedroom. Bedrooms have closets." And then the reason the wardrobe was empty hit him. It was easier to move if it was empty. He started pushing against it. It scraped against the wood floor.

Kendall came up beside him, and they both put their weight behind it. It slid a few feet, revealing a closet door.

Adam's heart was jackhammering in his chest. His hand shook as he reached out to turn the knob. He paused for a split second. Did he really want to see what was inside? If Frankie was in there, what condition would she be in? And was he prepared to find her that way?

He turned the knob, half expecting it to be stuck or locked, but the door opened with ease. It was dark inside. Kendall turned on her flashlight app and shone the beam inside.

Two round eyes met him. She scampered to the back of the closet.

"Frankie?"

The girl shook her head. Kendall pushed Adam out of the way and got down on her knees. "It's okay, sweetheart. We're not here to hurt you. My name's Kendall. I'm an FBI agent, and I'm here to take you home."

All the hope that had flooded Adam earlier was washed away like a tidal wave. Sadness, fear, and helplessness were drowning him, and he was desperate for air.

"Do you want to come out?" Kendall asked, reaching her hand out for the girl. Kendall backed up and stood. A small hand, covered in grime, slid into Kendall's. "How about we get you out of here and into the fresh air? Can you tell me your name?"

"Isla," came a whispered reply.

"Hi, Isla. We're so happy we found you."

Adam followed the two out to the front yard. Kendall led Isla to an ambulance that had just pulled up. A female paramedic came out of the back, holding a teddy bear, and handed it to the girl. She wrapped Isla in a blanket while the girl clung to the bear like it was a lifeline.

"These people are going to make sure you're okay. Do you hurt anywhere?" Kendall's voice was still soft and singsong-y.

Isla shook her head.

"Do you know your last name?"

"McMillan."

"How long have you been here?"

She shrugged.

"Do you remember what day it was when you were taken?"

"Tuesday, I think." She looked at the paramedics who were flitting about her, trying to check her out without disturbing her too much. "I want my mommy."

Kendall glanced at Adam. He pulled out his phone and walked away, placing a call to Jake. "We found a girl. Her name is Isla McMillan. She thinks she was taken on Tuesday. Can't confirm if it was this past Tuesday."

"We'll locate her parents and have them meet her at the hospital," Jake said.

The call wasn't going to Mark and Poppy. And just like that, Adam was consumed with regret and failure.

CHAPTER

45

ISLA MCMILLAN'S BODY shook uncontrollably despite being wrapped in a blanket.

"Do you remember if there were other girls here like you?" Kendall asked. "Did you see any other kids?"

She shook her head no but said, "I heard a girl. I think she got out, though."

A small ball of hope swelled in Kendall. "Why do you think that?"

"I heard her voice. I think she was in the backyard. The man was yelling at her to 'Get back here.' She was screaming at him, but I don't know what she said."

"Do you know if the girl got away?"

"I think so—"

If the girl was Frankie, perhaps she had escaped. Kendall needed to make sure the woods behind the house were searched. Would a K9 unit be able to get there before dark? Night was setting in, and the temps would drop. A girl in the woods not dressed properly could freeze.

"—'cause it was all loud, and then it was quiet," Isla said.

Dread filled Kendall. *Fuck!* She glanced toward where Adam stood on the driveway, his back to her, talking on the phone.

Turning back to Isla, she said, "These nice people are going to take you to the hospital. And Adam"—she pointed to him—"is making sure your mommy and daddy will be there, okay?"

Tears sprang into the girl's eyes as she nodded her head. Without warning, Isla flung her arms around Kendall's neck.

Kendall fought back tears. Another girl was going home to her family before she had been subjected to life-altering trauma. At any other time, this would've been cause for major merrymaking among her colleagues.

But Frankie was out there somewhere. And until she was found and could also be reunited with her family, any celebration was on hold.

Kendall patted the girl's back and carefully extracted herself. There was still work to do, and she couldn't afford to be distracted.

The paramedic sat Isla on the gurney. The doors closed, and the ambulance headed down the street.

46

Friday night
68:46:05 hours missing

ADAM ENDED THE call and slid his phone into his pocket.
So much was happening, so many emotions were swirling
through his head, he wasn't sure what was real and what was a
bad dream. It was a horrible thing to be disappointed that a missing child was going to be reunited with her family.

But the child wasn't Frankie. And that nearly ripped his heart out.
He could feel the despair and impatience taking over his thoughts.
He'd had a great deal of anticipation when he learned Frankie was
here. It had grown to a fever pitch when he opened the closet door.

And then hope had plummeted like an elevator free-falling from
the top floor of a tall building. He wasn't sure how many times he
could handle the ups and downs associated with finding his niece.

It wasn't supposed to be like this. He was a cop. He came from a
family of cops. Mark was a firefighter. They had instilled in Frankie
the need to be aware of her surroundings. Don't accept rides from
strangers. If something doesn't feel right, trust your gut and stay away.

He had failed his niece. Failed his brother. And he had no
idea where to go from here.

He scrubbed his face and took a deep breath.

*Get over the self-flagellation, Taylor. Your little pity party isn't
going to find your niece.*

So what if she wasn't there. She could be at a different house. They just needed to get the Schultzes to spill what they knew.

There was still reason to hope.

He glanced around. Where the hell was Kendall?

There was movement at Turner's house, which was curious, since Adam knew Turner was sitting in a cell at the Denver PD. And the search of his house had concluded over an hour before. So who was hiding out at his place? Whoever it was didn't want to be discovered. He was behind the curtain, only part of his face visible.

Adam knew who it was. He turned and headed for the back-yard. Once he was out of sight, he jogged to the back of Turner's house. As he suspected, there was a back door.

This was supremely stupid. There were plenty of cops around whom he could've engaged in a plan to capture the man with very little danger.

But Adam wanted—needed—to do this. Mitch Schultz was attempting to avoid capture. If he could hold out until all the cops left, he could escape and be enveloped in the criminal organization he was a part of, and he might never be caught.

And that didn't sit well with Adam.

Grasping the doorknob, he gently twisted, testing to see if the door was unlocked. When the knob turned, Adam sent up a prayer of thanks and slowly opened the door, careful to not make any noise. Stepping into the kitchen, he tiptoed to the opening to the living room and flattened himself against the wall. He counted to ten and then poked his head out.

Mitch was still looking out the window, completely oblivious to Adam only a few feet away from him.

Pulling his service weapon from the holster as quietly as possible, Adam grasped it in both hands. Slipping around the corner, he stepped softly, moving in behind Mitch, readying his gun. When he was a couple feet away, Mitch swung around, wielding a lamp, and smashed it into Adam's wrist.

The gun skittered across the floor.

Fuck.

Mitch barreled toward him. Adam crouched into a wrestling stance. As soon as Mitch was close enough, Adam wrapped his arms around the man's legs and attempted to lift him off the ground.

Mitch fell back, grabbed Adam by the lapels, and rolled over until he was on top of him. His fist slammed into Adam's jaw.

Adam thrust his midsection upward. Mitch was caught off guard, tilted to the side, and Adam was able to get out from under him.

It was then that Adam decided he was an idiot for not having backup. Frantic, he searched around the floor for his gun. He located it, which was good, except it was about a foot away from Mitch. Luckily, it didn't appear the man had noticed it yet.

But Adam had stared at it a bit too long. Mitch followed his gaze, his eyes widening when he spotted the prize on the floor near his feet.

Shit, shit, shit.

Adam charged at Mitch as he was bending over to pick up the weapon. He hit the man and pushed him back. Adam's legs were moving; he felt like he was back in high school, hitting guys and tackling them.

They hit the window with enough force to shatter it. Time slowed as they flew through air. Adam hit the hard ground in the front yard, pain rippling through his entire body.

Mitch jumped up, hands balled into fists, arms up, feet apart in a boxer's stance. Adam was tired of this bullshit. Lifting his arms, he waited for Mitch to take the first swing before tagging him on the side of the head with his fist. Mitch followed with an uppercut that caught Adam's chin and thrust his head back.

Adam dodged a fist to the face, caught Mitch off guard, and rammed his knee into the man's groin. Mitch dropped to his knees, hands protecting himself from another shot. Tears sprang to his eyes. Adam hoped he had driven the man's balls up into his throat. With a final left hook, he sent Mitch sprawling to the ground.

As soon as the fight was over, a gaggle of cops showed up to help.

"Get him booked for child trafficking, kidnapping, and assault on a police officer."

Adam ran back into the house and retrieved his gun. He glanced out the kitchen window into the backyard next door. Kendall had dropped to her knees.

Adam holstered his gun as he ran out the back door. Either Kendall was hurt, or she had found something.

CHAPTER

47

HEADING FOR THE backyard before Adam noticed she was
gone, Kendall surveyed the area until she found what she
suspected would be there. Sprinting across the lawn, she noted
the grass hadn't been cut, but it wasn't long enough to mask the
area. Along the edge of the yard, against the tree line, was a spot
where the dirt looked as if it had been recently displaced. As if
someone had been digging. Planting. Or burying.

She dropped to her knees and started digging with her hands.
Another agent joined her, and then another, and soon there were
a handful of agents searching through the earth for something
that didn't belong.

The smell of earthiness filled the air. The farther down she
dug, the colder the dirt became, numbing the tips of her fingers.

And then she felt it. Fabric. She brushed away the dirt, ran
her hand along the edge, searching for . . . searching for the one
thing she was desperate *not* to find. The fabric gave way to flesh,
and within another moment, Kendall was holding a small hand
in hers.

When the agents saw, they began to work faster, as if ignited
by a flame. The torso was cleared of soil, revealing a black sweatshirt. Kendall brushed the left breast, unconsciously holding her

breath, praying she was wrong. But there it was: a cat with long, snarling teeth and a paw set to strike, claws out. Around it was *Lakewood Panthers Hockey*.

And lying across her shoulder was a lock of brown hair. The same color as Frankie's. She fell back, sitting next to the body of her friend's niece and covering her mouth with her forearm. Tears flooded her eyes, failure and sadness and heartache suffocated her like a boa constrictor.

"Kendall?" Adam called to her.

She looked over her shoulder. His gaze locked on hers, internalizing the despair on her face. The tears threatening to roll down her cheeks. He took off running toward her at full speed.

In a flash, she was on her feet, darting across the yard, intent on stopping him. Her hands wrapped around his upper arms. Every ounce of strength she had, she put into holding him back.

"No, Adam."

"Kendall, let me go." He fought against her, but she held her ground.

"Is it . . . is it her?"

Kendall swallowed hard. It was an answer without her having to speak. And it was enough to get Adam moving toward the grave.

"No." She pushed him back, forced him to look at her. "Adam, you don't want to see her this way."

CHAPTER

48

Friday night
2:16:32 hours found

ADAM HAD BEEN waiting for the day when he could call his brother, Mark, and tell him Frankie had been found. There would be tears of happiness, thankfulness. Not sorrow and pain. Adam had never allowed himself to consider they wouldn't find his niece alive.

Mark and Poppy insisted on coming to the police station. They didn't believe him. They needed more information. Maybe he was wrong. Maybe there had been a horrible mistake. Were they sure she was dead? Had they taken her to the hospital?

"I need to see her," Poppy said. "I need to see my baby."

Adam shook his head. The last thing Poppy should see were the remains of her only child. Not even Adam had been prepared for what he had forced Kendall to show him.

"Don't shake your head at me, Adam." Poppy slammed her fist against his chest. "Don't tell me no. She's my daughter, and I want to see her. I need to see her and to touch her. And look into her eyes, kiss her cheek."

Adam couldn't take it. Tears flowed down his face. He couldn't speak. He couldn't explain to Poppy why she couldn't do that. How what she was asking was physically impossible.

Kendall wrapped her arm around Poppy and gently pulled her away from Adam. "Poppy, there's a reason we can't let you see her. The medical examiner needs to be able to establish what happened to her."

"Okay," she whined. "But why can't I see her? I won't touch her. I just want to look at her face. Why can't I do that?"

Kendall led Poppy to a chair and helped her sit down. She glanced over her shoulder at Mark, somehow telepathically requesting he sit down next to his wife. He stumbled over and fell into the chair. His eyes were vacant. He wasn't crying; he hadn't uttered a word since they arrived. He was barely alive.

Kendall grasped both of Poppy's hands in hers. "What I'm about to tell you is going to be hard to hear, but I think it's the only way you will understand why you can't see Frankie." She visibly swallowed before speaking again. "Frankie suffered severe injuries to her head and face."

"I can handle the blood, Kendall. I just need to look at her."

"You won't recognize her."

"Yes, I will. I don't care how swollen she is, I'll know it's her."

Kendall looked back at Adam, and he knew she was asking him what she should do. It wasn't fair to her. She shouldn't be put in the position of completely shattering their hearts.

Adam came closer and knelt down next to Kendall. She released Poppy's hands so Adam could hold them. He closed his eyes, trying to find the words. Kendall's hand was on his shoulder, and she gave him a gentle squeeze.

"The extent of Frankie's injuries go beyond blood and swelling. She was beaten so badly . . ." Adam choked on his words. "There's nothing there to see."

Poppy's face contorted, agony etched into every part of her features. She inhaled, the sob silent, but on the exhale she wailed. Long. Loud. And the sound of her pain was like a hand reaching into his chest, slicing through skin, breaking bone, and ripping his heart from his chest.

Mark wrapped his arms around his wife and cradled her against his chest. He looked at Adam. "If she isn't recognizable, how do you know it's her?"

"The medical examiner made a preliminary ID based on age, hair, and the clothes she was wearing when last seen."

"They will be doing a DNA test, along with checking her dental records," Kendall said. "But at this point, with the information we have, it appears to be Frankie."

"Okay," Mark murmured. "Come on, Poppy, let's go home." He stood and helped his wife up.

"Let me drive you," Adam said. Although he wasn't in any better condition to drive.

"I'll have someone take them home," Kendall said.

They all turned toward the door and stepped out into the hallway. At the other end of the hall, a man and a woman were on their knees, sobbing. And in their arms was Isla.

Mark tried to direct Poppy away from the scene, but Poppy planted her feet and stared at the reunion. In her face, Adam saw warring emotions: happiness, pain, gratefulness, and misery.

"Is she okay?" Poppy asked Adam. "She wasn't hurt?"

"She's okay. Dehydrated and scared, but not physically injured."

Poppy nodded and wiped the tears from her face. "That's good. She's home and safe, and that's good."

"Yeah, it is," Adam agreed.

Poppy looked up into his face, her eyes so sad it made Adam physically ache for her. "Can you do something for me?"

"Of course."

"Can you tell them to hold on tight to her and tell her how much she is loved every single day of her life?"

Adam choked back a sob. "Yeah, Poppy. I can do that."

EPILOGUE

Sunday afternoon
40:02:56 hours found

THE SUN WAS shining, adding insult to the darkest period of Adam's life. A light breeze swirled around him, and he could've sworn he heard Frankie's giggle as the air whistled in his ear. He'd been hearing things like that often since her body was discovered in the shallow grave. Somehow, the sounds provided comfort and calm when the world was suddenly chaotic and depressing.

Poppy sat on the bench in the park, staring at the playground. It was the park Frankie had come to when she was barely walking.

Adam took a seat next to her and grabbed her hand in both of his. She was like ice, and Adam wondered if she would ever feel warmth again.

"You doing okay?" Adam asked.

"Yeah, I guess so." A small smile flitted across her face. "Do you remember that time, gosh, Frankie was what? Three? And she insisted on climbing the rope ladder? We kept telling her no and trying to get her off." Poppy balled her hands into fists and scrunched up her face like a petulant, determined child—which pretty much was the very definition of Frankie at three. "She grabbed a hold of the rope and hung on for dear life."

Of course Adam remembered the three adults trying to coax a precocious toddler into letting go. They had felt ridiculous and ineffective and completely at the whim of this bundle of energy.

Adam's father had once described Frankie as "full of piss and vinegar."

"Nothing was going to stop her from getting up that ladder," Adam said.

"And she almost made it."

"I remember she was mad at Mark for catching her."

A chuckle came from Poppy. "Not for long, though. Her daddy, her hero."

"You were too."

"Moms are different kinds of superheroes," she corrected him. "We had our ups and downs lately, but I knew she loved me, despite her protestations to the opposite." Poppy glanced over at him, a glint in her eye. "She was a shit liar."

"Yeah, she was."

She looked at their clasped hands. "I don't want to know what happened to her." She continued to stare at their hands, but her voice faltered. "She's gone, and that's hard enough to comprehend. I'm not sure I could handle the particulars."

He nodded but wasn't sure he would be able to completely shield her. The media had caught wind of the case before they had Frankie's body out of the ground. It was a bit surprising to find Poppy in public without some press hounding her. Luckily, most of the press was at the McMillans' home. But Adam knew they had been removed from their house somewhat clandestinely and were staying with a relative not far from where Mark and Poppy lived.

He understood where she was coming from, though. He wasn't sure he wanted to work on Frankie's case anymore. It was too hard to be detached and unbiased. Often he would find himself daydreaming about sneaking down to the jail and slitting Geneva's and Mitch's throats and watching them bleed to death.

"See that girl over there?" Poppy nodded toward the swings. "That's her," she said. "Isla. She's the reason I've been coming here the past couple of days. It's weird, but it helps me to see her. To know she survived. She could've been in a shallow grave next to Frankie—or worse."

It was difficult to look at the girl and not imagine all the ways she might have been abused if they hadn't found her in that closet. According to emails found on the Schultzes' computer,

Isla was supposed to have been "delivered" to her buyer the next day.

A woman walked up to Isla and sat in the swing next to her. Adam recognized her from the station as Isla's mother.

"I'm not envious her daughter lived," Poppy continued. "I know that seems like it would be a natural emotion to have. Or to be angry. But I'm not. How could I be angry or jealous or anything other than happy for all of them? It's not to say I wouldn't give anything to have Frankie here too. But not at the expense of another child. I'm so happy Isla will get to grow up, have a life, do amazing things. I would never want to sacrifice someone else's child so I could have mine."

She lifted her face to the sky and closed her eyes, inhaling deeply. "Mark wants me to give Luke a chance. Let him into our lives and make him a part of the family."

"How do you feel about it?"

"I think I will want that someday. But not now; it's too soon. It's ridiculous, I know, but it almost feels like I'm exchanging one kid for another. Like I'm betraying Frankie. I think I just need some time to wrap my head around everything that's happened."

Adam knew Mark had already met with Luke and told him to give Poppy some time.

"My life has changed so much. I lost a daughter I loved with every fiber of my being. And I gained a son I never wanted in my life. I'm trying to do the right thing after making monumental mistakes lately. But I need air. I need to feel like I can breathe again. Right now, it's as if I'm drowning in a river and I can't seem to get to shore. Every time my head gets above water, there's something pushing me back under. Until I get on firm ground, I can't move forward. It's not fair to Luke, I know. He's being punished for a crime he didn't commit. It's just . . ."

"Hard."

"Yeah."

Adam had been in a fog the past couple of days. Not sure what to do. Angry that the world was still going about its business when it should've stopped the minute Frankie's life ended.

Isla and her mother stood up from the swings and walked hand in hand toward the parking lot. Every few steps, the little girl would look behind her. Adam wondered if she would ever feel safe again. Or if she would go through life petrified that someone might take her. Or harm her. Or kill her.

God, he hoped not.

Mrs. McMillan glanced over at Poppy, raised her hand, and gave a small wave.

Poppy smiled and waved back. "I'm ready to go home."

ACKNOWLEDGMENTS

GETTING A BOOK written is hard work, but it is only one step in the journey to getting it published. Thanks to my fabulous editor, Terri Bischoff, who loves Kendall as much as I love writing her, and never ceases to make my writing better. And big kudos to the entire Crooked Lane team who do all the behind-the-scenes stuff to make a book its best. Thanks to my agent, Stephanie Phillips, for finding me this gig.

Thanks to my amazing writing friends who helped me kick-start this book. I'm lucky to have such wonderful friends in my corner, who understand the quirkiness of writing. And thanks to Lisa Regan and her famous dog, Mr. Phillip, for allowing me to add a cameo. Lisa and her assistant, Maureen, are always there with an encouraging word and always sharing my books with the world (and their readers).

Thank you to my wonderful publicist, Kim Weiss at PR by the Book, for tirelessly working to get my book in the hands of all the right people.

Social media is not my forte, so I am always elated when I come across a post I like and it happens to be mine. That wouldn't be possible without Courtney Klute at Sol Virtual Assistance, who understands the crazy world of social media and what works.

Thanks to my unofficial editor, Amanda Kale, who reads my stuff with a keen eye and helps me through the saggy middle. You are going to take the publishing and academic worlds by storm.

My best friend, LeighAnn Sughrue, is my biggest supporter and cheerleader. She makes me feel like I am actually as good as she says I am.

To Jim and Lori—thanks for the great material!

My husband, Chuck Sparks, is the reason I am able to do what I do. He doesn't always understand why I do things the way I do them, but he always accepts them and helps me as much as he can. For that I am eternally grateful. I'm lucky I get to spend my life with you.

For the times I just need the world to be quiet, I have the best pooches who give the most amazing snuggles. Love my dogs, Zoe and Win.

I'm probably forgetting a ton of people who I will remember after this goes to print and will kick myself for excluding them. Even though I am the most forgetful person in the world, I do appreciate all the people who have made this journey amazing.

Readers . . . you will never understand how much you mean to authors. You take a chance on our books, allow us into your homes, hearts, and minds, and there are no words to express how thankful we are that you do. Your reviews, messages, and emails are what help to keep me focused on what is important—telling my story and providing an escape for you when you need to turn off the world for a bit. I am humble and grateful for each one of you.